m

Beautiful, remote Melanie watched the other members of the group with love shining in her eyes.

Mitch could see the pleasure she took in their company; the careful, concerned way she rushed to help her mother, sparing her unnecessary labors.

And later, as they sat around singing old-time songs, it was Melanie who played for them. Tunes flowed easily through her fingers as they rippled lovingly over the notes, her voice blending in with a rich, deep harmony.

They're like her family, he thought. *That's why she works with senior citizens. A big, happy family that cares and shares their lives with each other.*

It was something he'd never known and something he intended to find out more about.

With the help of Miss Melanie Stewart, of course.

Books by Lois Richer

Love Inspired

A Will and a Wedding #8
*Faithfully Yours #15
*A Hopeful Heart #23

*Faith, Hope & Charity

LOIS RICHER

credits her love of writing to a childhood spent in a Sunday school where the King James Version of the Bible was taught. The majesty and clarity of the language in the Old Testament stories allowed her to create pictures in her own mind while growing up in a tiny prairie village where everyone strove to make ends meet. During her school years, she continued to find great solace in those words and in the church family that supported her in local speech festivals, Christmas concerts and little-theater productions. Later in college, her ability with language stood her in good stead as she majored in linguistics, studied the work of William Shakespeare and participated in a small drama group.

Today Lois lives in another tiny Canadian town with her husband, Barry, and two very vocal sons. And still her belief in a strong, vibrant God who cares more than we know predominates her life. "My writing," she says, "allows me to express just a few of the words God sends bubbling around in my brain. If I convey some of the wonder and amazement I feel when I think of God and His love, I've used my words to good effect."

A Hopeful Heart
Lois Richer

Published by Steeple Hill Books™

STEEPLE HILL BOOKS

Steeple
Hill™

ISBN 0-373-87023-X

A HOPEFUL HEART

Copyright © 1998 by Lois Richer

Therefore I say unto you, Take no thought for your life, what ye shall eat, or what ye shall drink; nor yet for your body, what ye shall put on.... Consider the lilies of the field, how they grow; they toil not, neither do they spin: And yet I say unto you, That even Solomon in all his glory was not arrayed like one of these. Wherefore, if God so clothe the grass of the field, which today is, and tomorrow is cast into the oven, *shall He* not much more *clothe* you, O ye of little faith?

—*Matthew* 6:25-30

This book is dedicated to my grandpa John, and to Papa Richer. Both of them would have loved Melanie's refreshing attitude toward seniors and her efforts to improve the lives of those spending their last years in a nursing home. To you who devote your days and nights to caring for someone's spouse, mother, grandparent or friend, may I say "Thank you." Your labors do not go unappreciated.

Chapter One

Melanie Stewart slipped out of her battered tan car and slammed the door shut, hoping it would catch.

"You're doing fine, Bessie, old girl," she murmured, patting the ancient car's rusty fender. "I know. You need a paint job and new tires, but that will wait. It has to."

She grimaced at the thought of the number of high-priority items on her to-do list that seemed to multiply daily. Oh, for a little spare cash!

"The love of money is the root of all evil," she repeated to herself. "Remember that, and be glad for what you have."

With a sigh, Melanie blew her auburn bangs from her forehead, resigned to both her penurious state and the blistering July heat.

"Just a few dollars would sure be nice, though." She sighed, glancing heavenward. "Just a little spare cash could make a big difference to so many." Unbidden, images of the residents at the Sunset Retirement Home—*her* residents—rolled through her mind. "Give me a sign, Lord, please," she pleaded in a heartfelt prayer. "Just a little hint that better things are on the way."

"Oh, Melanie!" Mr. Jones strode jauntily down the street

toward her, whistling his usual happy tune as he pushed his delivery cart in front of Melanie's redbrick apartment building. "Afternoon, Melanie, my girl."

Fred Jones was a genial man who had been Mossbank's special-delivery officer for twenty years. He knew everyone in town and most of what went on. Melanie had long ceased to wonder how he kept the residents and their stories straight.

"Hi, Mr. Jones. How's your wife doing?" They exchanged the usual banter about the romance Melanie had helped along three years earlier. Then the older man thrust an ordinary white envelope with Official Notice stamped on the front of it into her hand.

"This looks pretty important, Melanie. Thought I'd better bring it over soon as you got off work. It was addressed to the nursing home, but I knew you'd be coming home about now. Sure hope it's good news." He grinned. "You've got a couple more wedding invitations, too. Reckon Cupid and you were real busy last winter," he said teasingly, watching her face flush.

His wiry tanned hand offered the shabby clipboard for her signature.

Melanie shook her head at the suggestion that she was the local matchmaker. In Fred's mind, the two latest invitations confirmed it, even if she hadn't meant to get involved.

"All I did was lend a little advice," she told him. When there was no response, she turned the plain white envelope over. There was nothing to identify it on the back. She peered at the strange letters on the front upper left corner—PJPB.

"Why do those initials seem so familiar?" she wondered. After a few moments of deep thought, Fred Jones answered her.

"It's probably just another of those form letters announcing you have won an unbelievable amount of money." He frowned. "Then, when you read the fine print, there is always a conditional *if* or *possibly* to free the sender of any misrepresentation." He shook his head gloomily and watched while

Melanie stuffed the envelope into the outside pocket of her tan leather bag. "Then again, maybe it's a letter from an admirer," he suggested slyly.

"Well, whatever it is, it will have to wait," she told him tiredly. "I need a shower and some supper. Thanks anyway, Mr. Jones."

Fred Jones grinned, waved his hand and strode off down the street to his next destination, still whistling, but this time it was "Here Comes the Bride."

Lethargically, Melanie forced her tired feet up the three stairs and into the blessed coolness of the air-conditioned foyer. The elevator took forever, so she slowly climbed the stairs.

As usual, the events of her day threatened to overwhelm her and she forcibly thrust them to the back of her mind, refusing to allow herself to dwell on the sad situations she often handled as director of Sunset Retirement Home.

At twenty-eight, she had never become resigned to the plight of seniors forced to enter a nursing home when they could no longer care for themselves. Empathy of a world-weary foster child, no doubt, she derided herself.

Melanie spent every minute of her workday trying to make their lives interesting and enjoyable. In short, she hoped to allow the residents the freedom to live as they wished with help nearby when necessary. Since her childish dreams of husband and children had never been fulfilled, the small community of Mossbank, North Dakota, but especially the residents at Sunset, had become her special family.

Melanie placed the letter on the hall table just as the phone rang.

"Oh, hi, Mom." She smiled at Charity Flowerday's excited rush of words. "Yes, Mother. I'm perfectly fine." She grinned at the familiar question. "I will eat supper, Mom. A lovely Chinese dinner that Shawna left for me. She's gone out on another date, I think."

"Aren't you going out, dear?"

Melanie burst out laughing.

"Me? No way. I'm dead tired and I just want to relax." She groaned inwardly. "No, Mother, I don't know Judge Conroy's grandson. You said he's moved here?"

Melanie eyed her letter longingly, knowing that her adoptive mother took a special interest in each and every newcomer to their small, closely knit town and would relay every morsel of information she'd found out about this most recent arrival. It seemed Charity had found yet another homeless chick to spread her wings over. For her own sake, Melanie just hoped this grandson was happily married.

"No, I hadn't heard anything, but then I don't know Judge Conroy all that well. If his grandson's been here for two weeks, I'll probably meet him at church soon. If I ever get another Sunday off!" Melanie smiled at the abrupt change of topic.

"Yes, Mother, I know there are some good men in the world. I just haven't met many of them, and those I think I might be interested in usually want my help to attract someone else." She smiled at the volume of reassurances that issued over the phone.

"Listen, Mother, I was just going to start dinner when you called. I have to go now. I'm starved. Have a good time with Faith and Hope. Bye, Mother."

The letter on the hall table stared at her all the while she ate her dinner. Knowing she could procrastinate no longer, Melanie finally carried her tea to the living room and sank into the depths of her overstuffed sofa. Yawning widely, she slit the slim envelope and drew out a single sheet of heavy white paper.

We are pleased to announce that M. Stewart of Mossbank, North Dakota, has been randomly selected by our computer as the grand prize winner of $50,000 in our recent Papa John's Peanut Butter contest.

This will advise you that prizes will be awarded

Thursday, July 15, during a televised announcement at WMIX-TV13. Please be at the station no later than 1:00 p.m. of that day. A company representative will contact you within the next few days to confirm your win and to give you additional information.

There was another paragraph offering congratulations and asking her not to talk to the press, but Melanie absorbed none of it. Her eyes read the words, but her mind couldn't comprehend their significance.

She turned it over to check for the usual qualifying sentences and found nothing. There was only a scrawled signature at the end of the letter which was identified as the CEO of Papa John's Peanut Butter. Stupidly, she stared at the embossed golden logo, afraid to believe it.

"He answered," she muttered to herself, dazed. "I've actually won some money!"

Melanie read the wonderful letter three times before her mind acknowledged and processed the information, and then she let out an unbridled squeal of joy.

"A grand prize winner," she mused, twisting one curling lock of her shoulder-length hair. "Thank you, Lord. As usual, Your timing is perfect. Maybe Mr. Henessey will get his wish after all. And of course, Mrs. Blair."

One by one, the residents of the special-care home flew through her thoughts. Many of the seniors had little or no family nearby. Some, like Mr. Henessey, had very little money for things that would make his last few years so enjoyable. A windfall of cash would be just the thing.

When Shawna sauntered through the door three hours later, Melanie had finished drawing up her list of future expenses. She pounced on her friend eagerly.

"I won, I won," she squeaked, thrusting the letter in front of Shawna's sunburned nose.

Her roommate was cool and efficient, well used to Melanie's bursts of excitement. Calmly she laid her jacket and purse on a nearby chair, wished her gaping date a good evening and closed the door on him firmly, then reached for the letter. After a careful scrutiny, she grabbed Melanie and they danced giddily around, laughing hilariously.

A week later, the thrill of excitement had not diminished as Melanie found herself ushered into the makeup room of WMIX, a Bismarck television station that specialized in North Dakota's news events. Melanie sat nervously while a teenage girl applied a thick layer of shadow and mascara. She felt butterflies dance an entire ballet through her midsection. Finally, eons later, a short, frumpy woman bustled into the room.

"M. Stewart?" Accepting the nod, the older woman wrapped her vivid purple nails around Melanie's arm and led her through a maze of corridors to a busy sound stage.

"Now, dear," she said over her shoulder, "we'll be broadcasting shortly. Don't move from this spot. When it's your turn, I'll be here to guide you on."

Like a plump, busy robin, the woman in the bright red shirt whisked through the menagerie of sound men, cameras and directors to the booth across the room.

From behind the curtain, Melanie saw part of the stage setting. A huge structure meant to represent a peanut butter jar full of gold coins sat front and center with the famous glittering golden letters PJPB on its side. Standing beside it was a man Melanie identified as Papa John, clad in his white shirt, bow tie, blue jeans and red suspenders. Snowy white hair looked exactly as it did on the commercials that flashed across the television screen every night.

In the last forty-eight hours, Melanie had spent valuable hours at work wracking her brain, trying to remember entering any contest to do with Papa John's Peanut Butter. Nothing specific came to mind, but then she had been in such a fog during a particularly low period in her life a few months ago. Right after poor old Mrs. Peters had passed away.

Suddenly the announcer's voice penetrated her thoughts.

"The winner is M. Stewart!"

Melanie felt a hand on her back propelling her forward. As she moved toward the grinning announcer, she noticed a tall, dark-haired man moving from the wings on the far side of the stage. Slim and muscular, he exuded the very essence of a man-about-town. He had rugged, chiseled features and the bluest eyes she had ever seen.

And those eyes were fixed firmly on her!

Melanie gave herself a mental shake and focused on the task ahead. Nervously, she wiped her sweaty palms on her skirt before moving to stand beside the announcer.

"M. Stewart," he boomed in his loud, TV personality voice.

"Yes," Melanie answered, and then heard a yes from directly behind her. Turning her head, she found those deep blue eyes glaring at her.

"I'm sorry, miss, but I think he asked for me." Low and rumbling, his voice rolled past her left ear as the man carefully but still rudely elbowed his way past.

"But my name is M. Stewart," Melanie insisted, wondering if the whole thing was a hoax. The announcer was obviously at a loss as he turned his perfectly groomed head from one to the other.

"I'm Melanie Stewart." Melanie was so nervous her voice slipped out in a soft squeak that no one seemed to hear.

Finally the director hissed from his seat in the sound room. The words were audible over the whole stage. "Do something!"

"I'm sorry, folks," the announcer said slowly, "but there seems to be a bit of a mix-up here. Our winner of the Papa John's Peanut Butter contest is M. Stewart. Sir, may I have your full name, please?"

The handsome interloper gracefully inclined his head as he stated clearly, "Mitchel Edward Stewart." His glittering blue eyes dared Melanie to top that.

"And you, miss. Your name is?" The microphone was

stuck in her face, and Melanie forced a tight rein on her temper as she answered.

"Melanie Clarice Stewart."

"Well, isn't this great. Are you two married?"

The stranger's dark head shook adamantly, his blue eyes hurling daggers at Melanie.

"I am not married and I have certainly never met Miss Stewart," he said, arrogantly dismissing Melanie's presence with a brush of his hand. "I was advised by telephone that I had won a contest and that I was obligated to be here today."

Melanie's simmering temper flashed to the surface. *Not so fast,* she thought, and tugged the rumpled letterhead from the pocket of her skirt, intent on wiping the smugly satisfied look from Mr. Mitchel Stewart's handsome countenance.

"I received this letter by special delivery," she said, waving the letter for all to see. Heat flooded her face as she stared into mocking blue eyes.

"I was to receive a phone call with further instructions, but—" She paused for .effect. Her tone was acidic in the extreme. "Apparently, that went astray."

Mitchel Stewart looked stunned at her words. Obviously he thought she was faking. Anger rushed through her as Melanie remembered all the things $50,000 could provide for her friends. There was no way this man was going to do her out of what was rightfully hers. She couldn't afford to let Mr. Pushy M. Stewart push her out of the running. If his name really was Stewart!

Just then, Papa John stepped into the spotlight. Taking the mike from the dumbfounded announcer's hand, he spoke into it in the soft, musical drawl known throughout North America.

"Now, folks. It looks like there's been some sort of mix-up here today. According to my information, our winner, M. Stewart, lives at 300 Oak Street in Mossbank, North Dakota."

His weathered face studied the two. Melanie spoke up.

"Yes, well, I work at that address. It's a nursing home. Sunset Retirement Home."

Clearly, Mitchel Stewart was not to be outdone. He stepped forward.

"I am also employed at 300 Oak Street."

Her anger grew as she glared at him, her eyes narrowed and searching. How could he do this to her? He was lying. She knew it. She knew all the tenants in the home, and she knew the employees, as well. He wasn't one of them.

"I started two weeks ago." He said it triumphantly, as if this was a game of one-upmanship. Melanie fumed.

"This sure is a puzzler, folks." Papa John scratched his head, obviously considering the next step.

One of the most popular television stations in North Dakota was broadcasting a lot of dead air, which was certainly not good for business, but it seemed no one could think of anything to say. Finally, the announcer stepped forward and spoke directly to the camera.

"Ladies and gentlemen, you have watched a newsmaking event on WMIX tonight. We apparently have two winners in the Papa John's Peanut Butter contest, both named M. Stewart and both living in Mossbank and working at 300 Oak Street." He smiled fatuously at both of them before glancing at the camera. "Keep tuned, and WMIX will keep you up to the minute with events as they happen."

As he gave the familiar station call letters, Melanie drooped with fatigue. Papa John moved to brush a gentle hand over hers.

"I'm real sorry about this, miss," he apologized. "I don't know what happened. There must have been some error. The selections were made by computer." Papa John grinned at her. "Couldn't have picked a better station, though, could I? WMIX. Mixed up, they should call it."

Melanie smiled weakly.

They both turned at the throat-clearing sound from Mitchel Stewart. The dark-haired man had absolutely no manners,

Melanie decided grimly. He stood peering down at both of them, eavesdropping on their conversation without any compunction. She turned her back to him deliberately as Papa John spoke again.

"I'm sorry about you, too, Mr. Stewart. I promise you that I will get this straightened out and let you know as soon as I can. Thank you both for making time to come down." The old man reached into his shirt pocket for a scrap of paper and a pen.

"Where can I reach you during the day, Miss Stewart?"

Melanie shuffled through her purse for a business card. She tried to ignore the tall man directly behind her.

"I am the director of care at Sunset," she told him, keeping her voice quiet.

"That's the one attached to the hospital," Papa John said, scribbling in odd, unreadable ink strokes. "I know about it from friends."

"Here's my address," Mitchel Stewart announced gruffly, unasked. "I'm often at the hospital, but I'll give you my card with office numbers." Trust him to butt in, Melanie thought.

A lean, muscular hand proffered a crisp white business card. His fingers were long and well cared for. The hands of a surgeon, Melanie guessed. Surgeons were usually arrogant. She turned to leave the two men.

"I have to get back to work," she murmured. "Nice to meet you, Papa John." Melanie glanced at the interloper, nodding dismissively.

As she strode out of the building, she wondered what would happen next when strong fingers closed about her arm.

"I'll walk with you," that firm, bossy voice declared. "If you don't mind, that is. It seems we have something in common besides our names." He smiled that thousand-watt grin that made her pulse flutter. "I didn't realize you worked at Sunset. Guess I didn't notice you."

Egotistical male, Melanie decided and tossed her gleaming curls. Her normally clear skin flushed with irritation in the bright sunlight. That was just what every woman wanted to hear—that she had been overlooked.

"Oh, no, I don't mind at all," she said with a touch of sarcasm. "Please feel free to tag along."

She was not a small woman, but Mitchel Stewart seemed to tower over her. Even with three-inch heels, her five-foot-five-inch stature seemed small and ineffective beside his height. She felt as if she was losing the upper hand in every confrontation with him.

She glared at him, tugging her arm out of his grasp as she stepped back, her body language telling him clearly not to invade her personal space.

"I don't appreciate being accosted in broad daylight, Mr. Stewart," she said through clenched teeth.

"Oh. Sorry. Do you appreciate it more after dark?" he quipped, grinning. "It was a little joke," he said, his smile noticeably drooping.

"Very little." Melanie was not amused. "I expect surgeons are so used to getting what they want, they never think of anyone else's wishes." Her normally calm, even tones were scathing.

"I expect they are."

He was trying to mollify her. She could hear it in his voice.

"You admit it?" Her dark eyes opened wide in disbelief. His impudence galled her.

Mitchel wasn't sure exactly what was going on. He had been aware of her dislike. It emanated from every pore of her well-shaped body. But right now it was as if there was another conversation going on. One that he knew absolutely nothing about.

He studied her small, tilted nose. It fit perfectly with her high-and-mighty attitude. The original attraction he had felt onstage had not abated. For some reason her dislike drew him like a magnet. He wondered if she would consider... Well, why not forge ahead?

Turning quickly, Mitchel folded her arm in his and began

striding toward the parking lot. Perforce the lady had to follow, although not happily.

"Will you stop dragging me about?" she demanded. As she tried to push his muscle-hardened body away, her heel caught in a metal grating. Mitchel caught her as she swayed.

"Now look what you've done," he said, smiling sympathetically. "All I wanted was to help you to your car and ask you out for dinner. I wasn't expecting you to fall into my arms."

Melanie pursed her lips and refused to rise to the bait. He was too infuriating. Instead she walked away.

"Where are you going?"

She pointed her finger at the tan beater parked haphazardly in a stall just six feet away. His black eyebrow arched quizzically.

"Vice-president, Communications?" Mitchel's gleaming dark eyes frowned at her. "I thought you said you worked at the retirement home." Clearly puzzled, he stared at her for several moments before his face darkened ominously.

"I get it," he announced, teeth bared. "It was all just a ruse, wasn't it? Just for the money. Well, I'm not going to be part of your little con game." His glittering sapphire eyes stared at the placard in front of her car. "Goodbye, N. Landt."

He turned on his heel and strode furiously away, shoulders stiff with anger.

Melanie sighed, resigned to her fate. "It has been a difficult week, Lord," she mused. "Today isn't going so well, either. And it doesn't look like things will be improving anytime soon. I know I can't understand everything You do, so could You just help me get through today?"

Sighing, she fished her key ring out of the leather shoulder bag and unlocked the car door. Gently she eased herself into the car, glumly grateful that she'd made it through this far. She would probably drive to the home, enjoy a cup of fresh coffee and get down to what she knew best.

A light tapping on her window roused Melanie from her thoughts. Turning, she saw a tall blond Adonis dressed in an elegant black three-piece pinstripe standing outside her car. She rolled down the window.

"Yes?"

"I'm terribly sorry," he apologized, flashing a movie-perfect smile, "but you are parked in my spot. I'm Neal Landt."

It was too much. Melanie burst into laughter, paroxysms of hilarity shaking her narrow shoulders.

"I'm very sorry," she apologized as concern etched itself on his worried face. Quickly she explained the reason for her visit. "I was so afraid I'd be late, I pulled into the first empty spot and rushed into the studio. I'll move right away," she promised.

Melanie flicked on the car's engine and waved at the bemused young man staring after her. When she glanced back, Neal Landt was scribbling furiously as he leaned against his silver-gray Jaguar.

"I'll probably get a ticket for parking in his spot, the way today is going," she muttered, and tried to ignore the pain pulsing through her puffy ankle.

"Once I get to work," she promised herself. "I'll be okay then. In fact," she muttered in frustration, "the whole day would have progressed very well if I had just ignored the stupid letter and gone straight to work in the first place."

There are no free lunches, she remembered Charity lecturing. *Whatever you get in this life is exactly what you've worked for, dear. There's no such thing as something for nothing.*

"As usual, you are always right, Mother," Melanie lamented sadly. "Especially today. But oh, what we could have done with that prize!"

It really was too bad the ill-humored Mitchel Stewart had not been able to see the funny side of this whole situation, Melanie thought, her lips tilting up as her mind replayed the scene. Humming loudly, she pulled into traffic and headed for Mossbank, confident that a return to routine would put her on track.

The mass of paperwork beckoned, and Melanie knew she would have to tackle it soon, but there was one duty she couldn't neglect in her daily ritual. Anyway, she didn't want to. She enjoyed it too much.

Quickly she slid out of the navy suit she had worn for her television debut and into the spare pink uniform she kept for just such occasions. She surveyed herself in the narrow mirror she had hung on the back of her door.

"Oh, lovely." She grimaced, noting the caked lines of eyeshadow and heavy red lipstick. "Wait till the candy stripers see you in this getup."

She grabbed a brush and tugged it through her dark russet curls, allowing them to fall to her shoulders. A few tissues and some cream took off the goop they had plastered on her at the studio, and she cleansed her skin well before applying a light touch of blush and a hint of mascara. She hated a lot of makeup, and anyway, she never remembered to renew it.

Satisfied, Melanie walked out the door and into the group of residents gathered outside.

"Mrs. Christie." She smiled, gathering the woman's blue-veined hands in her own. "I do believe it's a special day for you today."

The toothless old woman squeezed Melanie's hand tightly and nodded. Tears of happiness pooled at the corners of the weary, wrinkled eyes.

"My grandson is coming," she whispered as if afraid to say the words aloud. "He's bringing his fiancée. Isn't it wonderful?"

"Yes, it is." Melanie smiled at her. "And you look lovely," she told the elderly woman sincerely.

Each resident had something special to say to her, and Melanie allowed them to speak freely. It was so important to them, this time of sharing. Many felt neglected and alone, and they needed someone to listen. It mattered not that she had heard these same stories a hundred times before. What was important was the telling, recalling the happiness of the past. For many it was their only pleasant time in an otherwise bleak existence.

Except for Mrs. Rivers.

"Good morning, Nettie. You look lovely today. As usual."

The old lady sat silently staring out the window, her hands full of contest entries, which she shuffled from one hand to the other. She refused to answer any of the questions Melanie asked. Contrary to the administrator's evaluation, Melanie believed the older woman could understand everything that was said to her. It was merely a problem of finding the right subject or the right person to get her to talk. And heaven knew, Melanie had tried quite a few. Today nothing seemed to budge the woman out of her self-imposed silence.

"Well, Mrs. Rivers, I hope you have a good day today."

Because the stack of work still had to be dealt with, Melanie finally gave in. It was now or never. She returned to her desk, sat down and immersed herself in work, tuning out everything but the unfinished schedules and part-time applications that needed immediate attention.

A disturbance in the outside office alerted her to the possibility of trouble sometime later. Raised in anger, the voice barely carried through the strong metal door. Melanie dropped her pen to listen.

It was a man's voice, she decided. Rather low, but obviously furious. She grinned when Bridget attempted to intercept the flow of angry words with little success.

When her focus would not return, Melanie finally gave in to curiosity, grimacing as she stood. She would settle this and then it was back to the grindstone, she promised herself. No sidetracking.

As she opened the door, a familiar voice ranted at Bridget.

"It's a hospital, for heaven's sake. We can't have people wandering around in areas they shouldn't be, looking for lunch. Someone will get hurt. Don't you feed these people regularly?''

His tones were scathingly critical of her overworked staff, and Melanie surged forward, prepared to do battle.

"Dr. Stewart, we know exactly what we are doing in this facility. Perhaps if the medical staff in *your* hospital had enough sense to close the doors behind them, *our* residents would not wander into the hospital."

Mitchel Stewart whirled to face her, his jaw slack with astonishment. He was as good-looking as Melanie remembered. Still formally dressed in the dark suit jacket and matching slacks, he exuded the posh doctor persona.

Only the tie at the neck of his pristine white shirt was loosened and slightly askew. Curling dark hairs peeked out from his throat. He looked every inch a playboy with his rumpled black hair and twinkling azure eyes.

"You!" he gasped, clearly shocked. "What are you doing here?"

"As I told you before, Dr. Stewart, this is where I am employed. Supposedly you are, also, although I must have missed seeing you around." Melanie assumed a haughty look before demanding, "Is there anything else, Doctor?"

"I am not a doctor," he told her loudly. "And yes, there certainly is. May I speak with you privately?"

"Not Dr. Stewart?" Melanie stretched her lips thinly, faking outrage. "You lied deliberately, to try to cheat me out of that money, didn't you?" she accused, hands on her hips.

When a telltale flush of red covered his jutting cheekbones, Melanie felt deep satisfaction. Self-righteous and smug, she delivered the final blow.

"I don't think I want to be part of your charade any longer, whoever you are."

Turning, Melanie flounced into her office in high dudgeon, feeling a virtuous superiority. He had asked for it.

''We're not quite finished, are we?'' His deep tones rumbled over her left shoulder.

''I've said everything I'm going to,'' she announced smugly and flopped into her desk chair.

''Good. Then *you* can hear *me* out.''

Chapter Two

"Ms. Stewart, it seems there has been more than one mix-up today."

He had never before seen a woman so furious and yet so determined not to say a word, Mitch decided in amusement. He fully expected her to blow a gasket.

"What do you want?" Her low voice barely masked her frustration.

"Look, I came to say I'm sorry." She looked slightly mollified at his calm, contrite tone, but the glitter of suspicion returned to her eyes when Bridget walked into her office with Sam Sinclair shuffling alongside her. Mitch ignored them.

"*And* I came to make sure you keep those patients out of the hospital. They could get hurt." She had that look again.

"Ms. Stewart—Melanie—I'm very sorry I accused you wrongly earlier today. Please forgive me." Deliberately, Mitch made his tones sweet as honey.

"Fine. You're forgiven." Her voice was frosty, unwelcoming, with a tinge of bitterness. "Now, please, will you get out of my office. Bridget, would you do the honors?"

Leaning back in her chair, Melanie glared at him. He watched her huge green eyes flicker with something like suspicion as she studied him. Mitch decided the faint pink of her uniform was certainly her color.

Her almost round face, with its dainty nose tipped at that disdainful angle, dared him to try her patience. Her mouth straightened into a thin, disapproving line.

Deliberately Mitch tamped his growing interest and firmed his resolve. He wasn't here looking for a date. He was here to make restitution. Melanie Stewart was going to understand his concerns one way or another.

"Now, if we can discuss this rationally."

"Oh, buzz off—" She stopped short of saying whatever else was on her mind, and Mitch almost laughed at the childish phrase.

Melanie was fiery and determined and willful, but she had a streak of decency in her that forbade the use of cuss words. It was unusual in this day and age and something he admired, Mitch admitted. But he wouldn't tell her that just yet.

Stretching her long legs, Melanie deliberately ignored him. To Mitch, that was the final straw. He opened the door and ordered, "Look, just look.

"They're wandering all over the place," he told her, pointing toward one sprightly old gentleman dressed in an ancient green suit, which bore a striking resemblance to the apparel of a leprechaun. "This place is out of control."

He watched as she spluttered angrily. But as residents watched, Melanie Stewart refused to acknowledge his tenuous grip on her small hand. Smiling and friendly, she greeted each one, losing the smile immediately when they passed.

"The hospital cannot afford to have someone injured or worse, simply because you allow these people to wander around at large. It's my job to ensure we don't get embroiled in any frivolous law suits." He pulled her along behind him through the hallways, past the interested spectators gathered outside their rooms.

"You're a lawyer?" The way she said his profession, Mitch figured it rated pretty low on her scale.

It also brought on another tirade.

"Of all the silly, idiotic, lying tricks…"

Mitch let her rant until they came to a tiny woman sitting quietly on a bench in the hall. Bending his lips to her ear, Mitch teased her.

"If you scare these folks into thinking you're having a conniption fit, they are going to get worked up. Just relax, will you?" He breathed in the soft, light fragrance she wore, enjoying its teasing allure.

"Conniption fit? I haven't heard that phrase for years!" She frowned at him. "Anyway, Mrs. Rivers never says anything."

As they drew nearer, the little woman murmured something. Melanie stared in amazement. In two years, Mrs. Rivers had never been heard to utter more than one word. Suddenly, at the sight of this lawyer, she was speaking?

"I beg your pardon," Melanie said, hoping the old lady would repeat herself.

The woman's bright gray eyes were riveted on them, and she spoke louder.

"It's so romantic," she breathed. "Just like a knight in shining armor. Oh, Melanie, at last you have found your true love."

Mitch bowed as low as possible, a huge grin crinkling his smug face. "Thank you, ma'am."

Turning, he marched Melanie back through the office to her inner sanctum, then gently pressed her stiff, angry body onto the leather couch. As he moved to stand, Mitch gently drew his lips across her soft, angry ones.

"Maybe she's right, Melanie." He grinned cheekily before tossing his jacket across his arm and moving to the door. He slid his dark eyes over her once more before murmuring, "We'll see." The door closed softly on his laughing face.

Melanie hissed with frustration through tightly pursed lips. "No, Mr. Know-It-All Stewart, we definitely will not see."

Her hand swiped across her mouth as she tried without success to erase the feel of his seeking mouth. She clenched her fist as the pool of awareness in her middle refused to go away.

"Cad. Liar. Overbearing male. Rude. Pushy. Thief...oh!" There simply were not enough words, she decided.

"Talking to someone?" Shawna poked her head around the door. "I thought I heard someone calling names." She grinned, eyeing her friend's heightened color.

"Could be," Melanie answered, forcing a smile. "The way today's been going, anything might happen." She looked at her roomie curiously. "What are you doing here?"

Shawna unpinned her glistening hair and shook it free of her confining nurse's cap. She wasn't wearing scrubs, Melanie noticed.

"Not operating today?"

"Oh, Mal is late again. You know, it's getting so that the man never manages to arrive in the operating room until at least an hour after his scheduled time." Mal was her pet name for a doctor on staff she particularly despised. Short for malpractice.

"Doesn't that sort of throw things off?" Melanie knew enough about the tightly funded medical world to know that time is money, especially in an operating room.

"Oh, yeah," Shawna agreed. "And I can tell you that the other doctors are getting pretty tired of hanging around waiting for him to get his act together."

"Did you pick up your check?" Her eyes were big and round with excitement. "Can I see it? The money, I mean."

Melanie sighed deeply. "I didn't get the money." When Shawna's jaw dropped open, Melanie's hand went up, forestalling her comments. "It seems that two invitations went out, both of them to an M. Stewart. Unfortunately there were two M. Stewarts in attendance. One Melanie, one Mitchel. He just left."

The paging system interrupted her.

"I've gotta go. Mal must be here. Why now?" Shawna muttered in frustration. "I can't wait to hear more." Stuffing her long hair under the cap, the operating room nurse left in a flurry, looking model perfect.

It didn't matter how much she tried after that, Melanie could not concentrate on the job. Part of it was her own fault, she acknowledged bitterly. But most of it was due to a certain lawyer and she put in time without accomplishing much.

"I'm calling it a day, Bridget. Can you handle everything?" Melanie watched as Bridget nodded, her face lit with a huge grin. "Don't mention him," she ordered grimly. "This is all his fault!"

Melanie strode out the door, then turned.

"And don't call my mother," she ordered wrathfully. "All I need are the fearsome threesome hanging around trying to nurse me through this illness."

"Melanie! You know Faith and Hope and your mother only want to help. Why, I'm sure if they knew about that handsome man that just left, they'd be very pleased."

"Considering that they've been trying to marry me off for years, I suppose so." Melanie grimaced. "My mother was even trying to set me up with Judge Conroy's grandson the other day." She shook her head in dismay.

"Yes, but—"

"I have to go home, Bridget. My feet are killing me. See you tomorrow." Melanie left, winding through the maze of curious and grinning residents to the parking lot.

"Lawyers!" One last epithet and she was finished thinking about Mitchel Stewart, she decided.

"But they said he was dead! Killed in action." Hope stared at her two best friends in agony. "I pleaded and I begged them to check again and again, but they said they were sure."

"Hope, dear, God still works miracles," Faith murmured, patting the pale, smooth hand. "And He is the final authority. Just calm down and let us think this through."

Charity peered at the two women sitting in her living room and wondered if it was true. Had Hope's fiancé returned from the dead after nearly twenty-five years?

"How did you find all this out?" she asked. "Did someone from the government phone you, Hope?" She remembered the television clip from last evening. "I have heard that they are still finding some MIAs. Perhaps Jean was one of those?"

Hope shook her blond head, dazed.

"No, I don't think so. The lady who phoned said he'd been quite ill. Apparently, during a high fever, he mentioned my name. Lately someone's been searching for him. She asked me all kinds of questions, Faith. Strange questions."

"Questions? Oh, piffle!" Faith's normally sunny face was dark with foreboding. "What kind of questions?"

"Oh, if I was married now. And the year Jean disappeared. If I'd ever heard from him while he was in Vietnam. Things like that."

"There have been some private efforts to investigate claims about MIAs," Charity murmured, watching her friend's sad face. "Perhaps that's it. Maybe a family member?"

"Charity, he didn't have any family. And besides—" Hope winced "—Jean wasn't missing in action. They said he died!" Her voice was full of remembered pain. "How could they make a mistake like that?"

"We don't know, dear. Perhaps we never will. But God knows. And He will use this to bless you, you can be sure of that."

Hope's unlined face was haggard as she stared at her closest friends.

"I don't know what to do," she confessed wearily. "I don't know where to turn."

"Well, I do," Faith declared firmly. "First we turn to the Lord, and then I'm going to give Harry Conroy a call. He's got contacts in Washington. Maybe he can find out something."

"You don't have to phone him, Faith. He's coming over for dinner. And bringing his grandson." Charity smiled slyly. "Melanie's coming, too. Why don't you both stay? Maybe we can figure something out together."

"I can stay." Faith beamed happily, clapping her hands.

"I just love fried chicken. And Arthur's away in Denver at that conference."

"Fried chicken," Hope murmured, a look of faint chagrin on her face. "Very well, I suppose one high-cholesterol meal won't hurt. Thank you, Charity. In fact, I'll help you. I can make a salad."

Charity peered at Faith with a look that asked the other woman for help.

"That's a good idea. A nice fresh green Caesar salad with croutons and cheese and lots of dressing. But first we pray," Faith ordered, and led off a heartfelt plea to her heavenly father.

After twenty-three laps, Melanie was definitely winded, but after thirty-two she was relaxed. The huge pool area was one of the apartment's perks she really enjoyed. Some people jogged, and some did aerobics. Melanie had always preferred swimming.

Slowly, she pulled herself out and walked the few steps to the whirling hot tub. She never could stand the overpowering temperature for very long, but it soothed and rejuvenated like no other remedy for stress. Eyes closed, she reclined and let the bubbling waters do their work.

"Miss Stewart, how nice to see you again."

Melanie blinked, almost believing the man standing in front of her was a dream. Goodness knows, he was certainly dream material. Tall and dark, clad in a black swimsuit, he exemplified male macho.

Melanie gulped as she moved her gaze from his strong, muscular legs to his lean hips and tapered waist, across the broad expanse of his golden chest covered in fine whorling black hairs to his sharply featured face. He was hunk material, all right, she told herself, trying to calm her thudding heart.

The time since their last meeting had not dulled her irrational attraction to him in the least.

"Mr. Stewart." It was a miracle anything emerged from

her parched throat. For the life of her, Melanie couldn't think of a thing to say.

"Still mad, huh?"

Grinning, Mitchel Stewart walked to the edge of the pool and dove into its still waters. The ripples that spread seemed amazingly like those circles of excitement that rippled through her. She watched him swim with even strokes, broad shoulders and muscular arms cutting cleanly through the water.

Melanie gave herself a mental shake and turned her eager eyes from watching his graceful form. Instead she sank deeper into the hot water, hoping it would ease new tension. She closed her eyes and deliberately blanked out his presence.

"May I join you?" The question was perfunctory. Mitchel Stewart didn't bother to wait for an answer. He sank down beside her, his thigh brushing hers. Melanie edged away, giving him more room.

His dark eyes twinkled at her as he spoke.

"Okay, you win," he declared. "I think you have sufficiently paid me back with Mrs. Strange and her daughter." A rueful look passed over his face. "Some would even say you're points ahead."

Melanie burst out laughing. Agatha Strange was a lonely old soul whose fondest wish was to have her spinster daughter married before the old woman passed on, as she phrased it. When Mrs. Strange had come to her with a problem about her will, Melanie's plan had hatched. Who better to handle the old girl than attorney extraordinaire Mitchel Stewart? Gleefully, she had told the elderly woman about Mitchel, while managing to imply that he was single and desperately looking for love.

Throughout the week, bits and pieces of their exchanges had been relayed to Melanie until even she felt sorry for the man. Deidre Strange, the daughter, was at least twenty years older than Mitchel and about sixty pounds heavier. Truly, a perfect match.

His big blue eyes gazed woefully into hers.

"Could we please start again?" He sounded like a little boy trying to atone for stealing the last chocolate chip cookie. Melanie couldn't help it, she grinned. He thrust out one large, tanned hand.

"Mitchel Stewart. Mitch to my friends. Just moved into the building." He began to list his many attributes. "Single, good health, age thirty-two, six foot four, one hundred eighty-five pounds, legal counsel to corporate accounts." His bright eyes sparkled mischievously. "Same information I gave Mrs. Strange."

Giggling, Melanie shook his hand as she answered.

"Melanie Stewart, no age and definitely no weight."

"Okay." He dragged the word out. "So, Melanie, what's your favorite food?"

She joined in the game easily enough. Mitch appeared to hold no ill feelings, and she had more than paid him back for his high-handedness.

Besides, she was a little embarrassed at her behavior. Her temper had always been a sore spot. Whenever she lost it, she invariably regretted her lack of control. Maybe she could redeem herself. She focused on the conversation.

"Chinese, especially the vegetables. What's yours?"

Mitch lounged comfortably beside her, his long legs stretched out. Dark head tipped back, he thought for a few minutes before answering. "Food."

Melanie frowned. "Pardon?"

"I like just about everything as long as someone else cooks it." His mouth slanted mockingly as he leered at her. "I can make a mean raspberry punch, though."

"Oh. Well, good," Melanie answered lamely, refusing to acknowledge the spark of awareness that flew each time he brushed against her.

It was the heat, she told herself. She should never have remained in the Jacuzzi for so long. The reason she had, of course, was her swimsuit.

It had been a lapse in judgment. She knew that. Her bust was too full and her hips too round to wear something this

defining. Nevertheless, the heat was unbearable, and she had
to leave. Now!

"Excuse me, I have to get out." Melanie moved slowly
and calmly up the stairs, aware of his eyes on her legs. Once
out of the heat, she could draw cooling air into her lungs.
She reached for her towel and quickly tugged it over her
shoulders, trying to ignore him as he sat there watching her.

"Did I drive you out?" His eyebrows tipped downward.

"Oh, no." Melanie cinched her towel a little tighter across
her shoulders. "I just can't take the heat." Her face flooded
with pink. She rushed to correct herself.

"Of the pool. I mean, the Jacuzzi. After a few minutes, the
heat really gets to me."

Mitch knew what she meant. The heat was getting to him,
too. He could feel it frying his brain to mush as he admired
the lovely Melanie.

He'd seen far skimpier suits on many of the local beaches,
but nothing that looked as elegantly attractive as this. Mitch
decided he much preferred it over the pink uniform she had
worn the other day. Her long auburn hair was curling wildly
around her shoulders and face, hugging the wide cheekbones
and delicately arched brows.

Flushing brightly, Melanie turned her back to him to gather
her belongings. As she did, her towel slipped to the floor.

What was wrong with the men in town, he wondered,
watching her. The woman was gorgeous, and apparently had
brains, too. Yet here she was, spending her evening alone.
Idly, he wondered if there was someone special in her life.

Mitch watched her pull on a white terry covering that just
grazed her thighs. When the heat began to addle his brain, he
moved out of the swirling hot tub to tug on the baggy jogging
pants he had tucked into his sports bag. Something was definitely going on between them, he decided, some spark of
interest he'd noticed from the first. And despite his best intentions, he was going to investigate the fiery redhead.

"How about going to dinner with me?" The phrasing

wasn't the greatest, he decided, but it was hard to make sense when your brain was the consistency of mashed potatoes.

She was slipping on shorts, and at his question, Melanie stood stock-still, perched like a startled flamingo on one leg. Her tousled hair tumbled around her face, huge green eyes questioning. She had a fresh, clean-scrubbed look he found very attractive.

"I don't—"

He cut her off before she could refuse.

"Please," he cajoled, tugging on a shirt. "You would really be doing me a favor." He tried to look forlorn and alone. "I just moved the last of my stuff in and I can't possibly do any more hard work today. I deserve a break. Please?"

She looked at him steadily, obviously gauging just how reliable he was. He was surprised himself at how anxious he was to get to know her better.

"All right," Melanie agreed finally. "But I think you'd better come with me. I agreed to have dinner with my mother tonight." If she thought she would turn him off by introducing her mother, she had been dead wrong.

"Is she a good cook?" Mitch asked warily, watching her gather her belongings.

"The best. You may need to do a few more laps when you're finished."

He looked affronted as he pulled on his clothes. One hand patted his washboard-flat stomach experimentally.

"I could stand to gain a few pounds. You think?" He cocked his head with that little-boy grace she was coming to recognize.

"No comment." Melanie giggled and went out. "I'll meet you downstairs in half an hour. Don't be late."

He wasn't late, but she was there before him, tapping one foot impatiently against the marble floor.

"I wondered if you'd changed your mind," she murmured, tossing her hair over her shoulders. Melanie stepped through the door and began to stride down the street. Mitch was forced to hurry to keep up with her.

"A woman who's on time," he muttered, huffing as he marched beside her. "Who would believe it?"

"Quite a few people, actually. It's just one of my failings."

"Why are we running when we could have taken the car?" Mitch panted, half-walking, half-jogging across the street.

"We're not running, we're walking. My mother lives only three blocks away. There's hardly any point in driving. Besides—" she grinned at him pointedly "—it's good exercise."

"I prefer swimming." He breathed, trying to look macho while his lungs burned. To his disgust, Melanie seemed totally unaffected by the speed race.

"Most out-of-shape people do prefer exercise that isn't weight bearing," she murmured without losing a step.

"Now just a minute! I am not—" Mitch felt himself collide with the pavement at the same moment his temperature hit boiling. There was a web of stabbing pain radiating from his left knee, and his pants were torn.

"Now look what you've done," he said furiously as he stood with some difficulty, pushing her helping hand away. "I'm not going out for dinner looking like this."

Her green eyes flashed with something he might have thought was sympathy. Except for her next words.

"Mm, lack of coordination, too. Don't ever take up jogging, Mr. Stewart. You're not the type."

"I don't think we have to worry about that," he said through clenched teeth as he brushed bits of gravel from his palms. "And I am not uncoordinated! If you didn't insist on making this the Indy 500..."

"Oh, now it's my fault! If that isn't just like a man! Blame it on me because I keep in shape and you don't. As if I or anyone else could make you exercise more. Men!" She spat the word with a telling glance that relegated him to one of the lower subspecies in the universe.

Mitch smiled grimly.

"I'm sorry," he muttered, limping at a pace that was still far too fast but considerably slower than her former fifty knots. "But I am a man. I wouldn't have come with you if I had known you hated men."

"I don't hate men," she said in exasperation. "I quite appreciate them." Her eyes flickered and he wondered if he could call that stretch of her lips a smile. "Some of you are even quite useful."

It was a put-down, sure as anything, and Mitch refused to let it pass.

"I think I understand why you're not, er, out tonight," he murmured under his breath. "You're a man-hater."

She stopped so quickly he crashed into her, the breath wheezing out of his chest at the contact. Melanie Stewart was mad. He could see it in her glinting green eyes. He could feel it in the tingle of electricity that pulsed through the air around them. But what really gave away her emotional state were the small, pointed fingernails buried in his arm.

"I am not stupid," she enunciated. "You think that if you make all these ridiculous accusations, I'll forget you're trying to swindle me out of that money, don't you? Well, Mr. Mitchel Stewart, or whatever your name is—" she snorted in pretended amusement "—it's not going to work."

Carefully, with extreme patience and not a little wincing, Mitch removed her talons from his shirtsleeve.

"I don't know why you keep saying that," he muttered fiercely. "My name *is* Mitchel Stewart. And I am not trying to swindle anyone out of anything." He peered at her, noting with interest the high spots of color on her cheeks. "Why is getting this money so important to you, anyway? Do you need cash that badly? I know the bank manager," he said, frowning at her rising color. "There's no need to be embarrassed about needing some help."

Melanie flushed more deeply. Her hands were balled into fists, but she raised her chin defiantly while her eyes hardened to cold intense chips of emerald.

"I don't want it for myself," she enunciated clearly. "I want to use it for some friends. They deserve to have some comfort in life, and this is my one chance to give it to them.

If you hadn't interfered, I would have the money by now and I'd be able to take care of them.''

"I might have a perfectly good use for that money myself,'' he told her angrily. "Someone I care about very much could use that cash right about now.''

"May the best woman or man win, then.'' Melanie snapped open a black wrought-iron gate with one hand and stepped through. "Well, are you coming or not?''

"Yes.'' He sighed. "I'm coming. And I still think you dislike men.''

"No, she doesn't,'' a bright voice chirped. "Piffle! Melanie is just one of those modern career girls who put most of their energies into their work. When she gets married, she'll bury herself in that, too.''

Mitch glanced up to see Faith Johnson's beaming face.

"Oh, hello. I didn't know you'd be here tonight.'' He grinned happily, pleased to see the beaming older woman. "Melanie didn't tell me.''

"Melanie didn't know,'' his companion muttered. She glanced from one to the other. "Do I take it you two know each other?''

"Of course we know each other. I was here for dinner last week with my grandfather. Wait a minute!'' He stared at her as the pieces began to fall into place. "You mean Mrs. Flowerday is your mother? But your names—''

"Are different because Melanie is adopted. My own very special daughter.'' Charity hugged the slim form to her ample bosom and patted Melanie's back. "I'm so glad you could come, darling. And you brought Harry's grandson! How marvelous. Do come in.''

"Actually I'm her foster daughter. Harry's grand—'' Melanie whirled to stare at Mitch, her eyes wide with dismay. "You mean you're Judge Conroy's grandson?''

Mitch bowed at the waist.

"The one and only.''

"Oh, no.''

No one else heard the softly breathed moan, Mitch was

sure, but he did. And he didn't like it. The female of the species generally appreciated his company. But Melanie Stewart was looking at him as if he was a worm crawling out of the woodwork.

"You knew all about this, didn't you," she asked angrily. "You'd think you would know better than to fall in with the fearsome threesome's plans."

"I don't have a clue—"

"That's for sure," she said, her eyes shooting daggers at him. "Try to act normally. And if you don't make any waves, we may just get out of this early enough to nip their match-making in the bud."

She stomped away to talk to the two other women seated in Charity's living room. Mitch shook his head in confusion and headed for the nearest easy chair, only remembering as he sat that this particular chair had a bad spring.

"Oof!"

"Did you say something, boy?" His grandfather emerged from the kitchen chewing on a bit of meat.

"No, Gramps. Well, yes, actually, I said it was good to sit down." Mitch watched as everyone turned to face him. "I meant after the walk over. You know, in the heat and every-thing." Why were they all staring at him as if he had two heads?

His grandfather looked at him pityingly, eyeing the tear at his pants with some disfavor.

"Practice not doing too well, son?" He reached in his pocket, and Mitch cringed, remembering the habit from long ago. Before the older man could pull out his wallet, Mitch launched into speech.

"No, it's going really well. The hospital was a good start, and I've found a number of new clients this week."

Judge Conroy shook his head.

"Then why wear those things? Doesn't look too good for an up-and-coming young lawyer."

Melanie laughed her light, bubbly laugh, which Mitch hadn't heard for ages.

"He kissed the pavement on the way over here. Tore his pants and cut his knee." She grinned at the judge and winked. "Out of shape, I suspect."

"I am *not* out of shape." Mitch glared at her, gritting his teeth. "I tripped. It happens to lots of people."

"Oh, my dear! Let me see," Hope murmured, scurrying over to check the skin of his knee. "Come along, Mitchel. That needs cleaning."

The older woman had him firmly by the arm, and there was nothing Mitch could do but follow meekly. She plunked him on a chair and rolled up his pant leg efficiently.

"I remember this from my teaching days." Hope smiled. "How many Band-Aids did I use during those thirty years, I wonder? And the iodine!"

"I, er, I don't think I need iodine," Mitch murmured, trying not to remember his past and how that stuff stung. "Really, it's fine."

Hope looked at him with a knowing smile. "It's all right," she whispered, patting his hand. "Nowadays, the new stuff doesn't hurt nearly as much."

Mitch subsided, feeling a fool. He sat meekly as she dabbed and cleaned and bandaged him until he looked like a trussed-up turkey. His pant leg wouldn't go over the massive bandage she had applied, so Hope Langford carefully cut it off, leaving him with one short and one long leg.

He stared at his legs, aghast at the sight of his mutilated trousers. He had never been so thoroughly humiliated in his entire life, and the evening hadn't even begun yet.

"Well, you couldn't very well wear them to work with a patch in the knee," Hope told him kindly, her blond head tipped. "This way you can get the other leg cut off and make shorts out of them." She waved the scissors thoughtfully. "Would you like me to do it?"

"No, thanks anyway," he said, backing out of the room. "You've done a wonderful job, though." Of ruining his only pair of designer pants, he added under his breath.

Mitch turned carefully to go to the living room and found

Melanie in his path, her gaze wide with disbelief as she studied him. Her mouth tilted in a slash of amusement, and her eyes sparkled with delight.

"Don't say a word," he warned her menacingly. "And if there's anyone who'll be leaving early, it's going to be me."

"How the mighty are fallen." She giggled, walking behind him as he limped to his chair. Her face cracked up when he jerked upward as the metal prong stabbed him in the rear again. "Shall I call Aunt Hope for you, Mitch?" She chortled.

"Oh, go away," he told her miserably. His eyes moved to the seniors huddled over the pictures on the coffee table. "What's going on there?"

"Oh, that. Hope has just received word that the man she was engaged to years ago may not have died in the Vietnam war, as she was told. My mother wants Judge Conroy to help them check into it." Melanie's face was sad. "I feel bad because Hope never forgot Jean."

"But where on earth has he been?"

"I don't know," Melanie told him. "Let's listen in and see what we can find out."

"But if he wasn't killed there, why did they think he was?" Hope demanded. "There must have been some proof of identity." She glanced at the judge for confirmation.

"I don't know, dear," the old man murmured, covering her hand with his tenderly. "But I'll do everything I can to help you find out." There was a silence while everyone considered the implications.

Moments later the two older ladies went with Melanie into the kitchen and Mitch, his grandfather and Hope sat in the living room. It seemed the other two had forgotten him completely, so Mitch listened to their conversation unashamedly.

"Do you still have feelings for this man, Hope?" his grandfather whispered, his salt-and-pepper head bent near hers.

"I don't know. I don't know what I feel anymore. Everything has changed, moved out of its familiar pattern. I just wish I knew for sure whether or not Jean was alive.'' She stared at the old pictures with tears in her eyes, her face a study in contrasts.

''All those years ago I just gave up,'' she whispered regretfully. ''Maybe, if I had kept searching, Jean and I would have had a future together.''

Judge Conroy patted the soft white hand with affection.

''It's in His hands,'' he murmured comfortingly. ''Let's leave it there while we do what we can, my dear.''

As he sat at the dinner table, munching on wonderful home-cooked fried chicken and the smoothest mashed potatoes he'd ever eaten, Mitch studied each person carefully.

His grandfather sat next to Hope, and he was paying an inordinate amount of attention to the woman, Mitch noted. They were laughing about the good times they'd shared and their plans for the seniors' retreat at Lucky Lake.

Hope Langford was a beautiful woman, with her smooth blond hair and clear blue eyes. She was quiet but thoughtful, replying to the comments only after she'd carefully considered her responses. Which was totally unlike her friend Faith, who seemed to bubble with excitement. Mitch knew that the older woman had recently been married, so perhaps that explained her effervescence.

Charity Flowerday sat next to him, insisting that he try seconds of everything and teasing him about his good appetite. But it was her arthritic hands that he noticed most. Although they were bent and worn, they expressed her tender concern in a thousand different ways. She ruffled his hair affectionately, offered a friendly pat to Faith's shoulder, soothed Hope's fears and pinched Melanie's ear. And all with those deformed hands.

And Melanie? Beautiful, remote Melanie sat silent in her chair, watching the other members of the group with love shining in her eyes. Mitch could see the pleasure she took in their company, the careful concerned way she rushed to help her mother, sparing her unnecessary labor.

And later, as they sat around singing old songs, it was

Melanie who played for them. Tunes that Mitch recognized from his grandfather's era flowed easily through her fingers as they rippled lovingly over the notes, her voice blending in with a rich, deep harmony.

They're like her family, he thought. *That's why she works with old people. A big, happy family that cares and shares their lives with each other.*

It was something he'd never known and always thought he wanted. It was something he intended to find out more about, Mitch decided firmly.

With the help of Miss Melanie Stewart, of course.

Chapter Three

Once his knee had healed, the pain of embarrassment had passed and he'd purchased a new pair of pants, Mitch asked Melanie out for dinner. Chinese food. They sat across from one another in one of the local cafés without speaking as they waited for their meal of stir-fried Chinese vegetables and the deep-fried shrimp he'd insisted on. He figured Melanie could think of nothing to say—unlike their past encounter. Her fingers rolled the edge of her napkin. She took a sip of water.

"I like your dress." Mitch's low voice cut into her thoughts. His magnetic dark eyes gleamed in appreciation at the sweetheart neckline and fitted waist. "Green is certainly your color. That swimsuit was a knockout on you."

Blushing profusely, Melanie thanked him before hurrying to change the topic. "Have you heard anything from the contest people yet?" she asked.

Once more that wicked grin flashed at her, and once more her pulse started that rat-tatting that Mitchel Stewart always seemed to cause.

"Nope, not a word. Maybe they'll decide not to award it or to draw again. How did you enter?"

"I don't know." She laughed—that light, tinkling sound

he had come to associate with her. Shrugging, she confessed, "I don't even eat the stuff."

"What?" He gave an exaggerated gasp before he admitted, "Me, neither." His forehead was furrowed in thought. "How do you suppose they got our names, then?"

Melanie blushed again, and he wondered why. Gazing at her hands, she explained.

"A few months ago I was really down. One of our residents had died unexpectedly, and I...I was sort of depressed." Her green eyes were filled with sadness as she stared ahead. "Mrs. Peters was so lonely, you see. Her kids never came to see her except on a duty visit at Christmas that lasted all of five minutes. She needed to talk to them and feel that they still cared." Melanie heard her own voice harden.

"Apparently, all they needed was the check she always handed out. When she died, I phoned them and they were there in thirty minutes. Yet when she had been asking to see them only one week earlier, no one had the time to get away." Melanie waved across the table as she tried to help him understand.

"I remember the last thing she said to me. She wanted to buy a new dress," she told him sadly. Mitch's warm brown hand was wrapped around her clenched fingers. She glanced at him sadly. "She got her dress, but it was too late."

They sat there quietly eating the delicious food. Mitch had done nothing more than listen, but somehow his quiet strength helped, and after a minute or two she continued.

"Anyway, I was working with Mrs. Rivers by then and she was entering these contests. I thought, why not throw in a few of my own entries. Maybe a windfall of some kind could take some of the sting away and provide at least some of the essential equipment that so many need." She grinned self-deprecatingly. "That's been a hobbyhorse of mine for a while now."

"Why don't your pals just buy what they need? Surely some have money?"

Mitch's question was legitimate, and she tried to explain

the ways of those greedy families she had become familiar with.

"Well, many of them do have some assets when they enter the residence and they do get the help they need, as well as visits from caring families. But some of these folks are not mobile, and it's difficult for them to do their banking. Usually the family takes it over, and when they see how expensive it is to look after Grandma or Grandpa, many begin to resent every dime they lose."

"But the money isn't theirs," Mitch protested indignantly.

"I know, but when you begin to think of something as part of your inheritance…" Her voice died away. "Mr. Harcourt is one of those fellows who is quite capable of operating a motorized cart. It would get him out of the residence and to coffee with his friends. He's not wealthy and his family think it's a silly, wasteful expenditure, and so he sits, day after day, gradually growing more depressed."

The conversation had become dull and gloomy, and Melanie suddenly felt guilty for dumping all her problems on him.

"I'm sorry. This isn't a very happy subject, and I tend to harp." She smiled at him, trying to lift the tension. "Exactly what kind of law do you practice?"

He knew she was trying to lighten the atmosphere, and he went along with it. "Corporate. Litigations are my preference, although I do agreements for sale, probate wills, boring stuff like that." He grinned that sexy smile again, and Melanie felt her spirits lift.

"Do you ever practice family law?" Her inquiry was innocent enough, but his reaction was totally unexpected.

"No." Curt and abrupt, his answer did not encourage speculation.

"I'm sorry. I didn't mean…"

His charming smile was once again in place, a facade he hid behind, Melanie suddenly realized.

"I hate that end of the business," he told her. "Men and women who swore to love each other suddenly become bitter enemies, each trying to outdo the other in nastiness. Pulling children's lives apart so they can hurt each other.'' He shook his dark head. ''I won't be part of that.''

Melanie heard the underlying hurt and suspected that Mitch had been a product of just such a scenario, perhaps as a small child. He wasn't talking about it.

''Don't you want to get married yourself? Have a family someday?'' She studied him curiously, noting the flush on his high cheekbones.

''No. Well, yeah. Maybe. I'm not really the type.'' The words spilled out helter-skelter, and he frowned. ''If I ever did, I'd go into it with a no-escape clause. So far I haven't found anyone I want to be tied up that tightly with. What about you?''

''I always thought love and marriage would just happen, but lately work takes up more and more of my time, and truthfully, I just don't know how I could fit a family in with that.'' She grimaced. ''Those residents are important to me. I don't know if I could give them all up for a mere man.'' She grinned teasingly.

''We're not going into that man thing again, are we?'' He groaned. ''I already apologized three thousand times.''

''And that's not nearly enough.'' She smiled.

''You should talk! You called me out of shape, remember?''

''And?'' She raised one eyebrow meaningfully. ''If the shoe fits…''

''Time to go,'' he muttered, shaking his head. ''Before war breaks out.''

Melanie gratefully picked up her purse and moved to the door. She felt like a liar, because she knew she'd give up her so-called career in a minute for a loving husband and the warmth and comfort of a family of her own.

As they strolled along the street, Mitch took her hand in his and drew it through his arm.

''I think we'll make good neighbors.'' He grinned at her. ''The really neighborly thing to do would be to invite me in for coffee.''

The hint was hard to miss, and surprisingly enough, she didn't want to bid Mitch good-night just yet.

"Well, since you did take me out for dinner, I suppose it is the least I can do." Melanie deliberately made the invitation as unappealing as possible, pretty sure he would jump at it. She didn't want to seem too eager, after all!

They sat among the flickering candles on her patio, sipping the rich Colombian brew Melanie favored. In the dark, it seemed easier to talk.

"My mother often let me stay up in the summer and have chocolate milk on the porch. This reminds me of those times." Her voice was soft and filled with memories, and Mitch seemed loath to break the spell of quiet contentment.

"She probably wished I'd go to bed, but she and Hope and Faith never tried to talk me out of my daydreams. I will always be thankful for their love and care. I guess that's why I choose to work where I do." She smiled happily. "Seniors have so much life and love and knowledge to contribute, if only someone would take the time to listen."

"You were lucky," he told her. That hard tone had frozen the emotion in his rumbly voice. "Some kids never get the chance to experience any of that."

"But you had your grandfather. Didn't you ever come visit?" Melanie searched her mind, trying to remember Mitch from some foggy distant encounter.

"Not very often. We lived too far away, and my parents couldn't afford it. Gramps came to visit us once or twice a year for a week or so, but that's all. After I was on my own, I'd come out as often as I could get away. We kind of developed a bond then."

Melanie could tell the subject was closed, but she longed to ask him about his childhood, his parents, his background. One minute he was so charming and friendly, and the next he had closed up like a clam, cold and hard.

Soft music flowed on the evening air as someone on another patio below them enjoyed the cool evening air.

"Do you dance?" he asked suddenly.

Melanie stuttered over her answer. "Not very well. I, well, it's been ages, and…"

Tall and dark in his denim shirt and pants, he stood before her. She tipped her head to look at him.

"Don't tell me you're uncoordinated, Melanie, or I will be forced to make some remark that will draw the battle lines between us. Again. May I have this dance?" he asked. His eyes glinted in the candlelight. "I have to get my exercise, you know." And then Mitch tugged her gently from her chair without waiting for a response. "Here, put your arms around me like this."

Melanie let Mitch push her bare arms around his neck and then stood silent while he wrapped his around her slender waist. She was nervous and sure he knew it.

"No fancy moves," he reassured her. "Just swaying to the music."

They swayed gently, moving slowly to the music. As he held, she was aware of his warmth and strength, the spicy scent of his cologne and the momentary brush of his beard-roughened cheek on her own. Her skirt swished around her legs as his foot grazed hers. It was wonderful and exciting, and yet they did nothing but move leisurely around the tiny terrace.

She was relaxed, Mitch knew as he inched one hand a fraction lower on her hip. It felt so good to hold her like this, close but not too close, her soft presence filling the night air. His chin fit perfectly on top of her head, and he could just catch the soft, intriguing scent of her perfume. Against his neck, her silky hair caressed and enticed him. He bent his head and pressed the tiniest kiss to the soft skin of her collarbone.

Melanie Stewart was every inch a woman, soft and curvy, yet caring and concerned. She interested him. No one had ever said the things she had and been allowed to get away with it, and yet this fiery woman continued to hold his attention.

"What did you think of Hope's problem?" he asked finally, not wanting to break the companionable silence but needing to bring some reality into the evening.

"I don't know what to think. I'm afraid for her."

"Afraid?" He frowned. "For heaven's sake, why?"

Her finger absently played with the hair that just touched his collar as she moved slowly with him. Her touch bothered him, sending electric currents through his blood.

"Melanie?"

"She's waited so long. She'd almost let herself forget him. Did you know Hope has gone out with your grandfather a few times?"

Mitch jerked backward, staring at her in surprise. Suddenly, the little scene at Charity's made sense.

"You mean she's falling in love with him?" He frowned.

"I don't know, but something was happening between them. She was finally beginning to let go of the past and consider the future." Melanie heaved a sigh. "And now this."

"Makes you wonder who's in control of the universe, doesn't it?" he laughed.

"Oh, I know that God's in control," she told him seriously. "And whatever He has planned is more wonderful than any-thing we could ever imagine. It's just hard to understand right now."

"I never thought of God as personally interested in our lives," Mitch murmured. "I always think of Him as some far-off entity. In heaven, I guess." He shrugged.

Melanie smiled knowingly. "Well, I'm certain He's there, but He's also here with us, guiding us through our daily lives. I just have to keep praying that Hope won't be too badly hurt by all this."

She snuggled her head against his shoulder, and Mitch stared at the stars. Melanie Stewart made him think of all those things he wanted but could never have. Things like a wife, a home of his own, a family. Things he had no business dreaming about.

Pulling her a little closer, he guided her carefully across

the patio as the music died away. His left hand settled on her waist, and he tortured himself with the dream of someday holding someone who was special to him in just this way. In his ear there was a soft whisper.

"What?" he asked, missing the soft words.

"You move that hand any lower and you are in trouble."

Privately, Mitch thought he was in trouble anyway, but he decided to change strategies. His mouth touched hers softly in a whisper of a kiss that was over before it began. When she kissed him back, he followed the curve of her jaw with a tiny, feather-light brush of his mouth. His nose nuzzled the sensitive spot under one ear. That brought a tiny sigh from her. Then she edged away, pressing her palms gently against his chest.

"Thank you for a very nice evening." Her soft voice was primly correct, and he almost burst out laughing.

Nice? Talk about a nonresponse.

"You're more than welcome. And thank you for coming to dinner." He grinned at her, unabashed at the color flooding her face.

Bending, he pressed a kiss to her soft, pink mouth and one on a tiny freckle just below her eye. Then he whispered in her ear, "I enjoyed it. All of it."

When her face colored again, he grinned smugly. "You do blush a lot," he teased her. Then, lest he hurt her feelings, he told her the truth. "I like it on you."

They walked to the door side by side, saying nothing, both feeling the tension of the moment. At the door Mitch took her oval face in his hands and rubbed his thumb along her lips.

"Can we share dinner again?"

Waves of feeling swamped her, and Melanie was unable to think straight. A noncommittal answer, that was the best.

"Maybe," she temporized, unsure of anything but her surging heartbeat. "I don't know if I'll be able to afford it if I don't win that contest. You eat a lot."

He grinned. "Save your allowance then, because I'm going

to hold you to it," he promised. Mitch pressed one last kiss to her mouth. Then, sighing, he dragged himself away.

"Good night," he whispered, and pulled the door closed behind his tall figure.

"Good night," Melanie answered to no one at all. One slim hand touched her lips in wonder.

In a trance she moved through her nightly rituals, half dazed. Mitchel Stewart didn't seem nearly as irritating as he had two weeks ago. Nor as angry.

What Melanie recalled was the way his bad-boy looks had made her heart thump. And the black lock of hair that tumbled across his forehead. And his lazy blue eyes with their hidden flames. And the soft, caring touch of his hands.

Yawning widely, Melanie plumped her pillow and promptly fell asleep dreaming of Mitchel Stewart.

"You think this fellow is this Jean guy? The same one that Hope Langford was engaged to?" Mitch stared at his grandfather in dismay.

"Not only do I think he is the one, I'm pretty sure he plans to marry someone else. I've had someone looking into things for me. On the Q.T. of course." Harry Conroy rubbed his hand wearily across his stubbled cheek. "I'm stumped, laddie. I dursn't tell Hope about this. She's got her heart set on a reunion, and if this guy is what he seems, that isn't going to happen."

"What's his name?" Mitch asked curiously, flipping through the reports covering his grandfather's desk. "And where's he been for the past thirty years? Why didn't he let her know he was alive so she could move on?"

"I don't know, son. Those are all good questions that I'd like to ask the man myself. You don't go abandoning a woman like Hope without a darned good reason. Leave those papers be!" Harry sounded furious, and Mitch studied him with new eyes.

"You're pretty fond of Miss Langford, aren't you, Gramps?" he asked quietly.

"Fond of her? I've spent longer than I care to think about trying to get close to the woman. But she has this barrier she always puts up. Won't let people get too close. Leastways, not me." He frowned.

Harry Conroy peered at his grandson. Over the years he'd gained a pretty good knowledge of human nature, and he used it to good advantage now.

"I think you're interested in Charity's daughter, too. Aren't you, boy?" The faded gray eyes sparkled with hidden knowledge. "I was afraid it would never happen," he declared happily.

"It hasn't," Mitch assured him quietly. "I'm not looking to get married, Gramps. You know that. Neither is she. Sure, I like Melanie. She's sharp and witty."

"Not too hard to look at, either," his grandfather added.

"No, she isn't," Mitch agreed with a grin. "But she's dedicated to her career as much as I am to mine."

Harry snorted. "Hogwash," he bellowed with disgust. "You're still thinking about your parents, aren't you, Mitch?" He shook his head. "Those two didn't have a marriage, they had a battle zone. That's not the way it's supposed to work, boy."

"From what I saw at Mercer, Lloyd and Jones, that's the way it usually works," Mitch told him soberly.

"I knew you didn't like Chicago, Mitch, but I always thought you liked your work."

"I hated my work there," Mitch said hoarsely. "Bottom man on the pole wasn't the problem. I had to take whatever they assigned, and it was always family court." He shuddered at the memory. "I still see the looks in the kids' eyes, Gramps. So tired. And scared."

"Well, I'm proud of you for getting yourself out of there, son." Harry wiped a tear away. "It's a sad thing to see a family torn apart, that's for sure. But it doesn't have to happen to you. All marriages aren't bad. Your gran and I shared some pretty happy years." Harry stared across his desk, his eyes focused on some memory Mitch couldn't share.

"You never knew her, Mitch, but she was the kindest, gentlest woman God ever created."

"Sort of like Hope, you mean?" Mitch watched, stunned, as his grandfather's head reared back and his round belly shook with laughter.

"Good heavens, no! Hope is nothing like your grandmother. If she thinks I deserve it, she can tear a strip off me. Most times, it serves me right." He chuckled.

"Mom must have taken after your Anna, then." When Harry frowned, Mitch rushed to make his meaning clear. "You know what Dad was like, Gramps. He never had a decent word to say to anyone, Mom included. Most of the time he was screaming vile things at her. And she took it all without telling him off. Not once as long as I hung around can I remember a time when she would retaliate."

"No, she wouldn't have," Harry whispered sadly. "That was our fault. Anna and I knew your ma saw the court cases come and go, and we were afraid she would learn that retribution often paid. So we taught her that fighting back never solved anything." He stared at the picture of the young laughing girl on his desk. "I regret that now."

"There's no point in regrets, Gramps." Mitch smiled bitterly. "We can only learn from the past, and what I learned from my old man and his successors is that marriage tears people up."

"I'm sorry 'bout that, too, my boy," Harry whispered as the door slammed behind his grandson. "Because I think marriage is the best darn institution God ever invented."

He sat staring at his oak-lined office for a long moment before rousing himself to action.

"I wonder," he murmured, shrugging into his black robes for the last session of the day. He pressed the newfangled speed dial his secretary had shown him how to use.

"Hello, Hope? I need to talk to you about something." He waited for her response, a smile curving his lips. "I thought maybe we could go for a picnic. Haven't had one of those in years."

When she started to protest he cut her off.

"I'm due in court now, my dear. Let's just plan to leave around six. I'll pick you up. Wear pants." Harry hung up the phone with a huge smile on his round face.

Yes, siree, this was going to be an interesting date!

"Jessica, I cannot afford to reprimand you again. This is the last time." Melanie watched as the young woman's face turned sullen.

"But, Melanie, Mrs. Lindstrom was—"

"I cannot condone your actions regardless of what our residents do or say." She cut her trainee off. "Your treatment of Mrs. Lindstrom was callous and disrespectful, and we do not allow that here." She searched Jessica's pretty face for some sign of remorse. "Do you understand what I'm saying?"

"I guess so." The voice was petulant.

Melanie refused to allow herself any softening. The bullying tactics she had just witnessed were unforgivable.

"I'll make it perfectly clear, then, so that we both understand the way things go at Sunset." She waited until Jessica's sullen blue gaze met hers and then she laid down the law.

"This is your last warning, Jessica. Our residents are seniors, yes, and sometimes they need help. But force will not be used on anyone unless he or she is a danger to themselves or someone else. Okay?"

"But she was pulling my hair! Don't I have any rights?"

Melanie sighed, knowing the teenager would have to be relocated.

"Jessica, please. You were forcing her into the bath. She hates water. She's afraid."

"Well, how was I s'posed to know that?" The young woman had shifted from cranky to defiant, her lip curling with disgust. Suddenly, Melanie was tired of the whole thing.

"I guess you would actually have to talk to her, like a real person, and then let her talk back to find it out," she answered acidly, unwilling to go over the same material again.

Melanie knew she was venting some of her foul mood on the trainee, but Jessica deserved it. She would have dumped on Mitchel Stewart, too, if he had been around. He had been at the bottom of a lot of her problems lately!

She waved Jessica away tiredly as she raked a hand through her disheveled curls. Her secretary walked in with a cup of coffee and a commiserating smile.

"What happened to decency and courtesy, Bridget?" She sipped a mouthful of the refreshing brew and closed her eyes. When there was no response, Melanie opened them again. The woman just kept watching her. What now? she wondered.

"I'm sorry, Mel, but Mr. Northrup is slipping away fast. Hospital phoned to say you should come over if you want to talk to him once more."

Melanie got up immediately and moved to the door. Jonathan Northrup had been at Sunset even longer than she had. He had been her inspiration and hope for so long. It would be hard to say goodbye. The only consolation was that they both knew they'd meet again in heaven. Still, it would be tough. She straightened her backbone and strode down the hall, not really hearing Bridget's voice as she gathered her thoughts.

"Mel, there's some fellow from Papa John's Peanut Butter wants to see you immediately. He's at the front desk."

The last few words were hollered at Melanie's disappearing figure. She need not have bothered, Bridget thought. She knew Melanie Stewart had her priorities straight. And Jonathan Northrup was certainly more important than some silly contest!

Half an hour later, Melanie closed the big hospital door. He was gone. Serene to the end, Jonathan had given her his final bit of advice.

"You have to get out and live, my dear. Old folks are selfish and depressing sometimes, and much as we enjoy all your efforts, you have to look after yourself. One day you'll find a man who, if you let him, can give you so much." He had stopped for a painful, wheezing breath. "Make sure you

have enough left of yourself to give back. That's all I ask."
His frail, veined hand had clasped hers one last time.

"Enjoy your life, my dear. You've given me so much happiness. See you in heaven."

"Yes, in heaven." A tear rolled down her cheek, but Melanie dashed it away angrily. She would not cry. Jonathan wouldn't have wanted it.

A deep voice spoke from behind her left shoulder.

"Are you all right, Melanie?"

Turning, Melanie found Mitch's tall, elegantly dressed figure behind her. He looked very handsome in his navy blue pinstriped suit, but it was his eyes that drew her. Dark and searching, they probed deep within, sharing her sorrow.

"He was someone special, wasn't he?" he asked softly as his arm moved across her shoulder. His hand was gently soothing on her back, and suddenly Melanie gave way.

Turning into his arms, she put her head on his shoulder and bawled like a baby.

"Oh, Mitch. He was my best friend."

He let her cry out her loss and feelings without saying anything. And as she cried, Melanie felt the stress and sadness slowly drain away.

"Thanks," she murmured, accepting the snowy white handkerchief he pulled from his pocket to wipe her eyes. She knew she had smudged her mascara, and her eyes must look like a raccoon's, but Mitch never said a word. Gently, he took the fabric from her and completed the cleanup himself before stuffing the square into his pocket.

Then he tipped her face to look at his.

"Have you time for a coffee?" he asked. "I need to talk to you."

His voice was so serious that Melanie stared at him for a minute before nodding.

"I suppose I can. I'll just tell Bridget I'll be in the cafeteria."

"Actually, I thought maybe we could go outside for some

privacy.'' He pointed to a carafe and two cups. ''And she already knows.''

Shrugging, Melanie accepted his outstretched hand and walked to the patio that nestled on a tiny bit of green lawn between the hospital and the nursing home. There were lounge chairs spread around, and she sank gratefully into one in the sun. She needed the warm sunshine and light to banish her gloomy feelings.

When Mitch handed her the steaming cup, his fingers brushed hers, and Melanie felt the sparks his touch always caused in her body. She watched as his intelligent blue eyes studied her face carefully before he sank into a chair.

''Okay,'' he began, dark eyes probing hers. ''I know my timing stinks, but I guess the best way to tell you this is to just get it over with.''

Melanie watched his chest expand as he sucked in a lungful of air. A wave of foreboding hung over her. What now, she wondered.

He began.

''A rep from Papa John's was in to the office to see me today.'' His blue eyes bored into her. ''From what I understand, they were also here to see you,'' he told her sourly. ''Apparently they have come to some decision regarding their grand prize.'' Mitch's face was flushed, and he fidgeted in his chair uncomfortably.

''Say it,'' she ordered, gripping the armrests. When he didn't speak, she answered for herself. ''I don't win, do I?''

''Melanie, just listen to me for—''

She ignored his pleading. All her grand ideas, all her plans. She felt her dreams dissolving around her.

''I thought it was probably too good to be true. After all, I don't even use their product. How could I possibly endorse it?'' She turned to him, eyes glittering. ''That's it, isn't it?''

''Melanie, can you be quiet for once?'' The usually calm, deep voice was hard and strident. ''Just let me speak, would you?''

Pursing her lips, Melanie leaned back and folded her arms

across her chest. Her soft curls flopped across her cheek, but she was too angry to notice.

Mitch, however, noticed. He noticed only too well.

Thoughts of their evening together flooded his mind until he could almost feel her in his arms, feel her silky hair against his cheek, taste her soft mouth.

Shaking his head sharply, Mitch ignored the heat that was building in his brain and forced himself to concentrate on getting this right. It would not be easy.

"Melanie, they have both our entries now. And the home address you put on yours seems to be my apartment. Number 108. The winner lives at number 108." He waited for her to assimilate the information. When she said nothing, he tried again.

"I said—"

She stopped him immediately.

"I'm not a child, Mitch. I know what it means. It means I don't win, right?"

Her reddish gold head was tilted to the sun. As he watched, a single tear trickled from the corner of her eye.

"Not exactly," he told her.

She studied him curiously, intrigued by his mysterious manner. When he said nothing, she punched him lightly on the shoulder.

"Explain." She gave the command with all the imperious demands of royalty. He smiled at her dictatorial tone.

"I, er, I kind of told them that we lived in the same building. That, uh, we were roommates. Well, almost."

Mitchel Stewart had never seen anyone move that fast. In microseconds she was standing over him, hands on her hips as she glared at him.

"You...you fibber! You cheat! You liar!" Then she stopped. Her huge green eyes blinked twice before crinkling in puzzlement. "Why?"

"It seems that my contest entry has no apartment number on it. My name, however, is on the lease for apartment 108."

"And?" Melanie was completely puzzled by his strange attitude.

"Well, your name does not appear on any lease. Just Shawna's." He met her glittering gaze squarely. "And there is no phone number listed in your name."

"I know that. I only moved in after another of her roommates was married. We share the phone bill." It was clear to Mitch that Melanie didn't understand what he was telling her.

"But your entry says you live in my apartment. If you are not in fact living in apartment 108, your entry is null and void because you have misrepresented yourself."

He watched her absorb the information. Her small hands rested idly on his shoulders as she thought.

"How do you know this?" she demanded.

"I'm a lawyer, remember? Corporate law. Well," he said smugly, "I asked this rep guy for a copy of their contest rules."

He waited for her approval. In vain. Melanie merely glared at him. "And?"

"They must award the prize if we can both be shown to be living in apartment 108." As dismay flooded her beautiful face, Mitch quickly changed his wording. "That is, if you and I are both living in apartment 108."

He was triumphantly pleased with himself. Mitchel had made it his business to find out about Melanie Stewart in the past few days, and he could understand how badly she needed that money. Sunset Retirement Home was an underfunded, overworked nursing home that was following the patterns of business all over the world by cutting back.

Several of his golfing buddies had relayed horror stories about the place before Melanie had taken over, and Mitchel found out she was well respected in her field. The simple, humanitarian changes she had wrought in her tenure as director of care had resulted in Sunset becoming one of the choice locations for those requiring the services they provided.

At the same time, he had watched her surreptitiously with

a number of her clients. Melanie was unfailingly polite and courteous with everyone, but her seniors seemed her closest friends. Even Mrs. Strange had spoken glowingly of Melanie's special interest in each resident's needs.

"Don't you see?" he demanded, anxious for her to understand his contribution in all this. "If you move some of your stuff to my spare room and stay there for a few nights, they'll know you're living there, and you'll get your share of the money."

She looked as if he had hit her with a Mack truck, Mitch decided. The color was coming back to her face, but he didn't think that was a good sign. Mostly due to the sharp fingernails digging into his shoulder blades.

He lifted her hands away, careful to keep the lethal pink nails far from his eyes. She looked steamed, and with her temper, she would probably scratch his eyes out.

"Let go of me, you lecherous, manipulating, overbearing..." As the stream of vitriolic descriptives flowed from her soft peach lips, Mitch twisted her arms behind her back.

He disliked using force, but he wanted to preserve the skin on his face, as well. He let her blow off steam, but when she had not stopped a few moments later, his temper peaked.

Using the method he most favored, Mitch pulled her stiff, unyielding body close and pressed his lips against hers, stemming the tide of outrage. And he kept kissing her even when she stopped fighting him. Only when she finally started kissing him back did he pull away.

Women! Why didn't he smarten up? Surely after Sam's dirty tricks, he should be prepared for the way they operated.

"Listen, Ms. Stewart. I don't need a roommate so badly that I would go to these extremes. I've told you before, I don't intend to get married. Not now. Maybe not ever."

Mitch let go of her arms and stood back, furious that he had allowed himself to become so involved in someone else's affairs. That's what he got for trying to help!

"You know," he added, upset with himself for the stupid idea that had streaked into his head an hour ago, "I can use twenty-five grand for a few little schemes of my own. You're not the only person who has things to do, people you want to help out. And if you back out now, they will redraw the names.'' Mitch's dark eyes glared at her accusingly. "I'll lose out altogether because of your mistake." He told himself to calm down. Useless.

"I know how much you want that money. So do I. And this is the only way I could think of for you to share in it." Turning, he strode away, stopping only to add, "Sorry I interfered in your life," before yanking the door open and walking through it.

Melanie sank into the deck chair, her knees rubbery. Shocked, confused, dazed. Life was a perplexing whirl, and she wasn't sure of anything anymore. He had been trying to help, in a strange, rather unusual way. He wanted her to have the money, or at least some of it. But there was no way she was moving in with the guy. Get real!

"You're still there, directing me, aren't You, Lord?" she murmured brokenly. "Please give a sign. You know how much we need that money."

Glancing at her watch, Melanie decided that nothing made sense anymore and got up to return to work. As she gathered the cups and thermos, she permitted a tiny smile to tilt the corners of her mouth. Actually, Mitchel Stewart was kind of sweet. In a bossy, rude sort of way.

"He invited her to move in with him?" Hope fumed. Her eyes were wide open. "What a horrible young man!"

"He's not horrible at all," Charity murmured, threading the wool through her knitting machine. "Dear Mitchel was just trying to help. In a bizarre, unorthodox sort of way." She slid the carriage back and forth a few times experimentally and then began an even, steady rhythm that soon produced a width of white lacy fabric.

"Melanie was so hurt when her mother abandoned her. It took ages, remember, to get her to open up. That terrible childhood should have toughened her up, but instead she became more withdrawn.'' Charity smiled in remembrance. ''My Melanie was the child who always needed an extra hug or a few extra words of praise.''

''I remember,'' Hope murmured. ''She'd work so hard in school, doing far more than was necessary for any project I assigned.'' Her eyes stared into the past. ''She was always the one who lent a helping hand, stuck up for the little kid being bullied.''

Charity nodded. ''It was almost as if she was too insecure and afraid to believe in the love that Peter and I offered. When he died, I think she felt it was her fault for leaning on him so much.''

''Well, I want her to be happy,'' Hope added stoutly. ''But I don't want her to be hurt. And Mitchel will do that. He's had a terrible childhood, you know. Harry told me some of it.'' She filled them in on the few details she knew. ''Melanie needs someone strong with a solid background. Someone she can lean on. Not somebody with problems of his own!''

''I don't know why you're so concerned, Hope.'' Charity smiled as she started another color. ''Melanie is a good girl. She wouldn't allow anything untoward to happen. And they would only be sharing the kitchen.''

Hopes eyes were huge with disbelief.

''You mean you *condone* this crazy idea?'' She gasped. ''But you're her mother.''

''I know that, dear. And I'm not saying I condone anything. I have only her good at heart. But Melanie is too self-contained. She's always pushing everyone but her seniors away. She's missing out on the best parts of life, and I want her to find happiness with someone her own age.'' She shrugged. ''Maybe if she and Mitch do share an apartment, she'll realize the world is full of more than grumpy old men. It does have two bedrooms, you know.'' Charity's warm brown eyes twinkled. She delighted in her friend's shocked look.

''Oh, my,'' Faith breathed, her emerald green eyes glowing with excitement. ''And wouldn't it be romantic. Why, they could have a candlelight dinner without the whole town knowing about it." She stared into space, lost in a daydream.

"Well," Hope said, "I'm ashamed of you, Charity Flowerday. And there's no way I'm going to allow Melanie's good reputation to be soiled by such a tawdry situation. I'm going to do my duty by the girl." She picked up her purse and swept regally through the front door, the light of battle gleaming in the depths of her blue eyes. "We'll just see about this…arrangement," she muttered furiously.

When Judge Harry Conroy showed up promptly at six o'clock, Hope was ready for him. She wore a pair of navy slacks and a white blouse with a navy and white cardigan over her shoulders. She could barely control her temper as she waited for Harry to open her car door and her greeting wasn't as welcoming as it could have been.

"Is something the matter, Hope?" he asked at last. He started the car and pulled away from her house, then glanced at her curiously. "I mean, have you heard more about Jean or something?"

"Good heavenly days, no," she snapped irritably. "I hadn't even thought about that. Don't have time." She turned to face him angrily. "Charity is set on sending her daughter traveling down the path of destruction, and I intend to see that she doesn't do it."

"Charity is?" the judge murmured, puzzled. "But I thought…well, never mind that. What's Charity done now?"

"It's all because of that awful grandson of yours," Hope complained. "He flies into town, all handsome and debonair, and sweeps the girl off her feet."

"So you think he's handsome, do you?" Judge Conroy's eyes twinkled.

"Of course he's handsome," Hope spluttered. "You know very well he takes after you, Harry, and you were a heartbreaker at that age. You still are."

"Do tell," Harry murmured with a smile of appreciation, allowing himself to preen.

"But you had some scruples. You would never have up and asked a woman to live with you so cold-bloodedly."

Judge Conroy absently turned down the dirt road that led to the park beside the river where he'd courted his wife years ago. It wasn't much of a river now, of course. And he wasn't as young as he once was. But oh, my, things did sound promising!

"Mitch has asked someone to live with him?" he repeated softly. "That's strange. I didn't think the boy had any intention of getting married."

"He doesn't," Hope shrieked in exasperation. "He wants her to live in sin with him."

The judge stared at her as if she'd lost her marbles, sending Hope's blood pressure soaring.

"I hardly think Mitch would suggest—"

"Oh, yes, he would," she contradicted him. "I was visiting Nettie Rivers. We were sitting in her room, right by the window, and I distinctly heard him ask Melanie to move in with him." She slammed the door of the car and stomped to a clearing beside a tiny waterfall. "Well, I'm not having it," she spluttered, sinking down onto the blanket Harry spread. "Do you hear me?"

"Yes, dear," he murmured, trying to understand. It didn't sound at all like Mitch, but then the boy did have a mind of his own. "I'll talk to him," he promised, patting her hand commiseratingly.

"It won't do any good," Hope murmured, squeezing his hand gently. "But thank you. No, Charity's determined to go along with it all. She thinks Melanie needs to see what she's missing, working with old people all the time."

"Perhaps she's right about that, Hope. She is the girl's mother, after all. Charity wants to see Melanie happily married with her own children. So do I, for that matter." He stared at her. "Let's pray about it, dear. God can do anything. He can certainly handle this."

They bowed their heads, and Judge Conroy murmured a

short petition, asking for guidance and help for their friends and relatives.

"Do you feel better now, dear?" he asked, after they'd finished the low-fat potato salad, cold sliced chicken sandwiches with tomato, lettuce and spicy mustard. For dessert, there was fruit salad and hot, fragrant herbal tea.

"A little," Hope conceded. She stared into the woods. "I think I shall keep my eye on that situation. Perhaps I can be of help."

"But won't you be busy contacting the authorities about Jean?" he asked softly, knowing it wouldn't hurt her to discuss her past love. To the judge's immense surprise, Hope shook her head.

"No," she told him firmly. "I've decided to turn that over to the Lord. Jean has been gone for a long time. It's very doubtful that he's survived at all, but if, for some strange reason, he turns up alive, I'll be happy and I'll learn to deal with it. Somehow."

"What are you going to do?" Harry asked with a frown.

"Exactly what I've been doing for the past twenty-five years," Hope told him with a smile. "Take each day as it comes and plan on making it the best yet."

"Good," he agreed after a moment. "And I'll be here to share them with you."

"You have been for a long time now," she murmured, staring at his bald head as if she hadn't noticed it before. "We've had some good times, haven't we, Harry? You and Anna and I. She was my very best friend, you know. I always felt as if she was my sister."

Harry frowned.

"Well, I don't feel like your brother," he muttered. To his delight she giggled, leaning nearer to kiss him on one cheek.

"You don't look like him, either," she assured him, laughing. She jumped to her feet and tugged his arm. "Come on, lazybones. I let you feed me all that delicious food. The least you can do is help me walk it off."

"All right," he agreed meekly. "But I carefully planned a

low-fat meal, just as you prefer. You know that. As long as we just walk. I'm too old for anything else.''

Hope's blue eyes twinkled with mischief.

''Really?'' she asked. ''That's too bad.''

Harry let her lead him down the path, resisting an urge to kiss her then and there. But no, he decided. He'd bide his time. They were just beginning to get closer, and she was only starting to come to terms with the possibility of Jean's reappearance. Everything looked positive, but he'd keep mentioning things to the Lord, just the same. A little heavenly guidance couldn't hurt, he decided, hearing Hope's sudden burst of laughter.

Chapter Four

"Have a nice day, folks. Enjoy that sun."

Mitchel Edward Stewart was not having a *nice* day, despite the radio announcer's bland wish. He had risen with a splitting headache on his first day off in weeks. The coffeemaker had refused to cooperate, and his doughnut supply was tapped out.

It should have been simple. Everything was so carefully planned. He would pick up some supplies from downtown and then he was heading out for a day at the beach. Sun, sand and surf, that's what he needed. Maybe even a cold root beer.

Sighing, he stared balefully at his bright red sports car once more. Apparently, some things were not to be. The expensive engine refused to respond to his orders, and since anything under the hood of an automobile gave him hives, Mitch had called the shop.

"Nope, can't touch it today." The youngster's voice was less than helpful. At least he thought it was. You could barely hear over the crashing of some heavy metal band in the background.

"Pardon?"

"No can do, dude."

"And why is that?" Mitchel had forced a tight rein of control on his temper and prayed for strength. Impudent little brat!

"Mechanic's out sick. Have a good one!" With a click, the kid had hung up on him, leaving Mitchel to bite out a particularly choice epithet that divulged his irritation with the world in general.

"Something I said?"

He groaned, recognizing her voice immediately. Why now, why today? He turned to face Miss Melanie Stewart, a flush of red hinting at his turmoil.

"Hi." There. Let her make something of that.

"Car problems?"

His reply was curt and succinct. "Yeah."

"Can I look?"

He stared at her. "Why?"

Green eyes glared at him as she slapped her hands on her hips. "Gee, I don't know. I thought I could steal a few spark plugs or maybe even the air filter."

Whew, talk about cranky! Without a word Mitch popped the hood and watched Melanie lean over to peer inside. His stomach dropped as his gaze followed her long legs to the white cuffed shorts that covered her shapely bottom. A tiny bit of skin peeked out between her waistline and the cropped red T-shirt she wore. He couldn't stop staring.

"Hmm, distributor cap's shot." She turned her head to glance at him. "You need a mechanic."

"Thank you for your assistance, Miss Stewart," he said sarcastically. "I have already phoned one. He's out sick." Butter wouldn't melt in her mouth, he thought grumpily.

She shrugged and slammed the hood shut. Fortunately, she missed his knuckles by at least a millimeter.

"Okay, looks like you've got it covered."

He frowned. Was that supposed to mean something?

"Want a lift?" she offered, bending to pick up a large woven bag and a small cooler. "I'm going to the beach, but I could drop you somewhere."

Like in the river, he mused, well aware of her quick temper. Mitch decided he should not look a gift horse, or a gorgeous woman, in the mouth. Enough things had gone wrong today. Here was opportunity. Opportunity didn't knock that often. He shouldn't turn it down. Besides, she might invite him to share whatever was in that cooler, and he didn't want to miss out on a decent meal.

Mitch assembled his features into his best hangdog look and muttered, "Well, I was going there, too, but now, with no wheels…" He asked deferentially, "Are you sure it would be okay?"

To his delight, she burst out laughing, her green eyes glinting in the sunshine. Seconds later they were hidden behind huge round sunglasses.

"You don't do humble really well." She giggled. "In fact, it's downright pathetic." She waved. "But I'll take pity on you anyway. Come on. You can hitch with me for today."

Mitch watched the animation flood her features as she laughed at him and thought how pretty she was when she wasn't arguing with him. Of course, even then, with the light of battle turning her eyes that mossy color, Melanie still looked fantastic.

When she motioned to her old beater, his face dropped. Unfortunately, she noticed. Never missing a chance, Melanie poked fun at him.

"I know. It's a step down for you." She smirked. "But if you want to get to the beach today, this might be your only chance."

Embarrassed, Mitch got in while trying to come up with an appropriate apology. When nothing remotely suitable surfaced, he glued his lips shut and studied the dilapidated vehicle.

She read his silence correctly.

"Don't worry." She laughed. "Everybody thinks Bessie is gonna give up the ghost, but she always keeps going." Lovingly, Melanie patted the worn dashboard. "She's got the innards of a true champion."

"Champion what?" It wasn't nice, but she didn't take offence.

"She may not be pretty but at least she's running," she reminded him gently.

Mitchel tried not to stare as her shorts displayed those lovely long legs. He turned and stared straight ahead, trying not to ogle her. Sort of.

"Do you always go to the beach on Saturday?"

Good, Stewart, he congratulated himself. What a stimulating conversation!

"No, only in the summer, when I have time and it isn't raining." She laughed. "Other than that, I don't bother much."

Her curls were bound up in a ribbon on the top of her head. Mitch decided he'd like to undo that ribbon and run his fingers through the glowing silky mop.

"You are a smart aleck, you know that?" he muttered. His eyes opened wide as he caught sight of her feet. Her toenails were bright pink. Mitch suddenly realized they had an effect on his already racing pulse.

Gosh, he was in a bad way. It was just her toes, for goodness' sake. He forced himself to look out the window.

"Mitch?"

"Melanie?"

They spoke at the same time, each turning to stare at the other.

"You go first," he offered gallantly. The words he had wanted to say were stuck in his throat anyway.

"Well, as you know, I have sort of a temper." Mitch snorted at the obvious understatement, and Melanie had the grace to blush.

"Okay, I have a temper," she admitted.

"A terrible temper," Mitchel revised, tongue in cheek.

"Anyway…" She glared at him over her sunglasses. "I wanted to apologize for jumping to conclusions the other day. I know you were trying to help me, and I'm sorry I snapped at you."

Mitchel Stewart's mind had wandered to considering whether she would wear that swimsuit again. "Uh-huh," he muttered, lost in his daydream.

"If you are still offering, I would like to take you up on your offer of a residence. Just for a few weeks," she added quickly. And then, for his information, "No strings attached."

Privately grinning with glee, Mitch calmly asked, "What changed your mind?"

Her sea-colored eyes studied him suspiciously before she answered. "Well, I think I'm being evicted."

His head shot up in surprise. "For what?"

Melanie grinned. He could see that half-hidden little twitch that seemed to say "Gotcha!"

"Shawna eloped with her boyfriend last weekend, and now she wants her husband to move in with her." She grinned. "Not unreasonable, I suppose, but I think it's going to be just a little crowded with the three of us." Melanie shrugged nonchalantly. "Who am I to stand in the way of young love?"

He was getting to know her, and he recognized a put-on when he heard it from her pink glossy lips.

"Come on, Melanie!" Her big green eyes stared at him innocently. Mitch smirked. "What's the real reason? I know enough about that nurse to know she plans everything ahead. She'd no more elope than you would. And you would no more move in with a man than fly to the moon. I never expected that you'd go for my suggestion." He stared at her. "What's changed?"

Melanie sighed in defeat, and he knew she didn't really want to agree to his plan, at all.

"We got a notice that the owners want the top floor for their children, who will be going to school in the fall. They will pay us two months' rent if we vacate immediately so they can do some renovations before fall."

She shrugged her slim shoulders before continuing.

"I've been praying and praying that God would lead me in this contest thing. Then this came up. Right after you offered to let me stay there." Her sigh was not encouraging. "I guess God is trying to tell me something."

Mitch stared. "You think He wants you to have this money so badly He'd force you to move in with me? Wow!" He was teasing, but the laugh stopped in his throat as she turned those expressive eyes on him.

"I think He must be trying to tell me something," she said quietly. "I've been praying for ages and nothing happened. Now suddenly there's the contest and the opportunity to get some money for Sunset. I get evicted, and there you are offering to share your place." Her eyes were wide with amazement. "It's like a small miracle."

"I'm not sure…"

"Besides, there's nothing between us. Everyone knows that. And I work all kinds of hours. I just need somewhere as a base until I can find another apartment." Her head tilted toward him as she careened around a convertible full of rowdy teenagers. "So I gratefully accept your offer."

"You must know what it's like to find accommodation in this town." Mitch added that just to let her know how lucky she was and how magnanimous he was.

They talked terms and conditions all the way to the beach. Melanie could move in immediately. It would be every man for himself. No cooking, no cleaning, she told him. No garbage, no lewd propositions, he promised.

Eyebrows raised, Melanie asked what that meant.

"I only make proper propositions," he joked, eyeing her heightened color with interest.

Privately, Melanie wondered what the future would hold for them. Especially after an afternoon of Mitch's company. Her body hummed from the massaging action of his large hands as he obligingly applied sunscreen to her bare back. His big, strong fingers worked the oil into her skin, and she felt supple and exotic as the fragrance of coconuts wafted around them. Mitch had been insistent that she wear sunscreen.

"I've seen sun damage," was all he would say. "It's not pretty." She was aware of his appreciation of her swimsuit.

Melanie was flattered that he found her outfit every bit as interesting as before, but she regretted those extra ten pounds she had never shed. Not that they seemed to matter to Mitch. Shortly after rubbing in the oil, he had rushed away for a quick dip in the cold lake.

"Come on in," he had teased, dripping frigid drops of water on her toasty skin. He laughed when she shrieked, then razed her unmercifully about her squeamishness until Melanie could stand his teasing no longer.

"I knew you were a beach baby," he muttered. One dark blue eye had opened as he lazed on his towel. It traveled the course of her body, following the lines of her swimsuit. "I doubt if that thing even withstands more than a dip in the hot tub," he added, disgusted. "Afraid of a little natural water, probably."

When Melanie refused to answer, he continued the goading.

"You can't swim, can you? That bit at the apartment pool was all just a ruse to get my attention, wasn't it?"

Melanie *had* sat up at that, fury wrinkling her forehead as she glared at him.

"For your information, I don't need to attract anyone's attention." She straightened her spine in haughty disregard. "I would have you know I am an excellent swimmer. I simply refuse to subject myself to that frigid water in order to prove something to you." She arranged her beach chair more comfortably and leaned back, soaking up the sun's rays. "I merely wanted some free time away from the office. I would appreciate it if you could let me enjoy the day."

Melanie thought she had won their war of words until she heard him mutter something under his breath.

"Pardon?" she inquired superciliously.

"I said, you're chicken, just as I thought."

"You know," Melanie said, eyeing him severely, sunglasses pushed to the end of her nose, "if you ever win in court, it must be because of your bulldog tendencies."

She stretched out on her stomach, letting the warming heat of the sun penetrate her skin. There was blissful silence for about sixty seconds.

"What do you mean, bulldog tendencies?" His voice was strident. "Admit it, you are a chicken." Big blue eyes glimmered with excitement. "Bok, bok!" He flapped his arms.

Melanie was getting tired of his ridiculous juvenile games. She looked around the beach and found several pairs of interested eyes trained on them.

"Stop that," she ordered angrily. "Everyone is staring at you."

Mitch continued to chant louder and louder.

There was nothing else to do. He would not leave her alone, and she wouldn't get a moment's peace until she put an end to this stupidity.

Melanie stood gracefully and walked to the water's edge, dipping the end of one big toe into the water.

"Agh!" She sucked in her breath. It was freezing!

But when she turned around, Mitch was looming behind her. His eyes met hers, and he mouthed the word *chicken*.

Melanie sighed, resigned to her fate and fully aware that he would keep it up until she got wet. She strolled slowly into the water, getting a bit more of her heated skin wet with each step. She turned carefully, trying not to splash, and found Mitch directly behind her.

"I hope you're happy." She glared at him. "I have no feeling below my waist, and my hands are getting numb."

He grinned and dived into the smooth water beside her, splashing her hugely. When he stood up, streaming rivulets of chilly lake water running down his face, Melanie let him have it.

"You did that on purpose, you sadist. I'm soaked and I'm freezing. I do hope you feel better now."

She turned to go back to shore and found him blocking her way.

"I'm sorry, Melanie." His voice was deceptively soft as his chilly hand closed around her arm. Wide and innocent, his baby blues stared at her soulfully. "I really didn't know you couldn't swim."

"Of course I can swim, silly," Melanie told him, trying to stop her teeth from chattering. She wrapped her arms around her midriff, hugging herself for warmth.

Unfortunately the motion pushed her full breasts upward, accentuating the cleavage her suit displayed. She watched Mitch's blue eyes grow rounder in appreciation before she realized the reason. Her hands dropped to her sides in embarrassment.

His laughing gaze met hers. One black lock of hair dangled boyishly over his forehead. A wide smile slashed across his rugged, tanned face.

"You are just going to have to get in there and swim a few strokes to prove it," he whispered in her ear as his hands brushed up and down her arms to warm her.

Melanie glared at him even as her body recognized the heat flowing from his body. She moved closer. Just to get warm, she told herself. When his arms wrapped around her and she was pressed against the heat of his chest, she groaned at the warmth that was beginning to penetrate her skin.

"Come on, Melanie, let's swim."

It was the last thing she heard before Mitch's arms tightened like steel bands and he pulled her under the water.

Icy cold waves slapped against her and left her with two options: move or freeze to death. Melanie moved.

Breaking his tight hold on her, Melanie surprised Mitch with a move she had learned long ago in lifesaving class. In a few seconds he was flat on his back and going under. With one last shove, Melanie pushed him to the sandy bottom before swimming furiously away in a speedy crawl that had won her numerous competitions in high school.

Of course, Mitch demanded retribution. She just had not expected it to be a kiss. And when his cold lips pressed against hers, Melanie found that the fire building between them could not be doused, even by the freezing lake water. She kissed him back, returning his warm embraces until her blood was singing in response.

Mitch was the first to pull away.

"Okay, you win," he teased. "You can swim, and kiss." He grinned that devilish grin at her. "And you do both very well, I might add." Turning, he ducked under the water, surfacing twenty yards away to call out his challenge.

"I'll race you to the buoys," he dared her. His strong arms made a swath through the water. "Loser supplies supper," he told her when she caught up.

And so it had gone for the rest of the day. Teasing, talking, touching each other, but never getting too serious.

The long, lazy afternoon on the crowded beach presented a perfect opportunity for getting to know each other, but regardless of the many ploys she tried, Melanie gained very little personal information about Mitchel. It was frustrating and she was finally forced to admit defeat.

He lost their swimming contest and she left him to arrange their late supper, especially since he'd long ago finished off the sandwiches and pop she'd packed.

Ever resourceful, he'd come up with the very ingenious and inventive idea of hot dogs and chips, with chilled cans of iced tea to drink. As they sat around a campfire, replete with their feast, Melanie sensed he was deliberately shutting her out, refusing to answer her innocent questions. She turned a marshmallow, letting the coals toast it golden brown before popping it into her mouth.

Oh, he hadn't been rude about it. His answers had been polite enough, but, somehow, the subject of family was a closed book with Mitchel Stewart. And although he freely discussed his work, Mitch only let her see bits and pieces of the real man.

Melanie knew that he hailed from the East, that he had gone to school there and come to Mossbank a few weeks ago. She had learned a little about his schoolboy antics and that he loved to swim but wasn't very good at it.

But that was it. Mitch had told her nothing of his family or his past. And she wanted to know.

She gazed into the fire. Maybe a direct approach was the best. Plunge in and take the consequences. Somehow, the enveloping darkness gave her courage.

"Mitch?"

He sat on a log, staring vacantly into the flickering flames. The huge fire he had built had died down to an orange-red bed of coals. Wind danced across it, licking up a flame here or there.

"Hmm," he asked, staring languidly.

"Please, don't think I'm being nosy," she began, knowing darn well that nosy was exactly what she was being. "It's just that I would like to know a little more about you if we are going to be rooming together."

When his dark head jerked, Melanie held up a defensive hand.

"I know your reputation from my friends at the hospital, but…" Melanie hesitated, searching. "I don't know you." Her voice was soft, plaintive, a call for understanding.

Mitch had pulled a pair of tattered blue jean shorts over his swimsuit. Below the frayed cuffs, his long, muscular legs crossed and uncrossed as he fidgeted on the huge log. Finally he stood, towering over her in the gloom. Melanie could feel his blue eyes studying her. When he spoke, his voice was quiet but firm.

"Look. I've offered half of the prize money and a place to stay to make sure you can collect your half. Can we leave the personal histories out of it?"

He squatted in front of her and stared directly into her face. His voice was half-laughing, half-serious, but there was an underlying tenseness that Melanie couldn't ignore.

"I give you my word I'm not an ax murderer, or a psychotic, or any of those other terrible things you've been imagining." His white teeth glittered in the dark. Melanie thought immediately of a wolf and then remonstrated with her overactive imagination, sitting quietly when he continued.

"You are welcome to stay at my place for as long as you need to. But that's it. You go your way and I go mine."

His fingers closed around the soft flesh of her upper arms, drawing her upward. And Melanie allowed herself to be coaxed to his heat. He was like fire, and she a moth, drawn irresistibly to his flame. He attracted her with his hidden secrets and mysterious smile. His past was another facet of a man who occasionally let her see his generosity. And she would probably get burned, but right now Melanie could only concentrate on his touch.

"Don't get me wrong," he muttered as his eyes brushed her body, admiring her figure. "You're a very beautiful woman and I enjoy the view as much as the next red-blooded male." His hands slid down her back to the indentation of her waist, and he urged her closer.

"But I don't play games, and I have no intention of getting married just because I allow you to stay in my apartment."

"I never said I wanted to get married! Mitchel Stewart, you are the most egotistical, pushy, rude, overbearing—"

"You have said all this before," he reminded her. His hands were stuck carelessly into his back pockets as he studied her. "Get to the point."

With every atom of control she possessed, Melanie forced herself to refrain from violence. Curling her fingers into her palms, she sucked in a lungful of air.

"Look, buddy," she told him, poking a finger into his very broad, very bare chest. It confused her, that tingling sensation, so Melanie put her hand down and concentrated on the words.

"I will move into your apartment because I do need that money for my friends."

"We've already agreed on that." He chuckled, then bent to stuff the remains of their meal into the tiny cooler before dousing the fire.

"Right." Melanie tried to focus on her speech. "So I will stay there. But that's it. Not for anything else."

She tried to emphasize the words, but somehow they had

little effect on Mitch. He smiled that lazy, sexy smile and agreed with her quietly as he tugged her arm.

"Right, darlin'," he drawled as he pulled her along beside him through the warm sand. When they reached the car, he dropped everything on the pavement beside it and wrapped one lean brown hand around her neck.

"And nothin' anybody can say will change it," he drawled right before his grinning lips closed on hers.

Melanie knew his effusive charm was just a cover. Something that would draw her off course so Mitch would not have to answer any questions. And she would tell him that he couldn't just get away with this.

Soon.

With a sigh, Melanie decided she would tell him so right after she'd kissed him back. For a few delicious minutes she allowed herself to enjoy the feel of his lips tasting hers before she pulled away from his strong embrace and climbed dazedly into the car.

She knew there was something she wanted to say. But right now she couldn't remember what it was. Not on the long drive home, not when Mitch kissed her a very thorough goodnight outside her apartment and not when she was lying in her soft bed much later.

"Thanks for the sign, Lord," she whispered. "I'm taking this to mean that I should proceed full steam ahead. Now, if You could just work on his attitude a little."

A smile curved her soft, full lips as she drifted off. Yes, he had a bad attitude, all right. Tomorrow, she decided. She would remember to tell him off tomorrow.

"Oh. Uh, hello. Miss Langford, isn't it?" Mitch stared at the older blond woman in the doorway of his apartment. "Is there something I can do for you?"

Hope pressed past him without a word, her face drawn tight, lips pursed as she motioned to the items scattered at her feet.

"Actually there's quite a lot. But for right now, would you

mind bringing in my suitcases? I'll be sharing Melanie's room. You're not going to destroy my best friend's daughter's reputation as long as I can stop it!''

Mitch stared at her, his mind whirling. Was this what Gramps had meant this morning on the phone? What had he said? ''Hope has her feathers ruffled.'' Was that it? Apparently she was angry with him. Mitch groaned at the thought of this straitlaced busybody and her obviously mistaken impression of his and Melanie's unusual arrangement.

''Miss Langford, I assure you that there's nothing like that going on. Melanie and I—''

''Will have a chaperone,'' she interrupted smartly, straightening the cushions thrown haphazardly on his sofa. Her eyebrows lifted disdainfully at the coffee rings covering the glass surface of the coffee table. ''Melanie should be staying with her mother. And if it weren't for the missionaries Charity had already invited, I'm sure that's where she would be.''

Mitch watched transfixed as Miss Langford picked up a half-eaten box of doughnuts and dumped the whole lot in the trash.

''Hey! That was my breakfast,'' he told her, frowning resentfully. He decided to make a show of bravado, even though his knees were shaking. There was something about this woman that brooked no nonsense.

''Now, look here, Miss Langford. I'm letting Melanie use the spare room so she can get her half of the money for that nursing home she's so wrapped up in. That's all there is to it.''

''Fine.'' Hope Langford stared at the carpet, grimacing at the bits of lint and fluff. ''And while she's here, I'm here,'' she told him firmly. ''Please bring my things through to Melanie's room. I'd like to get settled in.''

Mitch found himself obeying even though the last thing he wanted was this neatness freak in his apartment. Fortunately his spare room had two single beds. He watched transfixed as Hope removed perfectly pressed clothes from the satchels and hung them in the minuscule closet that already housed a few of Melanie's uniforms.

His original houseguest had planned on moving the rest of her stuff tonight. It was going to be a tight squeeze in this dinky apartment, he decided, leaving Hope to pour himself another cup of coffee and contemplate the doughnuts in their box in the garbage can.

A really tight squeeze, if she was going to insist on chucking out his food supply. But how did you throw out an older woman determined to save the reputation of someone who didn't need it?

"Coffee is very hard on your stomach lining," Hope said in a stern voice. "I make a wonderful protein drink with raw eggs and yogurt that would give you lasting energy."

Mitch set down his cup hastily and grabbed his briefcase. He had to get out of here. Quickly.

"Er, uh, no, thanks," he mumbled, grabbing the doorknob like a lifeline. "I have to get to work. Early appointment." *At the convenience store across the street,* he thought. He almost had the door safely closed behind him.

"Young man?"

"Yes, ma'am," he answered, debating the propriety of a salute.

"I will need a key to this residence. There are several matters to be taken care of today and I will need to let myself in and out."

"Oh. Yes, of course." He thought. "I made a spare for Melanie yesterday. I think it's in the kitchen. In the drawer beside the sink. I'll get another cut this afternoon." He watched her carefully to see if that was all right with her, and when she nodded, he turned to escape.

"Have a nice day," she told him cheerfully.

No doubt all that happiness came from her power drink. He shuddered and climbed into his red Camaro with relief. Thank goodness it was running properly, at last. At work, Mitch could hardly wait to dial Melanie's work number.

When she answered, he almost bellowed at her over the phone.

"Thanks a lot," he shouted angrily.

"Mitch? Is that you?"

"Of course it's me." He tried, really tried to control his temper. "I'm just calling to say thank you."

"You're welcome," she answered politely. A few seconds later her puzzled voice came on the line. "For what?"

"Don't pretend you don't know. She arrived this morning, bag and baggage. All prepared to settle in for the duration."

He waited for her excuse; her plea for understanding for her aunt. He was all ready to shoot her excuses down, one by one.

Instead he heard:

"Have another cup of coffee, Mitchel, and call me back when you're awake and in your right mind. Okay, okay. I'll settle for awake." The telephone line went dead.

"Of all the overbearing, pushy women," he began, stuffing another chocolate-covered doughnut into his mouth.

"Mitch, your nine-thirty is here. Shall I show him in?" His secretary's eyebrows rose as she watched him nod and shove the doughnuts out of view. Amanda chuckled appreciatively. "Pigging out, are we?"

"Just show him in, will you, Amanda?" he muttered in frustration, trying to hide the sticky evidence.

Clarence Palmer had been a private investigator for thirty-five years. If there was a secret to be unearthed, Clarence knew exactly how to go about it. Mitch had known him for years and used his services several times, once for himself, to find the father he'd hated for so long.

He grabbed the older man's hand and slapped the thin back with pleasure.

"Clarence! Gee, it's good to see you again. Come on, sit down. Want a doughnut?"

"Mitch." Clarence nodded, peering at the doughnuts as he carefully wiped his hand on his handkerchief. "You still addicted to these things?'' His observant gaze scanned the package. ''Must be a bad day.'' He chuckled.

''Why do you say that?''

''Chocolate ones are all gone.'' Clarence grinned. He helped himself to a sugared doughnut and settled back in the leather chair. ''This a good time?'' he asked quietly.

''Yep, perfect.'' Mitch poured them both a cup of coffee and then leaned back, pen and paper at the ready. ''What have you got for me?''

With a swift economy of movement, Clarence whipped open his notepad and began.

''I got a lot of this stuff from your grandfather's contacts. Jean LeClerc. You want age, birthplace, all that?'' He waited for Mitch's negative reply, then continued. ''Okay. Vietnam vet, killed in action, or so they said. Actually, the other guy was pretty sure this Jean was wounded and kept in an enemy camp for years. The Viet Cong deliberately left some of his stuff to be found so he'd be presumed dead. You know the routine.''

Mitch nodded grimly. He did know. Very well, as it happened. He'd worked on a few cases involving fathers who had died in Vietnam. It wasn't pretty.

''Okay. Good old Jean came back but minus a few facts— like who he was. Met a volunteer at the vet hospital and they married. She had money and he put it to good use building an empire. Ever heard of Papa John?'' Clarence looked at him through his wire-rimmed glasses and saw Mitch's astonishment.

''This means something to you?''

''Yeah, it does.'' He stared at Clarence, seeing not him but the elderly white-haired man he'd met at the Bismarck television station. ''Let me get this straight. The Papa John's Peanut Butter magnate is Hope Langford's Jean LeClerc?''

''One and the same, we think. Only I'm not sure if *he* knows it. Legally his name is John Lexington. A nurse at the hospital said they called him that when he couldn't remember his name. He apparently responded to John, and they ad-libbed his last name.'' Clarence left half his doughnut on a napkin as he dug through his notes.

"Nurse Mary said he had lots of nightmares and kept mentioning the same words over and over. One of those words was *hope*. They didn't realize it could be a name until I offered it as an explanation. Apparently this guy was worried that someone would think he'd reneged on their deal. But whenever he woke up, he remembered nothing and couldn't tell them any more about what he was hoping for.''

"And she waited,'' Mitch muttered to himself. "She held on until she was sure he was dead. All this time she's been mourning his loss, and he's alive and well and married to someone else.'' He thought. "Have he and his wife any children?''

"Clarence shook his head. The wife's dead. Six years ago. Cancer. Long, drawn out and very painful.''

"And children?''

"One. A boy.''

"Can we talk to him?'' Mitch snatched his pen, prepared to write down the name and address.

"No. He's dead, too. Drive-by shooting. And it almost did the old man in last year. Some of my contacts in his company say he found solace in his loss with some woman. Don't have her name yet.''

"Wow!'' Mitch sighed, turning it all around and around in his mind, wondering what this new information would do to the prim and proper woman ensconced in his apartment.

"Want me to keep on digging?'' Clarence asked diffidently, as if it was none of his business either way.

"Heavens, yes.'' Mitch exhaled heavily. "The more we know, the better. I'd like to know who he's interested in and where she lives. I'd also like to know if he's remembered everything and is just too much of a coward to come and explain it all or if everything is still a blur.''

"Do what I can,'' Clarence assured him, snapping his notebook closed and rising to his feet in one practiced motion. "I'll check in when I've got something. See you, Mitch.''

And with those words, Clarence disappeared as silently as he'd shown up.

Mitch snatched his phone and stabbed out his grandfather's number.

"This is Mitch," he told the guardian secretary. "Is he there?" He listened, frowning. "As soon as he gets out of court, have him call me. It's important, Dora." He slammed the phone down in irritation and stood up to pace around his tiny office.

"Oh, Lord, oh, Lord," he groaned. "I know You're omnipotent and in control of everything. And You can make good things happen from bad." This was all so new to him. Mitch tried desperately to remember how the minister had told him to talk to God.

"Like a son talking to his father," Pastor Dave had told him.

Well, he hadn't had the typical father-son relationship, and he wasn't too sure just what that included, but Mitch decided to give it a try anyway.

"Father, I think a lot of people could be hurt by this. Please show me what to do. And help all those involved. Amen." Satisfied that he'd laid it all before the One who could deal with it, he returned to his desk and sat down.

A moment later, his head was bowed once more.

"And help me in this situation with Melanie so that neither of us get hurt. Just friends, that's all I want. Thank You," he murmured quietly.

It had finally happened, Mitch decided three weeks later.

He had begun to lose his sanity.

Thing was, he wasn't surprised. Not really. In fact, he'd half suspected she would be trouble. It had taken her just one week to move in and throw everything out of whack. Melanie Stewart had thoroughly upset his placid life, and now he was going nuts fantasizing about a woman he barely knew.

He tugged the pillow over his head, trying to drown out the sounds of Melanie in the shower. It was impossible. Jumping Jehoshaphat, those two women got up before dawn every blinking morning! And they didn't care who knew it, either.

Resigned, he placed the pillow behind his head and lay back, calmly accepting his fate. The way he figured it, he'd once done something really terrible and now it was payback time. Fine, he would take his punishment, but why did this torture have to begin so early?

It wasn't the panty hose hanging in the laundry room, slapping him in the face every night, that got to him. It wasn't that light but lingering scent she always wore that clung to everything in the apartment and refused to be doused by the strongest room deodorizer.

It wasn't even that she brought some of her residents to his apartment for a meal, a game of cards or just a night out— and more often than not, they conned him into playing crazy eights, too.

He could deal with all that, Mitch told himself firmly. He'd even managed to tolerate Hope's insistence on chaperoning every second of time they spent in the apartment.

But this daily trauma of pretending he wasn't aware when she showered, wasn't waiting for the faint hint of her lemony shampoo to carry to him, wasn't visualizing her rosy cheeks and that fresh-scrubbed look she wore so well—that's what was really getting to him.

"Blast it," he bellowed, without thinking, and then wished he had zipped his lip.

"Mitch?" she called quietly. "Are you okay?"

"I will be if I can ever get into the bathroom," he hollered, stubbing his toe on the nightstand as he reached for his shirt.

"I'm getting darned tired of taking cold showers," Mitch grumbled sourly twenty minutes later. Hope's short, economical showers after her early—emphasis on the early—walks would probably have left enough hot water for him.

But Melanie's extended steam baths left little but the most frigid of showers which were, of necessity, very short. He'd taken to shaving in his room because the mirrors in the bathroom were too steamed up to let him shave properly even if there had been room for his razor among the multicolored little bottles, vials and tubes. He couldn't figure it out. As far as he could tell, neither woman wore much makeup.

When at last Mitch sauntered into the kitchen, he was in no mood for pleasant conversation. He was desperately searching for a cup of coffee. Melanie did make good coffee, he'd give her that. That is, if he got any. More often than not, Hope would pour the ''vile black drug'' down the drain as soon as her niece was finished.

Today Melanie sat alone at the breakfast bar, staring vacantly out the window. In front of her was an empty cereal bowl testifying that she had already eaten. Bran flakes, no doubt. A shudder tickled Mitch's back.

''How can you eat that stuff?'' he demanded.

Melanie stared at him for a moment before answering.

''It's very healthy,'' she murmured as she strolled with that long-legged grace to the counter to rinse her bowl before bending to place it in the dishwasher.

Her slim, efficient body was immaculately clothed in blush-pink nylon, and she exuded freshness. By contrast, Mitch felt drained, lifeless. And he was beginning to hate the color pink.

''Maybe, but it tastes like dog food,'' he said grumpily, stuffing one of the doughnuts he'd bought the night before into his mouth. He glanced around to make sure Hope hadn't seen his secret stash.

''I wouldn't know.'' Her clear gaze surveyed his tired face. ''I have never tasted dog food.'' She smirked at him. ''It's a treat I'll leave you to savor.''

Mitch wanted to stick his tongue out, but he managed to control the urge. Barely.

''Boy, are you cranky. Something bothering you, Mitch?''

Butter wouldn't melt in her mouth. He scowled. Miss Perfect Stewart was no doubt well refreshed after her night on the town with pretty-boy Jeff, the blond doctor. No doubt they had gone out for a healthy meal of sushi, Mitch told himself jealously.

He was getting fed up with the parade of men who frequented his apartment. "Friends," she said, but Mitch wondered. Most of them phoned to ask her out for coffee, to take her for pizza or to a movie. A few even ended up in his living room getting advice about a birthday gift for their newest love. Young and old, they came to ask her advice about a new girlfriend. The kids took her to dinner, baseball games and all the church socials in town while they plied her with questions about the best way to handle their totally uncool parents. He never got a moment alone with her.

Mostly Mitch was really sick of the tall, ever-charming fellow from the television studio. Neal Landt was becoming a frequent visitor on the weekends. Charming and personable, he had openly admitted his interest in Melanie. The man had even asked Mitch for advice about her favorite meal!

"I want to make a good impression. You know how it is, old son. She's one very foxy lady."

Old son, indeed! Could the woman not see that Neal must have bleached his hair and his teeth to get them that white? Mitch forced his mind back to reality. That same woman was now sitting in his kitchen. Alone. Waiting.

"I was going to tell you—"

He turned toward the counter just as Melanie's elbow connected with his cup. The hot, sweet coffee splashed down the pristine white of his shirt. It was just enough to ignite his already red-hot temper.

"Blast it, woman, can't you be careful? It's not enough that you take over my apartment, use up all the hot water, constantly invite your seniors over and expect me to entertain them *and* run your Dear Melanie Advice Service from my telephone, now you've ruined my best white shirt."

Mitch's dark eyes flew to her face in time to catch the cascade of red suffusing it. Her jade eyes glittered sparks at him. He watched, mesmerized, as her temper flared and then he waited for the explosion.

Melanie jabbed her pink-tipped fingernail into the air, her voice betraying a tiny wobble, which she quickly corrected.

"What, exactly, is your problem?" she demanded. Her foot

moved as if to whack him in the shin. He jumped back. "You are the biggest dolt I've ever known. And the grumpiest. I'm terribly sorry I woke you, bear face. And I didn't intentionally ruin your shirt."

Mitch was pretty sure she wanted to stick her tongue out at him, but she didn't.

"Crawl back into your den till spring and sleep it off," she advised him angrily. "By then I'll be gone, thank goodness!" She rushed out the door.

Berating himself for his rotten attitude, Mitch moved after her. He hadn't really meant to say it. It was just…

"No, wait, Melanie." His voice was loud and strident, but she was gone. Only Mrs. Green from 106 stood in the hallway, frowning at him darkly.

"A den of iniquity, that's what it is," the elderly woman groused. "People coming and going at all hours. It's a good thing Hope Langford is watching out for that girl. Otherwise…" She shook her head doubtfully at Mitch's coffee-stained shirt and red face before returning to her apartment.

Slowly Mitch walked inside, pushing Melanie's strappy black heels out of his way. He remembered how great she had looked last night. Black stockings, black leather jacket and skirt, and these bits of leather on her feet. It had been a fifties car thing downtown, he remembered. She'd ridden with some punks in a convertible.

Mitchel kicked the heels away viciously. Didn't the woman pick anything up?

"Forget it, will you?" he ordered himself. "You're an idiot. A stupid, blithering idiot!"

His fist connected with the door frame in frustration as he realized he was thinking about her again and wishing he hadn't been so rude. When the throbbing pain finally translated itself to his brain, Mitchel Stewart decided it was time to do some serious regrouping. He stuffed another doughnut into his mouth and poured a fresh cup of coffee as he pondered his situation.

Okay, he admitted to his niggling conscience. He liked her

brash attitude and quick comebacks. A lot. And he wanted to get to know her. But after this morning's little fiasco, he doubted she wanted much to do with him, prize money or not. And he was going to have to figure a way to get past the hordes of people that always seemed to be around her.

"It's gonna take a lot of sucking up, Stewart," he told himself, then grinned. He knew he was feeling the sugar doughnuts hit his bloodstream, but suddenly he felt happier than he had in days. He had a plan, by George, and he was going to put it into practice today.

Whistling merrily, Mitch removed his sodden, coffee-stained shirt and replaced it with another.

"Fine." He grinned cheekily at himself in the mirror. "If she wants polite and restrained, that's what I will be. Decent. Upstanding. I can do that." At least he thought he could.

Melanie wasn't going to goad him into doing anything that would put her beloved money in danger. And if she didn't get that blasted cash for her old friends, nobody would lay it at his door.

There was a tiny voice in the back of his mind demanding to be heard. Was it really for the money that he'd talked her into staying here?

Mitch ignored the question. He straightened his shoulders. He had to get this cleared up. If she was staying, and he wasn't too sure about that, then he had some serious apologizing to do.

A gift, that was it. He'd give her something. He remembered something she had said about pets and old people being a natural. They weren't allowed here, but maybe at Sunset... Maybe that was the answer.

"Prepare for battle," he muttered to that little voice before grabbing his overstuffed briefcase and stomping out the door. His fingers snicked up the last doughnut on the way.

"Bran flakes, indeed!"

Chapter Five

"**J**unk-food junkie," Melanie muttered through tightly clenched teeth. Her heart sank as she spied Hope standing on the corner, waving madly. "Just what I need to make a lousy morning really complete," she muttered, staring at the woman's smiling face.

"Hi, Hope. Boy, you're up early."

She tried to infuse some enthusiasm into her voice while swallowing the little prick of conscience that reminded her that Hope had risen at precisely four fifty-eight, a full half hour before her own alarm went off.

"Yes, I had some thinking to do," Hope murmured, buckling herself in carefully after arching one eyebrow, then daintily removing a chocolate-bar wrapper from the seat with two perfectly shaped oval nails. "Could you give me a lift to the home, Melanie? It's my day to volunteer and I thought I'd get an early start."

"Yes, of course." Melanie steered into what passed for rush hour traffic in Mossbank and drove furiously through town.

"What did you say, dear?"

"Oh, nothing, Hope," Melanie lied, knowing perfectly

well what she had said and hoping against all the odds that her former Sunday school teacher wouldn't call her on it.

"You said, 'The man is a neat freak,'" Hope repeated, her voice serious. "I take it you're talking about Mitchel?"

"Oh, yeah." Melanie breathed, trying to stall all the unlovely things that begged release. "He was nattering at me again this morning. I accidentally bumped his arm and spilled his coffee. He's so rude!"

There was no point in holding back and getting ulcers, Melanie decided finally. Might as well lay it on the line.

"If I so much as put my feet up on the edge of the coffee table, he's there with a cloth, cleaning up." Melanie flicked the signal with more power than necessary and winced at Bessie's protest.

"If I have a glass of water, he waits, suspended at my side, ready to pounce the moment I set it down. Then he marches into the kitchen to put the glass in the dishwasher. As if I have some contagious disease!"

"Yes, he's become quite particular about things lately." Hope nodded, smiling happily. "And you could take a lesson from that, dear."

"I'm not messy," Melanie protested, her face flushed and angry. "I just like to relax for a while after work. It's not my fault he stepped on my keys last night. I didn't deliberately put them on the floor."

"He didn't say you had! He just asked you to be more careful. With the three of us, it is rather crowded, and you do tend toward accidents, my dear."

"I do not!" Melanie refused to back down when Hope's raised eyebrows begged her to reconsider. "Like what?"

"You left the lid off the blender two days ago, dear. When you started it, that tomato sauce flew everywhere. It took a long time to clean up." Hope's face was pensive. "I'm not sure it will ever come off the ceiling. Stipple is so dreadfully hard to clean, isn't it?"

"All right! One little accident. You're making it sound like a whole string of problems."

"Well, there was that business with the can of whipped cream, dear."

"I was trying to fix it! I didn't know he'd try to use it before I'd got the top back on properly." Melanie giggled in remembrance. "At least now we know what he'll look like when he gets old."

"And the barbecue? I don't think he'll be able to use the balcony without having some repairs done, Melanie. He also fell on your wet floor after the soap bottle broke. I'm glad he didn't break anything." Hope ticked an item off on her fingers. "You washed that white silk shirt of his with your red vest and put his watch down the garbage disposal." Hope looked sad. "There have been several problems, Melanie."

"And not all of them are my fault," Melanie complained, pulling into a parking spot. "That pizza last night, for instance. I'm allergic to shrimp, and yet he got it loaded."

"He didn't know, dear." Hope gathered her purse and sweater before brushing one hand over her hair. "You two always seem to be at loggerheads, and yet, really, I think if you'd admit it, you like each other."

"He hangs around in clothes a bag lady would reject and eats those horrible doughnuts nonstop," Melanie seethed. "And if I had a dollar for every file he's left strewn on the coffee table, or a quarter for the number of times he left his half-full coffee cup on the dishwasher instead of inside it, I could retire quite happily."

"Well, yes, it does seem to be the perfect case of a bachelor in a rut," Hope murmured. "Are you sure this money really means that much to you, dear? I mean, sometimes we ask the Lord for a sign and then we misinterpret things to our own benefit."

"But Hope," Melanie protested. "I've prayed and prayed about Sunset's needs, and every time I turn around, the answer is right there. Get that prize money and you can fill some of those needs." She stared at her friend. "Do you think I'm wrong?"

"I think you have to be very sure that this is God directing

Melanie and not you misconstruing what might just be chance.''

Melanie shook her head vehemently.

"I don't think that's what I'm doing, Hope. I've prayed so hard, and everything just seems to have fallen into place."

"Not quite," Hope murmured dryly. "I mean you two *are* only sharing the apartment to get the prize money, right?" She opened the door and got out, straightening her skirt carefully. "But I daresay all of that could all be corrected. In time."

Melanie wasn't sure whether to agree or not but was forestalled from answering by the simple expedient of Hope's departure. She strode toward the nursing home in long, determined steps. Sighing, Melanie gathered her briefcase and purse from the back seat, her mind replaying the scene in the apartment.

So he wanted to be alone, did he? Well, tough. He had asked her to stay and, nasty as he was, she wasn't moving until that check came. As she stared at her white fingers clenching the handle of her briefcase, Melanie just wished the money would come today. She released each finger, one by one.

Breathing deeply, she tried to view their situation from a distance. What was it about Mitch that made her so nervous? she asked herself.

Well, for one thing, his hands were constantly touching her, under her elbow, on her hand, brushing her waist. He made the blood flow hot and sweet through her body and then left her wanting more.

"But I detest him," she muttered, and knew that she lied. No man had ever made her feel so vulnerable. It scared her. In her world of old people, she was in control. Even her dates allowed her to set the tone of the evening. But when Mitch touched her, control moved out the window.

Control, she decided. That's what she really needed. An abundance of control. Unfortunately, it had never been her forte. She grimaced as the morning scene flashed through her mind.

No, she considered ruefully, there hadn't been much control there. She resolved to think happy thoughts. Mitch Stewart was not going to get under her skin again.

She hoped.

"I could use a little help with this decision, Lord," she murmured.

Once she entered the nursing home, Melanie tried to focus entirely on her clients. The shock came when she opened her office door after morning rounds with the doctors. Immediately her eyes began to water. She blew her nose several times before her senses cleared enough to spy the frail little woman seated on her sofa, cuddling a pure white angora kitten.

"Look, Melanie, a wonderful present arrived for you." Mrs. Rivers's soft voice was perfectly clear, and Melanie marveled at the sudden change in the woman.

The dim gray eyes were bright with excitement as Nettie stroked the cat's fur, cooing gently. Melanie wiped her eyes again, trying to stifle a sneeze.

"Just waid dere, Bissus Ribers. A'll be ride...achoo—bagk." Melanie hurried out the door to find Bridget. "Youb god to ged id oud ob here, Bwidget. I can'd bweade."

Melanie left her secretary to deal with the problem and strode quickly down the hall to the patio. Once in the fresh air, she sank into a chair, breathing deeply. Eventually, her nose began to drain and her eyes stopped watering.

It was there that Mitch found her ten minutes later.

"Taking a break?" he asked, eyeing her red eyes with curiosity. "What's the matter, Melanie? I'm sorry for what I said. I didn't mean to make you cry."

His voice was concerned, and Melanie was touched. After his angry diatribe earlier, she didn't expect him to be so solicitous. It made her feel even more guilty. He bent on his haunches, peering into her face, his long fingers brushing over her hand.

"You didn't," she muttered, trying to find that elusive control she had ordered herself to exert. "I'm fine, actually. It's just that somebody foolishly brought a cat into my office. I'm allergic to cats," she enlightened him, curious about the red stain that was flooding his face.

"It's too bad, too, because Mrs. Rivers is talking a mile a minute. That's something she's never done the whole time I've been here. Now I'll have to have the dratted thing taken away." She grimaced. "That'll set her back but good!"

Melanie was less than thrilled with having to handle such a touchy situation. The extra time and patience it would take to convince Mrs. Rivers of the unsuitability of the cat in a nursing home would probably not erase the loss she would feel when the animal went.

"Honestly! If people would only ask before they do something silly like this."

Mitch turned away to stare at the nearby flower bed. He seemed utterly absorbed in it, and Melanie wondered if he had heard a thing she had said. She was surprised when his low voice rumbled quietly.

"Maybe she could keep it in her room. You wouldn't have to go in there, and she would still have her companion."

Melanie stared at him.

"A cat in a nursing home?" she scoffed. "We're trying to keep a sterile atmosphere so our residents don't catch every bug that's going around. Do you know the diseases a cat carries?"

It was clearly not an option, Melanie decided, but Mitch pressed on, trying to convince her that he had a feasible solution to the problem.

"Maybe it's too sterile. Maybe those people would enjoy having someone else to be concerned about and care for." His dark eyes dared her to deny it.

It was a convincing argument, and Melanie knew it. The trade journals were full of articles about experiments involving pets in nursing homes that had been tried with excellent results. In fact, Sunset Home already had a parrot, exotic fish and a gerbil. But a cat?

"If it makes such a difference in her life, maybe it would help some of the other residents too," he coaxed, anxiously watching her face.

"I suppose it might work," Melanie conceded, considering options. "The litter box will have to stay in her room, though." She sneezed once more, shaking her head.

"There must still be some of those fibers on my clothes." She wiped her red nose and then leaned over to pluck one from Mitch's dark jacket. "Look, I've even spread them to you," she muttered in disgust.

Melanie sneezed one last time. "I only hope it doesn't cross my path again," she added grimly. Her wide green eyes perused Mitch's formally suited figure with a frown.

"What are you doing here, anyway?" she demanded, suddenly suspicious. Mitch held out a long white envelope.

"This came just after you left. By messenger. It's from Papa John," he told her, smiling sympathetically as she blew her nose in the fresh handkerchief he handed her.

"Well, what do they want now?" Melanie asked, tired of all the delays.

Her fingers tore open the envelope and she pulled out the single sheet of paper. Her face lit up with pleasure, eyes sparkling and pink lips grinning.

"Finally. They're going to award the prizes within two weeks," she told Mitch. "We'll be given the final decision within two weeks." She couldn't believe it.

Melanie jumped to her feet and, grabbing Mitch's hands, whirled around him like a top, spinning crazily out of control.

"Twenty-five thousand dollars! It's more than I ever dreamed of." Melanie hugged him happily before dancing off.

"Melanie." Mitch's low voice broke into her fanciful musings. Wide and green, her hazel eyes turned to study him curiously. "Things might not turn out the way you hoped."

Mitch kept his voice lightly cautious, hoping she would see the possibilities the company had left open in their letter. In fact, his legal brain had been perturbed at the gaps in the information Papa John had conveyed, but he didn't want to be the one to burst her bubble of joy.

Her arched brows quirked upward as her eyes opened wide to stare at him. He could see the awareness in her eyes and knew she was feeling the current snapping between them. Her pupils were dilated, but still she focused on him, allowing him to see into her soul.

"But it says right here," she said, reading the letter once more. Her eyes flew upward. "Don't you believe them?"

"Yes, of course." He felt constrained to agree. "It's just that I'll feel better when it's all settled." *A lot better,* he thought.

"So will I," Melanie burst out excitedly. Her eyes were glowing.

Mitch felt his heart drop to his highly polished loafers. She was too trusting, he decided. Melanie counted on that prize money to help her friends. She couldn't imagine not receiving it after all this time.

He, on the other hand, was well aware of just how swiftly her fortune could be rescinded in light of the errors that appeared on her application. Mitch made his decision. He wasn't going to be the one to erase the joy from her glowing face. His heart began its thudding beat as he stared into her rapt gaze. She was so beautiful. And so far beyond his reach.

The paging system disturbed their self-analysis, jolting each back to reality.

"I have got to get moving," Melanie told him. Her voice seemed breathy. She slipped around him to edge inside the building but his long legs caught up to her immediately.

"I'll walk you there," he offered, still dumbfounded by the depth of emotion he had seen in those deep eyes.

In her office, Melanie turned to call Bridget, allowing Mitch just enough time to scoop up the card he had included with the cat. It would not do to let her know the truth, he decided. Stuffing it into his pocket, he turned and came face to face with a grinning Bridget. She flicked her bright red nail at his lapel.

"Not such a good idea," she teased, laughing. "Next time try flowers."

Mitch tried to look nonchalant when Melanie called his name.

"Yes?" he answered, his blue eyes thoughtfully studying her.

"Aren't you going to work?" Melanie's impatient voice was like a douse of cold water. Glancing at his watch, Mitch strode to the door.

"Lord, yes. I've got to be in court in ten minutes. Gramps will probably cite me for contempt," he admitted. "See you later." With a wave he was gone, leaving Melanie to stare curiously after him.

She wasn't sure what it was all about, or even why he'd come. But, somehow, she felt as if Mitch had seen into her soul. Which probably was not good, given that Melanie seemed constantly attracted to his lean good looks.

Sighing, she turned to smile at a hovering Bridget, who stood inside the door with a box of tissues and a small vacuum. Now, for the cat.

Eight hours later, Melanie wished the cat was the sum total of her problems. She forced herself to sit and listen to the angry man deriding her and her staff for their inconsiderate lack of attention to the plight of families who came to visit the residents.

"Yes, Mr. Johnson, I realize that everyone works nowadays, but our clients need to eat their meals at a regularly scheduled time each day. We encourage them to come to the dining rooms on time, to eat with the others and to limit their snack foods." She waited for the next onslaught.

The blustering man's whining voice grew louder.

"But surely when we have made the effort to get here to see our mother, you could adjust the dinner hour somewhat?" His soulful brown eyes drooped with sadness.

Melanie's temper was wearing thin after forty minutes of his griping. There was still so much to be done before her daily to-do list was even halfway complete. She decided to set him straight and make her point without any pussyfooting around.

"Mr. Johnson," she said, her soft voice firm. "You have been to see your mother, what?" She consulted the open book in front of her. "Two times in the past month."

The man had the grace to turn red, but Melanie was relentless.

"Your mother is here every day of every week, all year long. She is hypoglycemic, which means that she has to eat regularly to maintain her blood sugar levels." She gave him her most severe nurse look. "Please don't ask me to adjust the routine of your mother and the other eighty-six residents, thirty-odd staff and an entire kitchen just so you can drop in for a visit once in a blue moon." She closed the big binder with a thud and stood in dismissal.

"I'm sorry, but you will have to wait until Mrs. Johnson is finished her meal or return at another time." Her tone suggested that she didn't particularly care which.

Grumbling and complaining, the man took his leave. Melanie sank into her chair with a groan.

"I didn't know we kept track of the residents' visitors." Bridget smirked from the doorway.

Grinning, Melanie held up the accounts ledger for housekeeping. "We don't, but it worked, so don't knock it." They giggled together for a few moments before Bridget spoke.

"You still need to call Mr. Richards's family about his clothes," she chided, glancing at her watch. "Or should I say lack of!" Bridget's round face beamed with mirth. "And then get out of here. It's after seven." She clucked at Melanie like a mother hen guarding her chick.

Two and a half hours later, at the end of a killer fourteen-hour day, Melanie reluctantly dragged her aching body into the apartment she shared with Mitch and Hope. Tossing her purse and sweater on the sofa, Melanie sprawled on the soft, cool comfort of Mitch's leather sofa, dreaming of a bubble bath.

"That's all I want," she mumbled wearily. "That and

someone to cook me a wonderful dinner," she elaborated, closing her eyes for just a moment.

"Melanie." A big hand was shaking her and Melanie wished it would go away. She pulled one eye open with the maximum effort and saw a pair of huge blue eyes peering into hers.

Not now, she prayed. She couldn't deal with a sexily rumpled corporate type right now. She shut her eye and resumed her fantasy.

"Oh, boy, you look bad." Mitch's deep voice rumbled beside her right ear, bringing her awake.

"I know, don't even say it," Melanie ordered halfheartedly. "I've been doing CPR on a resident." She glanced into his dark eyes. Tiredness caused the tears to course down her wan cheeks. "We lost him."

To his credit, Mitch never said a word. He just tugged her gently into his arms and let her bawl on his new blue shirt. When she was finished, he wiped her eyes gently and then sat on the sofa behind her, propping her up.

"Come on, lady." He urged her forward a little, his hands moving to her shoulders. "I'll give you a massage." His long, lean fingers kneaded the tensely knotted muscles in her shoulders. "You're dead on your feet."

Melanie was too tired to do anything but relax against him and let him do all the work.

"Mmm," she moaned, unable to move an inch. "I guess dreams really do come true." She tipped her head and peered at him from beneath lowered lids. "Did you bring dinner? Something yummy like chicken chop suey or moo goo gai pan?"

"You don't want much, do you?" he chuckled, squeezing the knots in her shoulder a little harder. "A masseuse, a meal. Can I get milady anything else?" His voice had assumed a butlerish English accent.

"That fifty thousand dollars would be nice," she muttered drowsily, arching as his strong thumbs found a particularly sensitive spot by her neck.

"I'm working on that," he told her, grinning. "But we need to talk first." He grunted as he probed the aching muscles of her upper arms.

"You are as strung out as a cat on a thin wire," Mitch muttered, kneading the tight knots of tension from her shoulders. "This is some stressful reaction coming from a nursing home."

Melanie wished he wouldn't mention cats, but she was too tired to lecture him so she eased into the sofa and sighed deeply.

"Melanie, what happened today to cause all this?" Mitch's quiet voice demanded a reply.

"The list is endless," she muttered. "One of the residents shed his clothes and took a stroll out-of-doors." Melanie could feel his knuckles manipulating the vertebrae in her back, and she curled her spine accommodatingly. "Unfortunately, several old dears had just completed a tea party with some of their friends, and the friends, members of the board, actually, were leaving the premises at the time. He flashed them."

The calm, sensible way she told the tale had Mitch nodding in agreement until he absorbed what she had said.

"Flashed them? You mean…" She didn't know why, but he sounded shocked.

"Uh-huh," she replied, stretching a little. "Could you move a bit to the right? Yes, that's it. Oh."

Mitch, to his credit, kept on working the muscles in her back as he appreciated the view. It wasn't every day he got this close to Melanie and he was pretty sure she wasn't about to stop him now. Not when her eyes were closed like that and she was breathing so deeply.

He had been dreaming about her for weeks, and he had no desire to end this contact with her, even if she was half-asleep. He was enjoying bringing her relief, he decided, as his fingers kneaded and manipulated the knotted muscles in her shoulders. She didn't seem to be protesting. He leaned forward for a better look and grinned.

Melanie lay asleep on the sofa, hair sprawled across her shoulders and over her face. Carefully, hoping not to wake her, Mitch slipped the silky strands off her cheek. A slow, satisfied smile tipped the corners of her wide mouth as she breathed a deep sigh of satisfaction.

"Thanks for the massage," she murmured. "I feel so much better."

Her mouth touched a tiny caress to the side of his neck in appreciation before her slim arms fell to her side. Curling like a sensuous kitten, Melanie nudged her foot against the end of the sofa, finding a more comfortable spot, before her huge eyes blinked shut. Seconds later she was blissfully snoring.

Mitch decided he could spend the evening just sitting there and watching her. She looked so peaceful, and there were none of those biting little witticisms coming out of her full pink lips. She looked adorable with her hair all mussed and her makeup completely gone.

He was in the process of easing a blanket over her, when he heard the key in the door. With a groan Mitch recalled Hope and her ridiculous assumptions about this arrangement. He knew he was going to have to move fast.

Mitch pushed Melanie up and propped her against the end of the sofa while he rearranged the cushions and smoothed the blanket over her. He had just straightened when Hope breezed through the door, a casserole in her arms and his grandfather following close behind.

"Hello," she greeted him happily. "I made my special tofu surprise this afternoon and I thought perhaps we could all share it." She trundled to the kitchen with the bowl held high.

"I suppose she wants us to eat our Wheaties and will serve spinach with it, too?" Mitch complained, glaring at his grandfather. "I'm not eating that stuff."

"You don't have to," Harry murmured. "Just pretend you're enjoying it and smile. I need some time to explain about Jean, and I was hoping it would be tonight." He stared at Melanie's slumped figure speculatively. "Will she wake up anytime soon?"

"I don't know." Mitch grinned. "She was pretty out of it after I gave her that mass—she was pretty tired," he amended. But his grandfather's eyes were glowing, and Mitch knew the old man had caught the slip.

"A massage? How kind of you. Never knew you to be so concerned about someone before," Harry murmured slyly.

The doorbell rang, signaling the arrival of Faith and Charity, who immediately began fussing over a groggy Melanie.

"My goodness, Melanie, you do look tired," Faith chirped cheerfully. "You should try some of that new tonic Arthur just got in. Liver tonic, I think it is." She shuddered. "Tastes vile but really restores your energy."

"Baloney!" Charity's brisk, no-nonsense tones were neither hushed nor quiet. "She doesn't need a tonic. Just some fresh air and a decent meal. Wake up, dear." She shook her daughter's shoulder briskly.

"Oh, is Melanie awake now?" Hope asked brightly from the kitchen doorway. Her spotless white apron was just as immaculate as the dress she wore beneath it. "My casserole will be ready in about fifteen minutes. We can all enjoy it together."

"Piffle! I hate—"

Charity's firm voice cut off Faith's protests.

"Mitch is taking Melanie out for dinner, Hope. Then they're going for a walk in the park or something. And Faith and I have already eaten." Mitch grinned at the frown Melanie's mother gave Faith. "But you and Harry go ahead. We'll just sit with you and visit."

Mitch was sure only he heard the whispered complaints between the two old ladies.

"You lied, Charity! I didn't have dinner yet."

"I didn't say you had." Charity's voice was cool. "I merely said we'd already eaten. Didn't you have breakfast and lunch today?" She waited while Faith nodded. "Then you've already eaten."

"But, Charity, I'm hungry," Faith wailed. "I've been weeding in your garden all afternoon, and I want my dinner."

"Badly enough to swallow her tofu casserole?" Charity muttered grimly. As enlightenment spread across Faith's countenance, Charity patted her hand. "We'll stop at Burger Heaven on the way home."

"Can I have fries?" Faith asked slyly, her nose curling as a strange odor wafted through the apartment.

Mitch wheeled and whispered in Faith's ear. When she nodded, he pressed a twenty into her hand.

Surprisingly, it took Melanie about five minutes to shower and change into a pair of white slacks and a cool blue top. Her hair was wreathed around her head in a coronet style that left the air free to caress her long, slim neck. Mitch decided he liked that style almost as much as he liked it when she left it loose and long.

"What did you give Faith twenty dollars for?" she demanded as soon as they left the apartment, the good wishes of the three ladies ringing behind them.

"To get rid of any of that *stuff* that's left," he told her. "You may be some kind of health nut, but I am not, repeat not, eating tofu casserole."

Quick as a wink, Melanie whipped open her tan leather bag and pulled out a ten, which she handed to him with a grin.

"Good thinking." She laughed. "I can't stand tofu myself. Particularly not after wading through those awful poached chicken breasts last night. They had no taste."

"Tell me about it." He chuckled. "Well, what's it to be? Artery-clogging fried chicken? Thirty fat grams of pizza? Or Faith's favorite—Burger Heaven?"

When Melanie beamed at him like that, Mitch wondered if it wasn't just about time to renounce his long-held beliefs on marriage and his aversion to it. Just about.

"None of the above. Let's try some lean, healthful Chinese food."

"Good idea! Like sweet and sour ribs and deep-fried chicken balls. Health food! Now that's my style." He pulled away from the curb with a roar and steered off down the street.

He couldn't help but join in her hoot of laughter. Nor could he avoid the sense of camaraderie that being with her brought. It was almost as if he belonged.

Chapter Six

"Please, God, just this once, don't let him be there."

Melanie prayed fervently but without much faith. Since that fateful day two weeks ago when her sane, orderly life had been traumatized by a back rub that had massaged away the aches but replaced them with desires that couldn't be fulfilled, Mitch Stewart had dominated her thoughts.

Lately, Mitch managed to be at their apartment whenever she was. Casually waiting, smiling that mysterious smile. As if he knew about the flicker of desire that curled in her stomach whenever she caught sight of his dark head.

And Melanie was more aware of him than any man she had known before. Regardless of what he thought, she did remember offering him a kiss as thanks for his help. She was pretty sure she'd seen desire in his eyes at that moment. And Melanie knew Mitch had wanted her as much as she had him.

She wanted permanence, someone to depend on, someone to build a future with. She had a sneaking suspicion Mitch might fill that bill very well, Melanie admitted. But Mitch had made it very clear that theirs was only a temporary arrangement. It would end, and they would go their separate ways.

When she left for work, his dark blue eyes stroked over her uniform, noting every detail. When she left on a date, his glance followed every curve and line of her outfit, mentally chiding her for leaving him alone with Hope. Oh, he never said a word, of course. But she was a master at reading that poor-little-me expression.

Of course, it's only for the money she was staying. At least, that's what she told herself.

Ruthlessly ignoring the tingle of electricity that jolted through her whenever his twinkling baby blues met hers, Melanie focused on work. She came in way too early and left later than ever and was still far behind in her work. She accepted every date she was offered, even though she spent most of the time sitting thinking about who Mitch was with while she listened to someone else's love life and their problems.

That's why Papa John's visit last night had been so unexpected. And so infuriating. Hope had gone out with Harry, leaving Melanie to tolerate the friendly arm Mitch placed around her shoulders just long enough to avert suspicion before she moved across the room, far away from his big hands. And when he sat right beside her on a sofa that could have easily held six, Melanie made an excuse to refill the tea, even though the pot was still more than half full.

"Oh, yes, we're great friends, Mel and I," he assured the old man, flashing that sexy smile guaranteed to weaken any woman's knees. "We share everything from breakfast cereals to our taste in music."

Mel had gaped at that. Mitch liked jazz while she preferred rock music from the past. And as far as she knew, he never ate breakfast. Unless you counted doughnuts.

The one thing they did share was their obvious lack of use of the old man's product. Melanie sincerely hoped he wouldn't ask for some, because she was positive there wasn't a jar of the stuff anywhere in the apartment. But then, as usual, Mitch was miles ahead. He proudly showed their half-empty jar of nutty peanut butter to a benignly smiling Papa John.

"This is great stuff, sir. I've enjoyed it every morning." Grinning ear to ear, Mitch proceeded to wax rhapsodic about peanut butter!

Melanie thought she would be sick.

"Did your children eat a lot of peanut butter when they were growing up?" Mitch had asked curiously.

When the elderly gentleman lost all his color, Melanie helped him sit down and offered him a cookie.

"I'm afraid my only son died," he whispered, his face chalk white with strain. "I have no other children."

"Oh, I'm so sorry," Melanie murmured, patting the blue-veined hand as she glared at Mitch. "It must be terrible to lose a child." To her disgust, Mitch continued on quite easily, as if nothing untoward had happened.

"Yes, I imagine it must be just like losing a parent," he said thoughtfully. "I used to know some people who lost a father in Vietnam. It was very sad."

Melanie didn't think it was possible, but the old man's color receded even further, leaving him pale and wan.

"I, er, I was in Vietnam, too," he murmured, his hand shaking as he sipped his tea. "I had an accident there."

"I'm so sorry." Melanie rushed to reassure him, wondering why Mitch kept probing at a subject that was obviously painful. She directed a glare in his general direction, but it did absolutely no good. Mitch kept right on asking questions that were none of his business.

"What kind of an accident?" he asked curiously. "Anything you can talk about?"

"I, er, that is, well, you see, I lost my memory." His eyes were distant, staring into the past. "I was hit with some flying debris when a comrade in the army stepped on a land mine." He peered at Mitch. "I still don't remember it all," he murmured. "But a friend of mine has been helping me understand that what's in the past isn't important."

"But what if there was someone, some family member

maybe, that had been waiting for you to return all these years?" Mitch's eyes were deeply intense as they studied their visitor. "Wouldn't you want them to know you're alive and okay?"

"Of course," Papa John murmured. He rubbed his chin and tried to explain himself. "But I just can't piece it all together. Not yet. Sometimes I get these pictures of someone, a woman…" He shook his head tiredly. "It's no good. I can never remember the dreams."

"Perhaps a hypnotist, or some specialist," Mitch offered quietly but Papa John shook his head.

"No," he said firmly. "I can't sit around waiting anymore. I made my wife wait too long before we were married, hoping I'd remember something from the past, some clue to who I was." His eyes filled with tears. "Because of that, we had so little time together."

"I'm sorry, Papa John," Melanie murmured. "We have no right pressing you like this." She frowned at Mitch. "This is obviously a painful subject and absolutely none of our business. I apologize for my friend." She laid special emphasis on the last word, warning Mitch silently that she wasn't finished with him.

"It's just that I'd like to help. If I could," Mitch added, his cheeks flushed. "I mean, could I conduct a search or something?"

Papa John smiled as he stood, towering over them.

"That's very kind," he said. "But you see there's almost nothing to go on. I don't remember any names from that time except John. I think that's mine. And a date," he added. "June twenty-first. I have no idea of the significance of that. And you young things don't want to be fussing about an old man like me. You've got too much living to do. I'd better get going."

Melanie ushered him to the door, murmuring a few polite words of farewell. The door flew open just as she grasped the handle, and an unusually flustered Hope came surging into the room, her hair wild and disorderly, her normally immaculate clothes rumpled and dirty.

"The nerve of that man," she sputtered, her voice full of dismay. "He actually asked me to marry him. At my age! Can you imagine it?"

Papa John observed Hope with a curious look, his eyes wide and questioning, obviously amazed that she found a marriage proposal so distasteful.

"He wants to get married right away! As if I would even countenance such a thing."

"But why not?" Mitch demanded. "Gramps and you make a fine couple, and I think you enjoy each other's company. Don't you?" His stare was speculative, his eyes narrowing as the older woman brushed aside a bright lock of hair.

"Of course I enjoy Harry's company," she burst out. "But I can't just suddenly decide to marry him. Not now, not with everything so up in the air."

"You know," Mitch told her seriously, his eyes fixed on the white-haired man in the doorway. "We were talking about that very thing and how a person shouldn't wait for something that might never happen. Isn't that right, sir?"

"Well, now, I'm not advising any rash decisions," the old man mumbled, staring at Hope's blond beauty, bushy eyebrows furrowed. "But there comes a time when you have to grasp opportunity with both hands and get on with your life. Before it's over."

Melanie suddenly noticed that Hope was staring at Papa John, her cheeks pale.

"Do I know you?" she whispered, peering into his eyes. "I feel somehow that I..."

"I'm sorry, Hope. I should have introduced you." Mitch was beaming at the two of them. "This is Papa John. You know, from the company awarding us the prize money." He turned to the man at the door. "This is our friend, Hope Langford."

They nodded at each other, but Hope had not lost that odd

look of speculation, and Melanie wondered for the hundredth time what was going on.

"Papa John Lexington," he told her succinctly, offering a quick little bow. "Most folks call me Big John." He turned to Melanie, who was standing dumbfounded as Mitch's muscular arm wound itself around her shoulders, pressing her against his side in a pose reminiscent of two young lovers.

"Any word on that prize money?" Mitch asked, snuggling Melanie's firm, unyielding form against his.

"It should be released any day now," Papa John murmured, still staring at Hope. "Strange, though, the entry forms having only the one initial. We don't think they were signed in either of your handwritings, either. We checked against the disclaimer we had you fill out." He was almost to the elevator before Hope's shrill tone stopped him.

"Wait a minute! Did you used to live near here? In a place called Sherman Oaks? You remind me…"

But Papa John was stepping into the elevator, shaking his white head.

"No, I'm afraid the name doesn't sound familiar," he told her. His gaze lighted on Mitch and Melanie still standing entwined. "Thank you for the tea. You'll be hearing from my company soon, very soon."

When the elevator doors finally closed on their guest, Melanie ducked out from Mitch's snug embrace to chastise him roundly.

"How could you?" she gasped. "He thinks we are in love with each other. He thinks we eat peanut butter. He thinks we actually like each other!" Her voice was squeaking, and Melanie fought for control.

"We could be, I do eat it, and we do like each other," he answered quietly before moving to clear away the dishes they'd used.

"But…but—" Melanie spluttered, unable to believe what she had just heard. She floundered, searching for words. "I never—that is, if we…I mean, darn it, will you stand still for a minute?"

She was frustrated at Mitch's calm acceptance of the situation. What did he mean, they could be in love? She had never given him any reason to think such a thing! Had she?

He did stop. Putting the tray on the ceramic kitchen counter, he placed his hands behind him as he leaned back to study her flushed face and wringing hands. His knowing grin made her palms itch to slap it away. This was no laughing matter!

"You know that you're as interested in me as I am in you," he told her. "We think alike. But if you want to keep pretending that there's nothing there…" He shrugged. "Fine. That's life. But you're only fooling yourself."

"I have no clue as to where you got this information," she told him spitefully. "But let me assure you that it is false. I am not attracted to you. You're too pushy and too bossy and—"

His big smile beamed teasingly at her.

"It's okay, Melanie. I don't expect you to own up to it. You never do." His blue eyes licked fire at her as he followed her figure to the cinched waist of her silky slacks.

"You're weird," she muttered angrily. "I don't understand where you get the wild idea that we think alike. I couldn't possibly think in nearly such a convoluted form as you." She glared at him. "Besides, I always own up to everything."

"Like this need you have to create big happy families wherever you go? Even if it means burning yourself out in overtime at Sunset with the residents?" His voice was low and intimate. "You know as well as I that you want your own family, and this is your way of creating one."

"You're being ridiculous." She bristled, angry at him for bringing the subject up. "I have family. I have Charity, remember?" She gasped when he shook his dark head.

"Yes, but is that enough? Can you deny that what you really want is to put down some roots of your own?" He chucked a finger under her chin. "There's nothing wrong with that, Melanie. What is wrong is to pretend you don't."

"I'm not pretending anything," she sputtered, turning

away. It was a lie. She'd dreamed of her own family for as long as she could remember, and it infuriated her to hear Mitch speak of it.

"Keep fooling yourself if you must," he murmured softly, pressing past her to move out of the tiny kitchen. "But you don't believe that lie any more than I do."

Melanie stood, transfixed. Was he right? Was she hiding behind the residents of Sunset, afraid to take a chance on her own dreams?

And even if she wanted to, Mitchel Stewart would hardly be her choice. He was more like a shark than the easygoing kind of man she preferred.

It was too touchy for discussion, she decided, and pursued his other claims, instead.

"You're a fine one to talk about denial," she complained. "You don't use their peanut butter!" She was furious at his temerity. He was going to jeopardize everything.

"Of course I do," Mitch countered, his voice smooth as silk. "It so happens that Papa John's peanut butter tastes really great on doughnuts." He pointed toward the half-empty container on the shelf. "That's my second jar."

Melanie gaped. She staggered to one of the kitchen chairs and sank into it gratefully. The thought of peanut butter on doughnuts made her gag, so she focused on his lean, taut body lounging against the counter. His legs were covered in disreputable old denim with strategically placed tears that gaped across both knees.

Melanie had no doubt those tears were from wear. He put the jeans on every chance he got, which was often enough. And that ragged old sweatshirt, too! Tonight he was dressed more sloppily than his usual relaxed attire. Why, the shoulders were so baggy, his shirt exposed more than it covered, and even on straight, it didn't cover an awful lot of his hair-roughened, muscular chest.

Melanie decided right then and there that it wasn't politic to focus on anything but his face. Not where her heartbeat was concerned. She forced herself to meet his sardonic gaze without flinching.

Blue eyes met hers, sparkling with suppressed laughter. He raked a hand through his wavy jet-black hair, and one irrepressible lock fell over his forehead. He looked very attractive in a jaunty sort of way. She felt her heartbeat speed up. It was time to go. Melanie turned, heading for the door.

"I'm going out," she murmured, hoping he wouldn't hear the little catch in her voice.

"Dressed like that, I expected so," he murmured, following her to the front room. "What is it this time? A teenage crush or counseling a reprobate husband?"

Melanie had a ton of sarcastic phrases, but she didn't get the chance to utter even one of the words that flew to her lips. Hope's soft voice broke in.

"That man," Hope murmured into the silence. "I...I think I might know him."

Melanie whirled to stare at her disbelievingly.

"Know Papa John?" She frowned. "How would you know him?"

"I'm not sure. He looks familiar." The blue eyes stared into the past. "I think he might be Jean." Her face fell as tears rolled down the clear alabaster skin, her eyes begging for understanding.

"But that's..." Melanie's mouth fell open when Mitch's fingers closed around her upper arm.

"Gramps and I think so, too," he told Hope gently. "I've been doing a bit of research on my own, and from what I can determine, Papa John might just be the guy we've been searching for."

"But he was reported dead." Hope's voice was faint and bemused. "They found his dog tags." She rubbed a hand across her forehead. "I don't understand this."

"I don't have a lot of information yet," Mitch told her, sitting beside her and enfolding her slim white hand in his big brown paw. "But when he was talking today, I got the impression that Papa John lost his memory and has never regained it." He patted her shoulder consolingly. "Gramps didn't want you to know until we were positive."

"Harry's known about this all along?" she whispered in confusion. "And he didn't tell me?"

"He didn't want to get your hopes up until we're absolutely sure. Unfortunately, I don't know if we ever will be. The guy still only remembers the name John and a date." Mitch shook his head in frustration. "It was so long ago, and there's so little information to go on."

"What was the date?" Hope whispered, her eyes huge and full of unshed tears.

"June twenty-first," he told her.

Melanie watched as joy flooded the older woman's countenance.

"He remembered that." Hope smiled gently, her tear-filled eyes sparkling. "Even with everything, he remembered the date."

Melanie looked to Mitch for an explanation, but he shrugged in confusion. They sat silent, waiting for Hope to explain. But she was clearly lost in her own world and not at all aware of them.

Carefully Melanie touched the older woman's shoulder, and when the blue eyes turned toward her, they were full of bemusement.

"June twenty-first was the day we were engaged," Hope told them tearfully. "Jean asked me to marry him and gave me this ring on June twenty-first." She fingered the diamond solitaire she'd worn on her right hand for two and a half decades.

Mitch tried to catch Melanie's eye and jerked his head toward the kitchen. When she frowned at him, he mouthed the word *kitchen* at her. Finally she nodded and got up from the sofa. Her eyes searched Hope's face for some sign, but the woman was staring, as if in a trance, across the room.

"Will she be okay, do you think?" she asked him, frowning. "Maybe we should call your grandfather."

Mitch shook his head thoughtfully, watching the concern that filled her green eyes.

"I don't think she'll want to see Gramps right now," he murmured, setting the kettle on the stove to boil. "But she does need her friends around her. Could you call your mother?"

"Yes," Melanie agreed, and dialed. "The fearsome three-some can band together and support each other like no one else ever could. Hello, Mother?"

Mitch listened as she explained the situation.

"You can? Great! Yes, bring Faith, too. She'll cheer her up." Melanie listened, then tipped her head, twirling a lock of glossy dark hair as she considered her mother's words.

"Well, I've got a date but I think Mitch will be here. Oh, just a minute." She turned to glance at Mitch, who was tapping her on the shoulder. "What?"

"I've got a date, too," he told her.

Her eyes widened, but she dutifully relayed the information to her mother.

"Yes, a movie just might do the trick. Thanks, Mom." She replaced the telephone and turned to stare at him. "They'll be right over," she told him.

The doorbell rang, and Mitch muttered something under his breath as he welcomed their latest guest. It was good old Jeff. Again. Tall, playboy Dr. Jeff, who never stopped grinning. Mitch endured the playful slap on the back, smiling halfheartedly as he noticed Jeff's fashionable outfit. So this was a real date!

"Jeff," he said without inflection. Mitch swallowed the gall that surged in his mouth. "Where are you going to-night?"

"Um, there's a performance at the local arts center. Operatic. We're going to opening night."

Mitch gulped down the sarcastic words at the warning look on Melanie's face. Manners, he told himself. That's what she wanted. Common decency. Assuming a politeness he didn't feel, Mitch smiled heartily.

"How nice. The opera." His black eyebrows surged upward when he turned to grin cheekily at Melanie. He tossed a handful of the freshly buttered popcorn he'd just pulled out of the microwave into his open mouth.

"Nala and I are going to stay here and watch a movie. Mushy old Cary Grant thing. So romantic." He stuffed some more popcorn in his mouth at the look in Melanie's eyes.

She was frowning, her gleaming head tipped to one side as she studied his face.

"Who's Nala?" Her voice was suspiciously abrupt, but Mitch gave no sign that he noticed.

"Oh, she's with Mercer, Metcalfe and Martens," he told her, naming a Bismarck firm. "Very bright, very smart, very high profile."

Right on cue, the doorbell rang, and Mitch opened it immediately, grabbing the tiny woman who stood quietly in the doorway. He wrapped her in an enthusiastic hug.

"This is Nala," he announced unnecessarily, watching Melanie all the while. Mitch swallowed his disappointment when his roommate showed nothing other than her usual courteous manners, greeting his date with a smile and a handshake before moving toward the door.

"Well, we had better be off," she murmured in her low voice. Her arm was threaded through Jeff's tuxedoed one. Mitch watched Melanie lips stretch in a happy smile. "Have a good evening."

"Yeah, you, too," he muttered. All discussion ceased as the elevator doors flew open and two elderly ladies swooped into the apartment.

"Are you all right, dear?" Charity murmured as she checked Hope's wan face and sad eyes. "Remember who's in control. He's never failed us yet."

"I know." Hope hugged Faith and then grasped Charity's arthritic hand in hers. "It's just been rather a shock." She stared at her friends. "I mean, if it is him." She shook her head in amazement.

"Then you'll deal with that, too," Faith told her sternly.

She eyed Melanie and Mitch with a frown. "I thought you two were going out somewhere?" she said.

"I am—" Melanie began, but Mitch cut her off. He didn't want these little old ladies thinking any more terrible thoughts about him.

"Melanie's going to the opera with Jeff, and Nala and I are going to watch a movie," he explained cheerfully.

Faith seemed upset by this.

"Oh, piffle! I thought surely you and Melanie would be together," she blurted. "Don't you like each other after all?"

"Like each other?" Hope's voice was full of scorn. "They can't stop bickering for five minutes. He eats doughnuts non-stop, and she leaves her stuff lying around. He likes to make packaged soup using every pot in the place. She detests whatever he makes—even when she likes it!" Hope shook her head in disgust. "It reminds me of my days at the junior high when everyone got a case of puppy love. I sorted out more disputes in those days." Her eyes searched her friends' for understanding. "But nothing I dealt with there was as petty as these two."

Mitch heard Melanie's weak voice. "Jeff, I, er, think we'd better go now. Good night, everyone."

Oh, sure, he thought, *leave me to take the heat for this, why don't you? If that isn't typical!*

But it seemed the ladies weren't hanging around.

"You need a break, dear. That's the best thing in the world for the worries. Take your mind off your problems and enjoy a bit of rest and relaxation." Faith was busy straightening up the apartment as she considered the possibilities Mossbank offered.

Which didn't take long, Mitch noticed with amusement.

"Why don't we go out to Fleming's Creek for a swim?"

He gaped at the gray-haired woman, wondering if anything he'd heard about her addled state had been exaggerated. Somehow, he couldn't see the fearsome threesome, as Melanie called the ladies, swimming in a creek.

"For heaven's sake, Faith, there hasn't been water in Fleming's Creek for ten years or more." Charity rolled her eyes.

"I've got it!" Faith's countenance shone with excitement. "The stock car races are on tonight. Let's go watch them."

Hope burst out laughing.

"I don't think I want to sit in all that dust and watch cars smashing into one another, but thank you for thinking of it, dear." She patted the rounded shoulder with affection. "No, I really think I'd just like to…"

As Mitch watched, Charity whispered something in her ear. He saw Hope's gaze flick over him first, then Nala. Her eyes grew round with something he couldn't define. She jumped to her feet, tugging at her wrinkled clothing.

"That's a wonderful idea, Charity. I'd love to rent a movie with you. I'll just change first, and then we can go."

"Go? Why do we need to go?" Faith sounded perplexed as her long fingers picked up the rented Cary Grant movie. "I love this one."

Mitch watched, mesmerized, as Charity shook her head at Hope and shooed her into the bedroom to change. Gently she lifted the black video box out of Faith's hands and replaced it on the television.

"You've seen this hundred of times, dear," she murmured, drawing Faith toward the door.

"I know. I really like how he falls in love with that young girl." She sighed. "It's so romantic!"

Mitch couldn't hear much of the rest but he did hear the excitement in Faith's voice when she said, "The Trevi Fountain, you mean? Ooh! I love the Trevi."

Within minutes, the three bustling sprites had scurried to the elevator, chattering a mile a minute. Hope glanced back just once, fixing Mitch with her sternest teacher look.

"I'll be late," she told him seriously. "Don't wait up."

And then with a swoosh of doors they were gone.

Nala stared at him openmouthed, her eyes wide with wonder.

"Mitch?"

"Yes?" He leaned down to straighten the mat at the front door. When there was a prolonged silence, he straightened.

"What," she whispered, awestruck, "was that?"

Chapter Seven

Four and a half hours later, Mitch finally acknowledged the truth. He had not fooled anyone, except maybe himself, anyway, with this crazy good-guy charade. Nala had her own ideas.

"You are in love with her," she said firmly.

Shocked, Mitch stared at his oldest friend. In love? Hardly. He'd never loved anyone. Melanie Stewart was gorgeous and full of energy, and he enjoyed her company. But love? Naught.

"I know what I'm talking about," Nala insisted. "And you are. Your eyes follow her around constantly. When you're not with her, you go all dopey daydreaming about her." She looked at him, her gray eyes bright with satisfaction. "It couldn't have happened to a more deserving fellow." She laughed.

"Nala, you know me." Mitch had appealed to her good sense. "You know I can't love anybody. Okay, I admit that I'm interested in her." He grinned sardonically. "In certain ways."

Nala merely swatted at his shoulder, brushing his argument aside.

"But love her? No. I don't know how," he told her.

"Nonsense," she insisted. "Okay, you've had some problems. Who hasn't? That doesn't mean you can't move beyond them."

They had argued good-naturedly for a long time. Eventually, Nala threw up her hands in frustration.

"I'm going home, Mitch. Your mind isn't here with me, anyway." She zipped her jacket as she spoke. "Just remember, you can run but you can't hide." Her soft lips had pressed gently against his forehead.

It was funny, Mitch mused. He had known Nala for years. She had pushed him through the bar exam when he would have given up. She was gorgeous, and fun, and bright. And he felt nothing when she kissed him. Zilch. Nada.

But when Melanie walked into the room, he could feel the air zap with energy, and the hairs on his arms stood at attention. He shook his head in defeat, disgusted with himself. Mitchel Stewart was mooning over a woman who shared his apartment because she wanted money. How trite!

Unfortunately, she wanted next to nothing to do with him personally. If he wanted her, he was going to have to make the first move, Mitch decided. But he wasn't in love with her, he assured himself. He couldn't love anyone. Not with a family history like his. What he could do was seize the moment, make the best of his time with Melanie.

"God is all-powerful, son," he remembered his grandfather saying just days ago. "He can work in ways you don't even know about. I know it was tough for you, but you've put your life in His hands now. Let Him show you what He has in store for you."

"Well, God," Mitch murmured, terribly self-conscious. "I don't know what to do. I'm not the marrying type, you know that. And Melanie Stewart definitely is. All she talks about is families and children." He stared at his hands before closing his eyes.

"Is it wrong for me to go out with her, date her, knowing that there isn't any future in it?"

There wasn't any answer. No still, small voice urged him to stay away from Melanie, and no one boomed, "Go for it!" in the silence of his apartment. Was it really so wrong to want to share a special meal with her, to share an evening that wasn't filled with problems? No answers came.

Sighing, Mitch decided he would start tomorrow. He would ask her out to dinner. He would be charming and scintillating and all the other things men were supposed to be. He only hoped Melanie wouldn't hurt herself laughing too hard.

"What did you say?" Melanie asked, staring at him, her head tipped to one side, as she considered his mental status. There had to be some reason for this abrupt change of mind.

"You heard me," Mitch muttered. He stared straight at her with those turbulent blue eyes. "Will you have dinner with me tonight?"

"Why?" Melanie felt like a ship suddenly freed of its moorings. The only thing that remained calm in her crazy world was the steady regard of his inscrutable eyes, fastened intently on her face.

"Because I want us to." He reached past her for the coffeepot. He drank thirstily before daring to face her again.

Melanie moved skittishly away from Mitch. He seemed different this morning. Sort of doggedly determined. And out of sorts, as usual. She eyed his rumpled T-shirt and baggy jogging shorts. Another ragged outfit.

"I suppose I could," she temporized. Suddenly, suspicion moved in. "Is this about the money?" she demanded.

"Oh, for Pete's sake, I just asked you out for a simple dinner. Does Jeff have to go through all this to get a date?"

Melanie's mouth hung open in astonishment. She was positive she hadn't understood correctly. "A date? You are asking me for a date?"

"Yeah, a date. I'd like to remind you that you have been on one before, as I've had cause to notice. And no, I don't want your advice to the lovelorn." He frowned. "What's so peculiar about going out with me?"

Mitch was affronted, Melanie could tell. And his patience was wearing thinner by the moment. Not that he appeared to have much tolerance for anyone or anything before nine o'clock, even on the best of days.

Well, why not? Melanie asked herself. She had wondered about him for long enough. Maybe they could talk civilly. Share a nice meal. Then he would open up about his past.

His dark hair glimmered in the shaft of sunlight falling through the kitchen window. Melanie noticed the way he leaned against the cupboard, tiredly rubbing the knot of tension in the back of his neck. She decided to help him out.

"Rough night?" she asked quietly, her fingers kneading the knot in his neck. She tugged on his arm. "Sit down. I can spare five minutes this morning."

Melanie let her fingers press and poke, hearing his quiet moan when she found a knot of tension.

It was utterly unexpected, this sudden change of heart. Why would Mitch want to have dinner with her? Was there some reason he wasn't telling her about?

Yeah, right, Melanie. Like he's totally in love with you forever and ever. Get real!

She stifled the mocking voice and decided to take the plunge. *You can't define every single move you make in this life,* she reprimanded her laughing subconscious.

"All right," she agreed, hoping this meant a truce in their ongoing warfare. "I will have dinner with you. Where?"

Her arched eyebrows shot up when he mentioned a very prestigious restaurant in a nearby city. It was famed for its haute cuisine. She pondered, wondering if she could find something semiformal on her lunch hour.

But the real issue haunted her. It wasn't like him. It wasn't like him at all. And that unnerved her more than anything. She stared at him suspiciously.

"What's really going on, Mitch?" The question was automatic. And Melanie wished she hadn't said a word when he pushed away from her and stood jerkily.

Mitch sloshed another cup of coffee into his mug before

he glared at her. His eyes were an angry ice blue. He took one sip of the steaming black brew before thunking the coffee on the counter and crossing his arms.

"Nothing's going on. I thought perhaps we could have a calm, cordial meal together for once, without biting each other's heads off and without benefit of dear sweet Auntie Hope." He jerked his head toward the bedroom door, where Hope had just disappeared to change her clothes.

"Perhaps I was wrong. Perhaps we've gone as far as people like us can go." The words were a stinging assessment of their relationship's deterioration in the past few weeks.

Melanie felt guilty. Here he was trying to extend the olive branch, and she suspected his motives. She could at least meet him halfway, she decided.

"Well, I have a board meeting until around five, but I could be home shortly after that. Is that early enough to leave?" She tried to infuse warmth into her voice. Privately she wondered how they would survive the evening without scrapping through every course, but if he was willing to try, then so was she.

"If you're sure you can make it," Mitch answered brusquely, hitching up his jogging shorts before retrieving his coffee. "I think we should leave about six. I'll make reservations for seven-thirty. That should give us enough time. Okay?"

He glanced at her, and Melanie nodded. A little prick of awareness twigged her consciousness. Something was strange, she thought, but perhaps she should try to meet Mitch halfway. Who knows? Maybe they did have something in common.

Anyway, it was just dinner. Yeah, right, her mind mocked. Just dinner with the most attractive guy she'd met in years. A man who, incidentally, was sharing her apartment. Or vice versa.

Melanie shook her head. This was getting too complicated. It was just a friendly, casual meal out together. That was all.

They would be friendly and civil to each other, and she wouldn't have to cook. Nothing more.

By six o'clock, Melanie was beginning to doubt her intelligence in agreeing. Here she was swathed in black silk, and Mitch hadn't even come home yet, let alone showered or changed. She flicked through the channels on his big-screen TV three times before tossing the remote onto the sofa.

By quarter after the appointed hour, Melanie had decided to change into jeans and a T-shirt and forget the whole thing. It was a mistake to court trouble. She knew what Mitch was like. Unreliable came to mind. As did pushy and stubborn.

It was just that he was the best kisser she had ever met. Unbidden, the images floated through her mind of the first time he had visited her apartment and the way that evening had ended. And then at work, she remembered his comforting arms and the gentle coaxing kiss that had caused such internal uproar.

Firmly, Melanie dislodged the picture. She had no defense when his lips touched hers. And defenses were what she would need. She wasn't going to be swayed into a relationship with the man simply because they shared an apartment. Even if he was inordinately handsome and had allowed Hope to stay without saying a word of reprimand.

There was a strong smell of roses, and Melanie sniffed. Opening her eyes, she found Mitch squatting in front of her, holding out a beautiful bouquet of barely opened yellow roses. Melanie reached out to take them, burying her face in their sweet fragrance.

"You," she breathed, looking into his electric blue eyes, "are late."

"And you are welcome." He grinned his seductive smile. "You could thank me properly," he teased, pulling her out of the chair and into his arms. His hands pressed into the curve of her waist, belted above her jeans. He glanced down and his blue eyes widened to indigo orbs of admiration.

"Wow." He whistled. "You look very, uh, nice."

Melanie burst out laughing. He was trying, she would give him that. She curtsied. "Thank you, sir."

When his eyes darkened appreciatively, Melanie avoided his eyes and moved away to pull the silk wrap across her bare arms. Carefully she slipped her feet into the black heels she had chosen especially for tonight. A tiny black bag completed her outfit. She turned to face Mitch.

"I'm ready if you are." Her voice was husky as she took in the mouthwatering view of Mitchel Stewart in a black tuxedo. Long, tall and lean, he suited it perfectly. Even the black cummerbund at his waist and the pristine bow tie suited him.

"I think I might whistle myself," she murmured, wrapping her arm through his. He flashed his white teeth in a smile guaranteed to knock her socks off before brushing the everpresent lock of dark hair off his forehead.

"When did you get home?" she demanded. His behavior made her reverse all those terrible convictions she'd been reciting.

"Oh, I've been around, waiting for you." He had the look of a fox about to pounce on a poor innocent little mouse, she decided, mesmerized by his electric eyes. "Shall we?" he asked and Melanie strolled with him through the door and down to his waiting car. She eyed it with distrust before sliding in.

"I don't have my tool kit. Are you sure we'll get there in this thing?" she asked, gingerly doing up her seat belt. "That's the problem with these cars. They're all looks and no stamina."

He frowned down at her.

"Just because there was one little problem with my car does not mean you have to—" He stopped abruptly when Melanie raised her hands.

"I surrender. White flag. Sorry." She grinned at him, winking. "Let's call a truce. Just for tonight. Battle lines resume tomorrow."

And they did manage to discuss a few personal topics during the evening without coming to blows.

The restaurant was a new one, and Melanie eyed its sumptuous interior with wide eyes. The huge room glowed romantically in the subtle lights, silverware gleaming and immaculate linen perfectly folded. Handsome young men stood waiting on the sidelines in their black suits with crisply pressed shirts. In the background, a pianist added to the general ambience.

Melanie sighed in satisfaction as she pushed away her plate much later.

"I will never eat again," she pledged solemnly. "The salmon was excellent. And those tiny potatoes. Mmm." She smiled across the table at Mitch. "Everything was perfect."

Her plate was whisked away. Seconds later Kramer, their waiter, returned with a dessert tray that swept away all her good intentions. Mitch immediately chose the French silk pie while Melanie took her time drooling over everything before deciding on the lemon pistachio cheesecake.

"Do you come here often?" she asked, closing her eyes as her taste buds reacted to the sensational flavor.

When there was no answer, she opened her eyes to find him staring at her. Melanie tried to fill the silence gaping between them.

"I can see why you swim if you drop in here frequently. There have to be about seven thousand calories in this sliver." She shrugged. "And it's worth every one."

"No, I've never been here before," Mitch answered. "And I know what you mean. I don't think thirty laps is going to kill off this pie." Suddenly he grinned. "We'll have to think of something else."

Melanie's face colored as she considered kissing those lips again. Not that she would, but it *was* an interesting thought. Still, she refused to be baited into voicing those very personal thoughts.

"You mean dancing?" she asked innocently.

Mitch kept grinning. That, of course, prompted thoughts of

the two of them together as a couple. To her dismay, that wasn't such a terrible picture at all.

"You seem to have settled into the apartment okay," he said quietly.

"Do I?" She laughed nervously. "I have to tell you, I still feel strange. It's a bit like lying to get something and then watching everything you say and do so you don't trip yourself up. That's the part that keeps bothering me." She shifted uneasily. "If there was another way to get that money for Sunset, believe me, I'd take it. Besides, they did say we were winners and sent the letters out, so I'm not trying to swindle anyone." She sighed.

"It is strange, though. The entry form said Sunset's address for both of us. I can't imagine how I made such a mistake."

"It's baffling, all right, but then the whole thing has been downright bizarre from the very beginning." His voice was low and full of something. What was it? Humor?

They lingered over coffee, enjoying the hauntingly familiar music and the mellow flavor of perfectly roasted Colombian beans. Melanie sat gazing at the couples moving slowly around the shining parquet floor before Mitch finally asked the question she'd been waiting for.

"Would you like to dance?"

"Yes." She rose from her chair with alacrity. "Remember, though, I'm not very good at dancing. Still, it shouldn't be too difficult. Everyone is just swaying to the music." And holding their partner in their arms, her subconscious whispered.

"Not difficult at all," he murmured as he pulled her a little closer against his chest. Melanie drew in a breath of air and held it as his hand slid down her back.

They moved slowly around the dance floor, brushing occasionally against the other couples. For once Melanie allowed herself to relax and enjoy the sensation. After all, what could happen with all these people around?

Which was probably how she came to find herself cradled in Mitch's strong arms as they swayed together on the terrace.

She could smell the fragrant lily of the valley blooming in the pots nearby. And the delicate scent of gypsophila in full flower, growing wild around the edge of the brick patio, carried its heavy perfume through the night air.

"Isn't it a beautiful night?" she whispered, gazing at the star-studded sky. "It's nights like this when it's difficult for me to believe that anyone would think God doesn't exist. You can see so much beauty in His creation."

She felt Mitch's hands in her hair.

"There's beautiful and then there is beautiful," he murmured, sliding the ebony combs that held the upswept curls in place. With a swish they fell in a cascade of russet, tumbling wildly around her bare shoulders. One fat ringlet curved against the end of his index finger and clung there.

"You have beautiful hair, Melanie. It's so soft and silky." He buried his face in the gleaming tresses as his hands raked through the curls. One finger gently lifted a lock, and he replaced it with his lips.

"Your skin is like satin," he murmured, trailing a path upward to the pulsing cord in her neck.

Melanie couldn't say a word. Her breath was trapped somewhere between her throat and her mouth as she stood silent under his tender caress.

When at last his lips covered hers, she answered his question with all her pent-up longings, holding him closely as she ran her fingers down his hard, smooth back.

"Ah, young lovers. How sweet."

The mocking tones of an elderly woman watching them from the terrace grated on her nerves, and Melanie pulled away from Mitch abruptly. His body shielded her from their visitors, and Melanie used the opportunity to gather her hair in some semblance of its earlier style. Her fingers shoved the combs in roughly, stabbing her scalp with their sharp points.

In an effort to break the tension crackling between them, Melanie glanced at her watch, searching for something mundane to say. She was stunned to see it was already eleven.

"Good gracious." Her voice sounded suddenly breathless.

She wondered if he knew she had been daydreaming about them. "I've got to get in early tomorrow. Would you mind if we left now?"

Reluctantly, Mitch guided her to their table. He shoved his credit card into his wallet before lifting her shawl from the chair.

"How much earlier do you have to get up?" he asked dourly, obviously envisioning being awakened in the wee morning hours. "You're already up before the birds."

"Don't worry," she told him gaily as he wrapped her shawl about her shoulders. "I won't wake you."

"Yeah, right." It was very faint, but Melanie clearly heard the muttered response. She wisely left the remark alone.

They rode home silently, except for the soft jazz sounds playing on the car's CD. For once Melanie didn't mind the music, letting it flow around her like a blanket. As they neared the apartment block, Melanie turned toward Mitch.

"Thank you again for a lovely evening," she told him sincerely. "I think I understand that legal brain of yours a little better now after listening to some of those college stunts."

Mitch snorted derisively. His dark eyes widened as he grinned at her.

"Somehow, I think that is a dubious compliment from a woman who rigged a wheelchair to collapse while her instructor demonstrated its use."

Melanie shrugged, widening her eyes to stare innocently up at him.

"Can I help it if I'm mechanical?" Her tones were the sweet, honeyed ones she used in the boardroom. They hadn't gained her much sympathy there, either, she reflected as Mitch's derisive tones followed her.

"Poor little thing!"

Mitch unlocked the apartment door and ushered her inside. Hope was nowhere to be seen. Melanie slipped out of her heels and curled her toes in the plush carpet. Suddenly the silence between them gaped uncomfortably.

"Uh, well, good night. And thanks again." Even to herself, Melanie knew she sounded like an embarrassed schoolgirl.

"Melanie." Mitch's deep voice urged her to stay even as his hand on her arm stopped her flight. Dark and brooding, his eyes moved across her face.

"I enjoyed being with you, Melanie. I'm glad we could share tonight." His voice was softly sensuous in the quiet apartment. "I want you to know that I enjoy having you as my roommate."

Mitch slid his hands up her arms slowly. His voice continued to surround her like a thick, numbing fog.

"I'm sorry I've been such a bear to live with. Forgive me?" He bent his head low enough to press a tiny kiss to the rapidly pulsing cord along her neck.

Melanie gulped, searching for the right words. It was hard to think with Mitch's spicy after-shave tickling her nose, reminding her. She finally muttered, "I like you, too," but her voice was squeaky. Probably because his hands were tangling in her hair, massaging her tingling scalp in a way that made Melanie's knees go rubbery. That misty voice was covering her in a haze of longing that begged for more of his touch.

His soft lips pressed a tiny caress to the corner of her mouth as Melanie felt his arms go round her. Then he was kissing her harder. And she was kissing him back.

It was crazy, Melanie thought. She couldn't get involved with this man. She had things to do. A mission. She wrapped her arms around his neck and let herself relax just a bit. "This can't be so wrong, can it?" she asked herself.

"I have wanted to do this for so long," Mitch told her. His hands slipped over the smooth skin of her arms, transmitting little sparks all along the way. "You have beautiful hair," he breathed, his hands moving up to luxuriate in the strands he'd loosened.

"Oh, Melanie," he murmured, "I knew a date with you would be sheer torture." His lips took hers once more in a kiss that threatened to send Melanie to outer space.

And somewhere, in her deepest thoughts, she relayed a

message heavenward. *Oh, Lord, if this is wrong; if You don't want this, please tell me now.*

Eons later—or was it only seconds—Melanie became drowsily aware that Mitch had stopped the gentle, tender movements of his hands. She lifted her head when he moved away from her, chilled by the cool air of the apartment on her skin. Dimly she heard a buzzing sound, but her befuddled senses couldn't seem to identify the source.

Mitch pushed the shiny auburn strands off her shoulders and pressed a tiny kiss to the corner of her mouth.

"Someone has incredibly bad timing," he muttered, frowning. "I guess we should be thankful it wasn't Hope and that she didn't burst right in." Muttering dire predictions, he stalked to the door and swung it open, ready to lambaste the intruder. Instead his mouth hung open in amazement. Not a word left his lips.

Their visitor, on the other hand, suffered no such affliction. She wedged her tiny jeans-clad form through the narrow opening Mitch's body allowed and stood facing Melanie. Her gamine features were enhanced by the short, spiky black hair that framed her face. Deep blue eyes crinkled when she smiled, standing on tiptoes to kiss his chin.

Then she strode to Melanie and thrust out her hand.

"Hi," she greeted her brightly. "You must be Melanie. I'm Sara. Mitch's ex."

Chapter Eight

"Oh, Father, I need Your help."

Melanie prayed desperately for the floor to cave in. Since it didn't, she decided to brazen it out. If this was God's answer, it was a pretty clear one. She felt disoriented, confused. She'd been on cloud nine. Now she slammed into old terra firma with a vengeance. She should have known better than to expect someone who looked like Mitch to be free and available, and indisputably she should have known he wouldn't be interested in her, plain, boring Melanie.

Melanie felt exposed, her desire for this man revealed for this interloper to see. It was humiliating to realize how much she had wanted him to be Mr. Right, and now to see how little she obviously meant to him.

Although she knew her lips bore the imprint of his kisses, Melanie decided to leave the room with as much dignity as she could muster. She also decided to get out of her outfit. Maybe some of the embarrassment would fall away with a change of clothes.

"I'll leave you two alone, then," she murmured, moving toward her bedroom. "Good night." The quiet words took every ounce of pride she had left.

"Sara," Mitch exploded as soon as Melanie had closed the door. "What in the world are you doing here?" His tone was not welcoming.

"Breaking up a cozy little tête-à-tête, by the looks of it." Sara grinned unrepentantly. She shook one finger at him. "Living together? Mitchel Stewart, I am aghast and dismayed that you've dropped your standards."

Mitchel could have cheerfully strangled her, but he sighed deeply and decided instead to find out what had made this visit so necessary. Sara's surprises were well-known. But first things first, he resolved.

He'd watched Melanie's face when Sara had dropped her bombshell, and Mitch knew he would have to talk to her. He had no intention of letting Melanie go that easily. Why, he wasn't sure, but it was somehow important that she know he hadn't been lying to her, that she was the woman he'd wanted to be with this evening.

After settling Sara with a cup of coffee at the kitchen counter, he knocked loudly on Melanie's door and then, when he heard her tell him to go away, disobeyed and opened it.

She was standing in front of her closet arranging the black dress on a padded hanger. Her makeup had been removed, and her long hair hung in loose waves down her back. He noticed she was swathed head to toe in flannelette. The sight had a ridiculously unsettling effect on him. It was her face that caught his attention, however. It was pinched and white. Her huge green eyes stared at him, pools of color in her wan complexion.

"I don't think this is a good idea—"

He cut her off. "Well, tough, because I do." In two strides he reached her. Gently he fastened a hand around her arm. "Sit down for a minute, Melanie. I want to talk to you about Sara."

"None of this is any of my business," she murmured, trying to pull away.

Mitch wasn't having any. He would blasted well nip this in the bud. He grimaced. Then maybe they could go back to where they were before Sara had thrown a wrench into things. Much as he hated disclosing his personal life, Sara's arrival had left him little choice.

"Melanie, Sara isn't my ex-wife, she's my ex-sister. Sort of." He could see disbelief cloud the clear green of her eyes, and he rushed to explain.

"My mother was married to Sara's father when we were kids. They got a divorce before they killed each other, thank heavens. But when each of them got married again and we were split up, Sara was heartbroken." He took a deep breath. It was still painful seventeen years later.

"She always had this family thing," he told her, as if she didn't. "Sara was only ten at the time, and she needed a friend. The only way I could console her was by telling her we would still be related, and she clung to the relationship. She still uses it whenever she needs a hand, or a shoulder to cry on."

Mitch brushed the soft curls on her shoulder. One curling tendril fastened itself around his finger.

"If she's here, it must mean something has happened. She wouldn't come to me unless she had nowhere else to go."

He tipped her rounded chin up, forcing her sad eyes to meet his. He smiled gently and brushed a feather-light kiss on the corner of her mouth. The sizzle was still there, he mused, pulling his mouth from hers with difficulty.

"I promised I'd be here if she ever needed me, Melanie, and I can't renege. Can you understand that?" He deliberately held her wide-eyed gaze with his, letting her see into his soul. He hoped somehow that she would understand, but he held his breath just in case.

The bedside clock ticked loudly in the silence of the room while Melanie watched him. Finally, her soft hand closed around his as it cupped her chin.

"Go," was all she said, but it was enough.

Mitch leaned down to press one more kiss on her full, inviting lips.

"Thank you," he whispered. When she kissed him back,

he was drawn into a maelstrom of heat that burned in its intensity. Finally, he forced his head up. Getting off the bed, he straightened his backbone and walked resolutely to the door. Before he pulled it open, Mitch stopped and turned to face her.

"We are not finished our earlier discussion," he said quietly. "Not by a long shot. And one of these days we are going to finish what we start." Then he turned and walked through the door, pulling it softly closed behind himself.

Two hours later Mitch decided that life couldn't get much more complicated. He had given Sara his bedroom and now he searched for some comfortable spot on the sofa. He was beginning to realize comfort was not one of the assets built into this piece of furniture.

But worse, he kept seeing Melanie sitting on her bed, wearing her pyjamas, her face full of something he didn't want to define. A picture of Hope's astonished look when she'd let herself in an hour ago and found yet another female in residence was more than enough to scare away what little sleep he thought he might gather.

Enough!

Mitch rolled over and decided to focus on the previous evening and the conversation he and Melanie had shared. He'd been impressed with her plans for the nursing home. The money from Papa John's ridiculous contest would go a long way toward her dream of installing those new bed monitors she had described.

Mitch had been appalled when Melanie described how some patients were restrained from injuring themselves and others.

"That's inhumane," he told her, outraged at the idea of anyone being restrained in a chair or bed.

"Yes, it is," she agreed. "That's why I'm trying to change the way we deal with residents. But the monitors are new and very expensive." She'd studied her hands.

"There is a lift that I've requested from the board several times, which lifts the resident out of the bathtub without endangering him. And a special type of whirlpool for those with arthritis.'' She ticked the items off on her fingers. ''And it sure would be nice to get a stock of those new bed linens that would replace our present five layers of cotton. All that washing means we need a large laundry staff, and our bills are horrendous.''

To Mitch, the list was unending.

''Is the place that far behind?'' His question had irked her.

''I haven't even told you about the van I want, to take residents on excursions to the park or whatever.'' She smiled. ''And we need a big-screen television that the visually impaired can see without squinting.'' Melanie had enlightened him with several more plans, her hair shimmering red sparks in the low light of the restaurant.

''Mitchel, there is a terrific need to update old machinery everywhere, including the special care homes. More and more, we are trying to keep seniors in their homes for as long as possible, with the help of visiting nurses and live-in care, but our population is aging, and the costs keep soaring.''

He had seen Melanie's green eyes flash fire with the intensity of her feelings. He watched her face, fascinated by its mobility as she described the home.

''But it's more than monetary needs. It's also a perception of the way we treat senior citizens.'' Her long fingers had pleated and folded the pale green napkin carefully as she spoke.

''So many people today think that older people have lost their ability to hear and see and feel. They are rude and condescending to people who were once someone's boyfriend, lover, coworker or friend. They have dehumanized our parents and grandparents into statistics. That's something I won't tolerate.''

Her tone had been fierce, and Mitch was amazed at the amount of feeling Melanie had shown. It was clear that each resident was an individual to her, important in his or her own way. He had seen it well enough in the visitors she invited to the apartment, or had taken on long drives through the countryside. Just yesterday he'd watched her feed ice cream to a man who drooled continually. Melanie simply wiped his chin matter-of-factly and kept right on feeding him, talking all the while.

Mitch sympathized with her opinions. In his own work, Mitch had watched as some of his clients tried to bully their parents into choices they clearly didn't desire. All for the sake of money. It was a poor excuse, he knew that from firsthand experience.

He was seriously attracted to her, Mitch decided, thunking his pillow once more. He had known that for a long time but had refused to acknowledge their growing chemistry because there was a part of him that steadfastly resisted becoming involved in a serious relationship. He had been involved with his heart once before.

When the one person he had really trusted had walked away without a backward glance, Mitch had been stuck with pain unlike anything he'd ever known. But this thing with Melanie was different somehow. Wasn't it? She would never do what Sam had done. But no matter how he phrased it, his mind stubbornly resisted and told Mitch exactly what happened when you got involved. You got hurt.

And no doubt that little voice was right. He had watched his mother's marriages go down the tubes for most of his childhood. He had experienced the pain and destruction that went along with it, all in the name of love. His father's brutality had convinced him that love was not to be desired. No way would he do that to another person.

Life didn't come with guarantees, and there was no way he would subject another human being to the feeling of loss and abandonment he had known. He would enjoy Melanie's companionship, yes, but his heart would remain untouched. He repeated it, just to make sure his subconscious absorbed all that.

And yet as he lay there rolling the pictures through his mind, an inner voice questioned his truthfulness. Wasn't it possible that he was already losing his detachment?

Unbidden, the tape in his mind showed a giggling Melanie as she had tossed a laughing little boy in the air. Mitch had come home to find her baby-sitting her friend's child one evening last week. He'd felt a funny tremor in his throat, a sort of tightening as he watched the two of them romp together. Her face had been alive with pleasure as she enjoyed the little boy's hug. Her eyes lit with an inner light before she set him down to continue their game.

For a moment, he'd almost thought that child was himself, years ago. It was exactly the scene he had always wanted to remember from his own youth and never would. Somehow that expression of love and devotion signified the kind of caring he had ached to have someone show him, but never had.

He tossed the thought aside grimly.

Don't get sentimental, buddy, he told himself. *Your life was about as far from her picture-perfect world as it got. And it isn't going to change just because you've gone all syrupy over one beautiful nurse.*

Mitch turned over on the uncomfortable sofa, refusing to examine more closely what he felt. He hit the pillow one last time, deciding to get some sleep. Which wouldn't be easy considering the way the sofa cushions separated under his ribs.

"Lord, You know how I feel about this. And You know what's inside of me, creating this ache for someone to be close to. Please help me to know the right road."

At three-thirty Mitch switched everything end for end, then lay down on the puffy unstable cushions once more. He still had Sara's problem to deal with, he reminded himself. It would be a long day before he got that little issue settled to everyone's satisfaction.

It was probably going to be even longer before he got another chance to be alone with the woman in the next room. Mitch decided to forget everything but the picture he had in his mind of Melanie in that black fluffy outfit she had worn tonight. A smile curved his lips.

Yes, sirree, that was quite a woman.

"Melanie, Thomas McCabe peed in his juice glass again!" Bridget was not amused.

Melanie faced Bridget, thinking out loud. "I have always deplored using diapers on adults just because it's not convenient for the staff members to be kept constantly running to assist them." Her face tightened. "But in Thomas's case, I might be persuaded to reconsider. At least the dishes would be safe."

Melanie heard Bridget's laughter bubble out behind her as she reluctantly left the applications she was perusing to deal with the recalcitrant Mr. McCabe.

Of course, she didn't get back to work immediately because, for the tenth time that day, one of their most uncooperative residents refused to lay off the buzzer beside his bed. She sucked in a deep breath, ready to lay it on the line, when the piercing shriek of a door alarm went off. Since she was nearest, Melanie headed for the exit at top speed, warily checking left and right to see who had activated it.

She used her master key to silence the bell before heading out the door. She came face to face with Mitch. He was red with embarrassment as his sapphire blue eyes guiltily met hers. He shuffled from one foot to the other, jiggling his black leather briefcase impatiently.

"Melanie." His low, husky greeting caused a flare of excitement within her, which she forced herself to ignore.

"What, exactly, are you doing?" she demanded, fixing him with her fiercest glare. When a worried RN stuck her head out the door, Melanie assured her that everything was fine. "Mr. Stewart merely lost his way," she said. "Please leave the door unlocked. I'll set it when I go back in."

Melanie planted her hands on her hips. "Well?"

"Yes, well, uh, Mrs. Rivers, um, do you see her?" He was peering into the shrubbery like Inspector Clousseau.

Melanie was not amused. She thought of those interviews that needed doing if she wasn't to spend another weekend covering several part-time shifts on the floor. Not to mention the reports due two weeks ago. And she hadn't even started charting the med orders that awaited processing after this morning's rounds.

"Time is of the essence here, Mitch. Exactly what do you want?"

He looked over his shoulder to be sure no one was listening. "Mrs. Rivers phoned my office, asking me to be here at two-thirty sharp. She said it was urgent and a secret. She left specific directions to meet her here." He looked around the courtyard again. A small frown pleated his forehead. "At least I think it was here," he mused.

Melanie burst out laughing.

"Nettie Rivers suffers from memory loss, Mitch. She may very well have made an appointment, but chances are she's totally forgotten what it was about." Something clicked in Melanie's mind. "Did you activate the alarm or was it already going?" Her voice was sharp with anxiety.

Mitch grinned self-consciously, brushing a hand through his black locks. Melanie privately thought he looked even cuter all mussed up.

"I guess I set it off," he admitted. "That means she couldn't be out here, right?"

"Right." Melanie tugged on his wool-suited arm. "Come on, Mitch, time to move on. Nettie is probably on her way to the dining room or already drinking her afternoon coffee as we speak."

She pulled him through the door and set the alarm. Brushing the fall of hair off her neck, she sighed.

"I could do with a cup myself." As Melanie strode energetically down the hall, Mitch moved to catch up.

"Where's her room?" he asked. "I'm curious to see if it has all been a hoax. My secretary said the old girl sounded pretty impatient."

Melanie stared at him. "Nettie's room is down this corridor, then turn right." She turned to speak to one of the special care aides, and when she turned back, Mitch had disappeared down the hall. Shrugging, she moved wearily toward the dining room. She had just poured herself a cup of coffee when he returned.

"Can I join you?" he asked warily, noticing the lines of tiredness around her eyes.

"Help yourself," she told him, waving toward the trolley nearby. She was absolutely not going to wait on him. Not today, when her feet felt like lead.

As they drank their coffee, Mitch told her more about the unusual phone call.

"My secretary said she was whispering. I'm afraid I couldn't get here when she wanted, so she said this afternoon would be fine." His blue eyes, wide open and boyishly touching, stared into hers.

Melanie told herself not to get mushy. There was a roomful of residents and staff surrounding her. Most of them had their eyes fixed on Mitch. She could imagine their thoughts.

"I just thought of something." Melanie motioned to one of the activities aides. "Didn't Nettie Rivers go out this afternoon?" she asked curiously.

The woman nodded, a grin creasing her full cheeks.

"A limo picked her up right after lunch. Very fancy. She won't be back till five or so. Your mother was with them."

"My mother?" Melanie frowned. Charity seldom went out with anyone but Faith and Hope, and certainly never in a limo. "And who is *them?*"

But the aide had no more information. She hurried away to rescue her bingo game. Melanie looked at Mitch, shrugging.

"I don't know what they're up to," she said thoughtfully. "But if the fearsome threesome are involved, it's liable to be complicated. Guess you got the times mixed up or misunderstood her."

"No," he told her seriously, "I know she specifically said two-thirty." He shrugged. "I'll come back at five," he told her. "Maybe she'll be back by then."

They sat talking for the rest of her break. Melanie asked

him questions about Sara, to which he relayed the barest information. He refused to give any details, and after a while Melanie gave up.

By the time she arrived home, Melanie's curiosity about the strange afternoon had soared. She made herself sit and talk amiably with Sara until Mitch came home, but the minute he was through the door she nabbed him.

"Did you find Nettie? What did she want?" But Mitch wasn't giving.

"Sorry, Mel, but it's client confidentiality. Can't discuss it." His eyes twinkled as he undid his flashy tie.

Melanie flushed with embarrassment. He was enjoying this, darn the man. Okay, she could play, too. Turning to Sara, she asked innocently, "What was it you were telling me about Mitch's girlfriends, Sara?" She grinned, satisfied when she saw his head whirl. Melanie winked at Sara, who caught on immediately.

"Well, they're all so cerebral, if you know what I mean. Brainy without an ounce of human kindness. There was this one…" Her voice trailed away as Mitch's bedroom door slammed shut. The conspirators looked at each other and burst out laughing.

Sara was a good sport, Melanie decided. Maybe his sister would help her try to understand what made Mitch tick, why he was so negative when it came to family and commitment.

"Sara, please don't think I'm trying to pry." Melanie began slowly, feeling her way. "But why is it that Mitch is so closed off, self-contained? What's his problem?"

Sara studied her, her dark head tilted to one side.

"I have a pact with him," she told Melanie in soft undertones. "I don't break his privacy, and he reciprocates. But in your case…" Her blue eyes searched Melanie's. "In your case I'm going to make an exception." She took a deep breath and began the story.

"Mitch has been a loner for as long as I've known him," she told Melanie. "I suppose he's told you that we are not really related?"

Melanie nodded.

"Well, Mitch and I were so happy when our parents got together. We thought we would be a family, you see. He wanted that so badly for his mother." Her huge blue eyes were sparkling with unshed tears.

Melanie thought about what Mitch had told her of Sara's need for family. Now she knew Mitch had needed one, too.

Sara dashed her tears away and continued.

"As it turned out, there couldn't have been a worse move for our folks. They couldn't agree on anything. And they fought continuously. About everything." The younger woman was lost in thought.

"Can you tell me any more, Sara?" Melanie hesitated to ask, but any information she could add to her cache of knowledge about Mitch could help her understand him better. She leaned back in the hard kitchen chair as Sara resumed speaking. In her mind she began building a picture of a vulnerable little boy.

"I was ten and Mitch was fifteen. He was so happy to have a father who didn't beat his brains out. Problem was, he couldn't seem to relate to my dad." Sara brushed her short hair off her flushed face. "Not that I blame him. I had a little trouble there myself." Sara grinned that self-deprecating smile.

"Anyway, things between them went from bad to worse. Add to that our parents' total unhappiness with each other, and it's not a pretty story." Sadness flooded across her pretty face.

"Finally, of course, they divorced. Mitch was furious when his mother married again just one year after she got the papers. He came to see me once in a while, and I got the gist of his life at home. It was pretty bad."

Melanie watched with pity and sadness as disgust and loathing distorted Sara's face.

"It was her sixth marriage, and although she seemed to have finally found happiness, Mitch couldn't adjust. He and his stepfather argued continually. The guy was pretty straight and very tough, insisting that Mitch tow the mark one hundred percent. Mitch's mother sided with her husband. When she wasn't strung out on tranquilizers or booze, that is.''

Melanie put her hand on Sara's shoulder in consolation. It was obvious that Sara had felt Mitch's pain deeply. Still did.

''I suppose you knew that's why he doesn't drink?'' Her eyes were bright with curiosity as she watched Melanie. ''Mitch always said his mother did enough for both of them, and he won't touch the stuff. He won't even take an aspirin without being in severe pain.''

''I'm afraid I didn't notice,'' Melanie told her. ''All I have seen is this cold, hard side of him that he's convinced can't be changed. If you push too hard, he shuts you out.''

''Yes, that's exactly how he's always survived,'' Sara told her, a wistful smile on her face. ''I guess it's better than not surviving at all,'' she added. ''Fortunately, Mitch excelled at school, so his mother decided to send him to boarding school. Paid for by his stepfather. His mother was pregnant and sobering up by then, and they wanted him out of the way while she dealt with her problems.'' Sara's face was grim.

''You couldn't blame them for that. The woman needed help. But pretty soon a pattern began to develop. Every time he returned for holidays or school breaks, there was a child around whom his mother and stepfather doted on, and no place for him—or at least Mitch didn't think so. Eventually he didn't even try to fit in. He wasn't so hardheaded then, though.'' Sara's voice died away.

''That happened when Samantha Jones arrived.''

Melanie thought back on the few statements Mitch had made about himself. She didn't remember anyone named Jones.

''Who?'' Melanie tried to keep her curiosity under control.

''She was someone he fell for in law school. And he fell hard. Samantha had him wound around her little finger.'' Sara's voice was filled with disgust. ''Anything Sammy wanted, Sammy got. Mitch had to hold down two jobs just to get himself through law school, never mind provide the little baubles she constantly demanded. And don't forget he was studying all hours, as well.''

"I imagine it must have been difficult," Melanie said sympathetically.

"Difficult? It was darn near impossible. But he did it— until Samantha got him cutting back on his study time." Sara's eyes glittered angrily. "Poor little rich girl needed a date to Daddy's dinners!"

"Oh." Melanie cringed at Sara's sarcasm. "But couldn't he have refused?" she asked curiously.

"He did, at first. But Samantha wasn't giving up. And little by little, she took over his life. He was so totally besotted, Mitch never knew what hit him until he got his marks. He flunked the year." Sara moved to pour a glass of water. She drank slowly, her eyes deep pools of bitterness.

"Well?" Melanie demanded, finally getting an insight into what made Mitchel Stewart tick. "Go on."

"Mitch knew it was make-or-break time. No way was he going back to his stepfather. And by then his grandfather was encouraging him to buckle down. Mitch got his professors to agree to let him repeat the year, but he lost the funding that paid for his tuition."

"But couldn't Samantha help with that?" Melanie asked curiously. "Make him a loan or something?"

Sara snorted. "She had a new boy toy by then, Melanie. She had never been interested in Mitch other than his abilities as an escort to parties or showing her off on the dance floor. He was a hunk who could ferry her around. He wouldn't stay at her wild parties, so she dropped him. She finally told him to his face exactly how little she thought of him." Sara shook her head sadly.

"But for Mitch, it was the final straw," she explained. "He had tried for years to be the son his mother wanted and never quite made the grade. Now a woman he thought really cared for him, someone he had based his future on, wanted him to be something he wasn't. When he wouldn't even pretend to do as she asked, Sammy turned her back on him." Sara's voice overflowed with disgust.

"In fact, she left him for his best friend. And Mitch was left to pull his life together. Alone." Sara wrapped her arms around herself as her big eyes fixed on Melanie.

"Well, he pulled out of it, passed the bar and went into practice. I was there the day he got his degree. He told me he was finished trying to find love. He cut himself off from his mother and stepfather, got his own life and never talked to any of them—except his grandfather, as far as I know."

"You mean his parents are still married?" Melanie asked curiously, caught up in the story of such a sad family.

"Oh, yes. His mother finally found a man she loved. Unfortunately, she lost her son." Her eyes were sad with regret.

"But Mitch…" Sara shook her head. "He's convinced himself that he can be totally enclosed. Because he lost the ability to trust his own feelings, he will not believe in anyone else's. He's frozen that side of his life. Now he doesn't make any commitments." She shook her head. "And so he is never disappointed."

Sara rubbed her tears away.

"I have got to get going. I'm going to buy a house here, and as soon as I do, the kids are coming. We're supposed to put the down payment on one I really like today and then we can move some stuff in. Mitch said he could help. See you later." Sara drummed her fingers on Mitch's door. "Come on, bro. You've got a heap of lifting to do today."

They left shortly after that, insulting each other with good-natured gibes.

Melanie sat on the hard kitchen stool and contemplated the little boy who had never received the affection he craved. Was all that male macho and freewheeling debonairness just a facade? She remembered his remarks about trust and knowing who you were and she cried for that needy child and the man he'd become. She could still hear his pain.

"You were lucky," he had said about her mother and the adoption. "Some kids never get to experience any of that."

Kids like him, she thought sadly. Kids who needed a hug so badly they ached. Bitterness welled within her at the childhood of pain that still clung to him.

Suddenly, the anger and frustration Melanie felt toward Mitch mellowed as she perceived his attitudes through a different light. Trust would come hard. And loving? Well, that would be very difficult. If it ever happened.

She knew there was something between them. It was there when he had wrapped his big arms around her last night. His kiss had not been cold and calculated. Instead he had touched her with sensitivity, gently nullifying all the inhibitions she had so carefully held. And he had asked for as much as he gave. Somewhere under that immaculate facade was a man who had a lot to give the world, if he would only let go. Then, later, he had asked for her trust.

Well, then, she would trust him, Melanie decided. She would explore the building relationship between them as far as he would let her. And if the time came when he no longer wanted her around, well, Melanie would deal with that, too.

Finally, she acknowledged what she had known for days.

She loved him.

And the emotion scared her to death. He'd been hurt, badly. And she had no experience in dealing with men like him. It had always been she who had been in control in the relationship. Now, suddenly, there was no control. Melanie felt as if her life was in free fall.

It was hopeless. It was wonderful. It was crazy. And Melanie had no idea how to act. She was living with a man who refused to discuss his past. They shared his apartment, rubbed shoulders daily. And they waited for prize money he would help her acquire. Meanwhile, he aided a stepsister who needed his help.

Melanie was convinced that Mitch had fooled himself. He was a man who had a lot of love to give, he just didn't know how. Somehow he needed to see that.

"Oh, there you are, dear. Had a good day?" Hope scurried in the door, her usual immaculate, efficient self. She was carrying several shopping bags but didn't offer to show the contents.

"Interesting," Melanie replied, with an astute glance at the parcels. "And you? I heard you were at Sunset today." She watched for a reaction and was rewarded when Hope's eyes widened in surprise.

"Oh, well, yes. The girls and I decided to go visiting."

"Did you? How nice. How long did you have Nettie out for?" she asked solicitously.

"Oh, well, you know how these tea things go. A couple of hours." Hope's normally pale skin was suffused with color.

"I see. Did you go in your car?"

"Oh, dear me, no," Hope said. "That is, we didn't need to. Papa John was there, and he took us all for a ride in his limousine. We went to the malt shop."

Melanie stared, her brain striving to assimilate the unlikely picture of the four older women and a silver haired, pot-bellied man daring to breach the sanctity of the teenagers' local haunt.

"Papa John was at Sunset?" Melanie frowned. "I never heard a word."

"Oh, my dear, he's been visiting Nettie for simply ages. They're quite good friends, you know. And he's ever so kind and gentle with her. Nettie speaks so freely when she's with him."

"But doesn't that bother you? I mean, Mitch told me he might be your Jean."

Hope shook her head. "Oh, he's not my Jean," she said softly. "I think my Jean died a long time ago. Papa John doesn't have Jean's French accent and doesn't express himself the same way at all."

"So you don't think..." Melanie hated to say the words.

"Do I still think he bears a resemblance to Jean?" Hope murmured thoughtfully. "Oh, he definitely does. But that's not exactly what I meant. You see—" She fiddled with a strand of hair. "Jean was that special person in my life all those years ago. We shared our hopes and dreams and there was nothing we didn't discuss.''

"And Papa John isn't like that?" Melanie tried to understand.

"Yes, he's like that all the time. But with Nettie. He really cares for her. And whatever he may or may not have once felt for me, I wouldn't dream of destroying the happiness they seem to have found.'' Hope looked up, tears rimming her eyes.

"Whatever Jean and I might once have had is past and buried. It hurts something fierce to say that, but it's true. I'm just beginning to realize that all these years I've been waiting for a fairy tale that couldn't possibly come true.'' She wiped away the tears with her hand in a most indelicate fashion.

"Maybe it could come true," Melanie persisted. "Maybe if he could just remember that you and he were once engaged…''

"Oh, you mustn't encourage that, dear. It would only make him feel sorry for me, obligated somehow. And he's not. Not anymore. No one is. All these years everyone has been so sympathetic.'' She glanced at the ring on her right hand thoughtfully.

"No, my Jean is gone, and I think it's time I removed this and started living in the present. That's what Papa John had to do when he returned from the war. He didn't have a past. And maybe that's for the best. Sometimes people get bogged down in the past.

"Don't you think the same might be true for you?" the older woman murmured.

"I, uh, don't know what you mean," Melanie insisted. "I'm not dreaming any fairy tales.''

Hope shook her head regretfully. Her voice was very gentle when she spoke. "Oh, Melanie, do you really think I don't remember how much you wanted a family? Why, you always used to dream up games about happy families with fathers and mothers and perfect children.'' She wiped away a tear. "Your mother, Faith and I used to pray that you would find your dream someday.'' She fixed Melanie with a stern glance that reminded Melanie of days spent in her class.

"Don't you think perhaps that time has come? With Mitch?"

"You mean you think I should ask him to marry me?" Melanie tried to fob off the question with a laugh. "He's told me numerous times that he's not the marrying type, Hope. And, truth to tell, I'm not sure I am, either. At least not to someone like him.''

"What's wrong with him? He's as handsome as a movie star, established in his law practice. He's even trying to help you get half that prize money, although I confess I wish that aspect would disappear.'' She chuckled. "A real prince, I'd say.''

"Maybe.'' Shrugging, Melanie got up to fill her coffee cup. "But he's also got a lot of baggage from the past.''

"We all carry baggage from the past, Melanie. Some of us just hang on to it longer than others.''

"Maybe,'' she said again. "But even though he is handsome, Hope, I still don't think Mitch is the type of man I need.'' Melanie wanted to nip this particular matchmaking idea in the bud.

"I want someone who is solid and dependable. I have enough bad history to deal with. Those kids I used to dream about…'' She paused, staring at the light fixture. "The truth is, they're a long way from my own childhood reality. I wouldn't know how to raise a child. Not properly. I have no history to draw on. And I won't be responsible for wrecking a child's life.''

Hope's soft, smooth hand covered hers and squeezed gently.

"I'm no expert, of course,'' she murmured. "But I've watched children and their families for years. And my conclusion is that nobody knows exactly the right way to raise a child. And every child is different from every other child, so there is no magic formula.''

"But that's precisely what—''

"God gave us this as a plan," Hope told her seriously, picking up her Bible from a nearby table. "The only formula we have is to ask for God's help, search His word and then apply some good common sense." She spread her hands wide. "And that's it. Except for loving them, of course. And that's usually not too hard for a new mother."

"Maybe," Melanie murmured doubtfully. "But it seems awfully risky to embark on such a thing with a person you barely know."

"Sometimes you have to take a leap of faith," Hope told her sternly. "And it's not really so frightening if you have God behind you, is it?"

"It's very frightening! How can I know that something is God's will and not just my own wants or needs?"

"You ask Him," Hope told her simply. "And then when He opens a way, you take it. Slowly. And trust that He will direct your footsteps through life." She glanced at her watch and stood. "I have to get going. I told your mother I'd have dinner with her." She patted Melanie's hand. "Think about it, Melanie. And pray for His will to guide you. God gives us desires for a reason and He wants to fill those secret wanting places more than we can imagine." Hope tugged on a sweater and moved toward the door.

"Don't waste the present, my dear. Trust me, it's not worth the pain when you find that life has moved on and left you standing alone in your ivory castle, waiting for some fantasy while the real thing walks right past."

Melanie sat for a long time, considering Hope's words. They whirled around her brain until she couldn't make sense of them anymore. Wearily, she set about making supper for Mitch, his sister and herself.

"Is he the one, Lord?" she asked. "But we're so different!" She closed her eyes. "I'm scared, Lord. Scared of getting hurt so badly that I won't be able to pick up the pieces. Please help me to know the right way."

Chapter Nine

"Well, girls, I have some news for you." Hope's voice was brimming with excitement as she burst through the door at Charity's cozy home. She glanced from Faith to Charity and sank into a nearby chair. "You two have been my dearest friends for so long now, I wanted you to be the first to know."

"Go on, then, tell us." Faith beamed, green eyes wide with excitement. "I just love surprises!"

"Yes, dear. Share it with us."

"I'm getting married!" Charity lost three stitches when her knitting needles fell to the floor, and Faith's mouth opened and closed like a fish gulping for air.

"Then it is Jean. I knew he'd come back." Into the shocked stillness, Faith's voice rang with joy. "Praise the Lord!"

"I don't know that Jean has come back, Faith, but I am going to marry Harry. In three weeks."

"Harry Conroy?" Charity squeaked, her brown eyes huge.

"Of course, Harry Conroy," Hope told her, frowning. "He's been asking me for years. Why are you surprised?"

"Because he's been asking you for years. What's suddenly changed that makes Harry so acceptable as a husband now and not ten years ago?'' Charity's expression was full of suspicion. "It's not because you're afraid this Papa John fellow is getting really fond of Nettie Rivers, is it? Hope, are you afraid you'll be left out?''

"Of course not! Charity Flowerday, have you ever known me to act so foolishly?'' Hope murmured in disgust.

"I have,'' Faith said, smiling with a delight. "Remember, it was when we had that new preacher. The one before Pastor Dave. He was so interested in you, Hope, making all those lovey-dovey eyes. And you wouldn't even give him the time of day.'' She twiddled her finger at Hope's reddening face. "He was so handsome—a real hunk.''

"Faith! Wherever did you learn such disgusting terminology?'' Hope asked indignantly. "And for your information, I had no desire whatsoever to become a minister's wife. I'm too outspoken for that. Besides,'' she mumbled, wringing her hands in exasperation, "he ate far too many sweets.''

"So does Harry,'' Charity reminded her friend with a knowing smile.

"Well, it's just different, that's all,'' Hope told them with a shrug. "Harry's been my friend for so long, he feels warm and kind. He doesn't care about my little foibles.''

"Just like my Arthur,'' Faith crowed proudly. She swept Hope into a tight, suffocating hug that wrinkled her best blouse. "I'm so happy for you, dear. Can I help with the wedding?''

"That's what I wanted to talk to you both about.'' Hope smiled, hugging Faith back. "I have a little plan in mind and I want you to help me carry it out.''

Faith jumped to her feet, clapping in excitement.

"I do so love your plans, Hope.'' She beamed happily. "You're always so organized and efficient. What shall I do, Hope, dear?''

"I think perhaps you'd better explain this plan first, Hope. I have a feeling it involves more than you and the judge. Am I correct?'' Charity waited for Hope's nod. "I daresay you have some notion of involving my daughter in it.''

Charity rose from her easy chair and stood frowning at her best friend.

"I do not want Melanie involved in one of your schemes, Hope. Something might go wrong, and my daughter would be very hurt. She knows what she wants out of life, she just hasn't found it yet."

"Oh, yes, she has," Hope murmured. She brushed a soothing hand over Charity's bent shoulder. "I'm not suggesting anything nasty. Just a little helping hand. That's all, I promise."

"And I'll give a helping hand, too," Faith offered. "After all, I did a pretty fair job of it with Gillian and Jeremy, didn't I?" She beamed with satisfaction.

"You did a wonderful job, Faith. And they make a very nice couple. Those two truly love each other." Hope's voice brimmed with tenderness as she smiled at her friend. "I couldn't have wished for a better man for my niece than your nephew."

"Good heavens." Charity breathed in astonishment. "You don't mean to say that you're trying to match up my daughter with Harry's grandson?" She shook her head. "Oh, Hope. I don't think it's a good idea at all. Melanie doesn't even *like* the man. It could all go so wrong and then everyone will be miserable."

"It's not going to go wrong," Hope said firmly. "Now, here's my plan. I intend to ask Melanie and Mitch to help us with our wedding." She detailed the arrangements carefully, and when she had finished all three women were smiling broadly.

"I knew you'd have a wonderful plan," Faith cheered. "You always do."

"And with a lot of help and several minor miracles from above," Charity added dourly, "you just might get it to work."

If she hoped to dampen the spirits of her friends, Charity acknowledged that it wasn't working.

"Well, then, let's ask for that help right now," Hope urged

them. "You might remember, Charity," she chided her friend. "God can do anything." And reverently they bowed their heads to ask their heavenly Father's help in carrying out Hope's wonderful plan.

Hello, Mother. I stopped by to ask you if I might move in with you for a while. Just until I can find another place."

Charity stared at her daughter standing drenched and glum-faced in the sudden downpour, still clad in her pink uniform.

"Darling, of course you can. You know that! Come in."

She urged her inside and waited while Melanie tried to dry herself off. "But I thought you had to stay at Mitch's until they awarded the prize money?"

"Originally that was the plan. But now his sister is here, and the house she bought isn't ready for her or the kids, and I think it's only fitting that Sara stay with her brother." She swooped her damp hair into a knot on the top of her head. "There's just not enough room."

Charity stared. "But I thought Hope was moving out?"

"She did. This morning. That's another reason I think I should leave. It doesn't seem right for me to be staying there now. And Sara and the kids need my room." Melanie peered at her mother suspiciously. "Is there some reason you don't want me to come home, Mother?"

"Of course not! The very idea!" Charity led the way into the same living room Melanie had spent her teen years, without notable success, to decorate to resemble the pictures in several fashionable magazines. "You know that you're welcome anytime."

"Thank you, Mother." Melanie hugged the thin shoulders gratefully. "I was hoping you'd say that, because I've got my stuff in the car outside."

She raced out to the car and returned with two huge suitcases and a paper sack that broke as she came in the door. Melanie blushed as her mother's eyes roved over the bits of tulle, tiny plastic cupids and packages of mints splayed across her floor.

"What in the world?" Charity's eyes were huge with amazement as she spotted white ribbon embossed with bells and tiny golden rings.

"They're for the reception. Hope wanted something for every guest. And the rings go around a little scroll that tells about the custom of marriage. It's really quite lovely."

"But the woman hasn't even chosen her invitations yet," Charity gasped. "Shouldn't that be first on the list?"

"I asked her the same thing," Melanie said, stretching to reach the last ring under the heavy oak bureau in the dining room. "She said, and I quote, 'It's being handled.'"

Melanie plopped into the badly sprung easy chair, edging carefully away from its protruding spring, and frowned at her adoptive parent.

"Mother, what do you really think of it all?"

"Darling, Hope is my very best friend." Charity smiled as she flicked a speck of dust off her coffee table. "I want her to be happy, so naturally I'm very pleased she's found someone to brighten her life."

"Yes, of course," Melanie agreed absently. "But why now? Why all of a sudden like this?"

"Melanie," Charity reprimanded her in a tone of voice Melanie was very familiar with. "Hope and Harry Conroy have been dating on and off for nearly fifteen years. I hardly think this is a *quick* decision. Besides, maybe she's begun to realize that each person only has a finite amount of days available to him."

"I think it has more to do with Jean and Papa John," Melanie murmured slyly, peering up between her lashes.

Charity frowned. "Why would they matter?"

"Hope thinks Papa John is Jean. And Papa John is attracted to Mrs. Rivers. He's always coming to visit her, brings her flowers, takes her for a drive. They even have long, involved conversations."

"Melanie!" Her mother scolded her with her eyes. "They are adults, entitled to their privacy. I thought you encouraged that at Sunset."

"Of course I encourage it," Melanie told her defensively. "But I can't help noticing, can I? Besides, what on earth do they have to discuss? They've hardly known each other long enough."

"Oh, darling." Charity laughed. "When you find your heart's mate, you discuss everything under the sun. You and Mitchel seem to have some of those same discussions," she said offhandedly.

To her disgust, Melanie felt her face color. She frowned. "We've only been discussing the wedding," she claimed stoutly. "For some reason, Judge Conroy has asked Mitch to help out with the wedding. Although what that lawyer knows about weddings could probably fit into a thimble with room left over for your finger."

The doorbell rang, preventing Charity from chastising her youngest child.

"Why, Mitchel! Do come in. How are you this evening, dear?"

Melanie straightened and whirled to face her nemesis, filled with foreboding. To her surprise he had a smile on his face.

"Hi, Mrs. Flowerday. I'm fine, thanks. I wondered if I could speak to Melanie for a moment. I happened to notice her car out front."

"Of course, dear. Come in and have a seat. I'm just going to pick up a loaf of bread from the grocery store. I never baked any today, you see." She glanced from one to the other of the young people. Realizing that they were paying her absolutely no mind whatsoever, she grasped her purse and headed out the door.

"Are they in there?" Hope whispered as soon as Charity had negotiated the stairs. "They're not fighting, are they?" she demanded in the next breath.

Charity wrapped her hand around Hope's thin elbow and drew her along the sidewalk.

"Now, Hope," she chastised in a smiling voice. "You were left to manage your own love life. Let's give them the same opportunity."

"Ha!" Hope's lips turned down in disgust. "I stayed with them for weeks in that apartment, and as far as I can tell, their minds never got close enough to *consider* marriage, let alone view the other as marriage material!"

"Perhaps, my dear Miss Busybody Hopeless," Charity said, using an old childhood nickname, "perhaps you don't see as clearly as you once did."

Melanie, meanwhile, was having trouble with her breathing. Instead of his usual grungy after-hours attire, Mitch was handsomely turned out in a pair of pressed white cuffed shorts and a shirt the exact shade of his cobalt blue eyes. He had on brand-new runners with white—*pristine* white—socks. His hair was tousled as though someone had just run a hand through it, and for the tiniest moment Melanie felt jealous.

"Hi," he murmured, his eyes moving over her wrinkled, still soggy uniform and the scraggly wad of hair pinned to the top of her head. "Have another rough day?"

"No," she informed him abruptly. "I got caught in the rain." She sucked in a deep breath of courage and then let it out in a whoosh. "I'm moving into my mother's for the next little while. You and Sara need the extra room, especially with the kids here now, too."

"I see." He looked almost sad, she decided. "It's a good thing I came over then, isn't it? Otherwise I might not have known." She would have started explaining, but he cut her off.

"Anyway, thanks for thinking of them. This house thing is going to take a little longer than either of us had realized." His eyes studied her carefully. "What's really behind your decision, Melanie?"

"I just didn't feel right about living there anymore," she told him softly. "Not after last Sunday's sermon about living a lie. And anyway, my mother's guests have left now. I always said I'd leave when I found another place." She refused to meet his glance.

"Could we talk as I unpack the car? I have a ton of things

to do for this wedding, and one of my best nurses just went on maternity leave. I may have to go back in.''

"Sure. Come on, I'll help you." And he did. Stoically, without complaint, he carted in box after box, ignoring the dust and mud spots on his clothes. "This isn't all of it, is it?" he asked after lugging the last box up the narrow stairs to her old bedroom.

"No, but I couldn't manage any more in one trip."

"Well, let's go get the rest of it, then. If you're anything like Sara, you can't do without even one of your possessions!"

It sounded like a good opening to an argument, but after his willing help, Melanie didn't have the heart to take him up on it. Besides, she was so hot and tired, she wanted to save every ounce of energy for lifting.

"Okay," she agreed. "Might as well get it over with."

"Might as well." Mitch spoke in a voice that Melanie wished was a little less enthusiastic. Did he want to be rid of her that badly?

Sara had just finished laying the table when they arrived. Melanie could hear the boisterous voices of children giggling and laughing in the other room. Since the children had only arrived that morning, Melanie hadn't had the chance to meet them yet. She moved curiously through the front door, wiping her hands on the seat of her pants. There were two of them, one boy and one girl. They were playing some type of tag, racing around and around the apartment, each trying to avoid the other.

"Becky and Ben," Sara sternly said. "This is an apartment, not the playground."

The two looked suitably chastened. Their black hair and wide blue eyes were identical. Sara spotted Melanie and grinned.

"These two are mine," she told her proudly. "Kids, this is Uncle Mitch's roommate, Melanie."

Mitch's mouth twitched at her words, but neither he nor

Melanie had any opportunity to remonstrate with Sara as one of the twins spoke.

"Are you Uncle Mitch's girlfriend?" Becky asked, her head tilted.

Melanie's cheeks flushed a dark red, but as she opened her mouth, the other child spoke.

"We always like Uncle Mitch's girlfriends. Are you getting married?"

Mitch's blue gaze met Melanie's head on. In his eyes, she could read the message clearly—*fat chance*. He chastised the children for their rudeness and then explained their situation.

"Melanie is a friend of mine. She was staying here until she could find her own place, but then you guys arrived and she decided to move out to give you more room. You be nice," he added sternly.

Both shrugged. "Okay," they agreed happily before moving to turn on the television.

Sara went to shower while the casserole cooked. Melanie was in the kitchen when she felt a long finger under her chin as Mitch tipped it up to look into her bright eyes.

"Sorry about that," he murmured, his hand cupping the curve of her jaw. "They tend to talk first and think later." His eyes twinkled at her. "You have to admit, though, they only asked what a lot of people in this town already think."

Melanie couldn't control the surge of red that colored her face.

"It's a good thing I'm going, then," she managed to say. "Maybe my departure will settle all the gossip down."

Mitch laughed at her embarrassment as his hand tugged her thickly curling hair. The caress was softly intimate, and Melanie felt the familiar thud of her heart as it pressed to jump out of her body.

"They'd worry even more if they knew about this."

She felt his gentle touch on her neck before his lips closed over hers. It was a softly questioning kiss, seeking an answer from her. Melanie kissed him back, then delicately pressed her lips against his stubbled cheek.

"Fortunately for your reputation, I don't kiss and tell." He dipped his head again, seeking the touch of her mouth. They would have continued but for the giggles that erupted.

"I told you she was his girlfriend," one knowledgeable voice whispered. "That's why they're kissing."

"Is not," the other said. "It's 'cause she's got a boo-boo. Uncle Mitch is making it all better." Nodding, the two continued their investigation of the apartment by returning to the living room.

Melanie tried to break away, but Mitch wouldn't let her. He tightened his arms around her waist.

"Do you have a boo-boo?" he asked quietly, his eyes dark and serious. "Tell me where it hurts."

Melanie considered his offer and then tapped a finger to her cheek. Her mother hadn't raised any fools, and if this was to be her last opportunity to be close to Mitch, she was grabbing it with both hands.

"Right here," she murmured. His lips pressed gently there. "And here," she added, and waited for his touch on her temple. "And here." Daringly she pressed a hand to her mouth, waiting with bated breath.

His eyes watched her, deep fathomless pools of blue, until finally his hand slid across her shoulder and his mouth brushed across her lips in a tender caress that made her heart ache.

"You're asking for trouble, Melanie Stewart," he murmured.

"No," she whispered. "Just a kiss. To make it all better."

He kissed her with more passion than she had dreamed possible. Melanie would have crumpled to the floor if his strong arms hadn't held her against the counter. When he finally moved his mouth, she tipped her head, giving him free access to the sensitive skin of her neck. And Mitch took advantage until the buzzing timer and loud voices drew him out of his lethargy.

"I'm not crazy about your timing," he muttered in her ear as they listened to the high-pitched squeals in the next room.

"But I am crazy about your…boo-boos." He grinned saucily, stepping away from her when she would have retaliated.

They could hear Sara chastising the children a few feet away. Reluctantly, Melanie turned off the timer and lifted out the steaming dish as her mind protested the end of their embrace.

"Later," he whispered in her ear, before his sister walked into the room.

Mitch raved about the Spanish rice dish, and the children ate everything on their plates, including the little bit of salad they were served and had deemed yucky. There was a great deal of frivolity during the meal, and Melanie felt Mitch's gaze on her warm face more than once. She was glad when they could resume carrying boxes. At least he couldn't stare at her all the time!

"You didn't have to do this," Sara murmured as she packed in the last of Melanie's knickknacks. "The kids and I could have gone to a hotel. Especially when it means you might lose the prize money."

"Don't be silly! Of course I'll stay with Mother for a little while. You guys need the room. I probably should have moved there in the first place," she muttered, getting in behind the wheel. "Missionaries or not."

"What! And spared me Hope's tofu casserole and your early, early morning rising?" Mitch teased, getting in beside her. "Not to mention bran flakes and all the odious comments about my health."

"Why are you in my car?" Melanie asked, frowning as his knee brushed hers. "You live here, remember?"

He bowed. "Yes, thank you. I do remember. Senility does not run in my family." He arched an assessing look at her. "But my car is at your mother's. Besides, I need to talk to you about something."

"Oh. I forgot." Melanie put Bessie into gear, waved goodbye to Sara and pulled away from the curb. She kept her lips closed and her eyes on the road ahead. But it was totally impossible to ignore the grinning giant next to her.

"What is that noise?" he asked at last, shifting gingerly in the narrow confines of his seat. "Is it going to blow up?"

"Not yet," Melanie said, refusing to rise to the bait. "Bessie needs her carb cleaned. I just haven't had time."

The car backfired, jolting Mitch out of his seat with a jerk.

"It needs to be retired," he muttered, casting her a baleful look. "I hadn't realized your love of seniors ran to cars."

"What did you want to talk about?" Melanie asked, ignoring the bait and changing the subject adroitly. "I left your key and half of next month's rent on the hall table."

"I don't want your money," he spluttered. As her eyebrows rose, he swallowed. Melanie watched his Adam's apple bob up and down several times before he cleared his throat and began again.

"I have the wedding invitations for Gramps and Hope," he told her. "I just wanted you to look them over. Hope said you would need to know the color scheme to order the flowers and stuff."

"*You* chose the colors? *And* the wedding invitations? Why?" Melanie couldn't absorb the idea of Mitch Stewart entering a bridal shop to pick out such a thing.

"Why?" He sounded indignant. "Because she asked me to, that's why. She's too busy trying to find a dress and bridesmaid dresses and deciding on a place for them to live. The invitations have to go out fairly quickly, you know." Mitch preened. "I picked out the most suitable and had them printed up by special order. I've also chosen a lot of the hall decorations."

Melanie pulled in beside his bright red sports car with a jerk and turned to stare at him.

"But I thought I was supposed to do all that," she protested weakly, unable to envision him choosing wedding decorations.

"No, you're supposed to do the church, the table favors, the caterer and the emcee. Forget the groomsmen, though.

Gramps already has everything picked out. And he won't change his mind."

Stunned, Melanie carried box after box into the house, glad that for once her mother wasn't home. She could never have explained this crazy situation. When they were finished, Mitch went out to his car and returned with yet another box. He carefully slit the tape and opened it, lifting out a smaller white box.

"Now, proof this and tell me if everything is okay."

Melanie stared at the pale green announcement with amazement. It was embossed with two pearlized calla lilies and elegant script, which invited the recipient to "Please Join Us."

She slid apart the two lilies and opened the heavy bond paper to see what syrupy sentiment Mitch had chosen. To her surprise, the invitation was beautifully worded.

"Miss Hope Langford and Judge Harry Conroy invite you to join them as they pledge their marriage vows to one another on August third at eleven o'clock a.m. in the sanctuary of Third Avenue Church. A buffet luncheon will be served in the community hall immediately following the ceremony. Your presence will be your gift to us."

Two embossed Hs were linked at the bottom.

"It's, uh, very nice," Melanie sputtered, astonished at this new image of Mitchel Stewart, wedding consultant.

"It did come out well, didn't it," he agreed happily. "I didn't want it to sound sappy or anything. I mean, they do have their dignity. And this is an important occasion for them. I want everything to be just right."

"So do I," Melanie told him, shaking herself mentally. "But I thought everything was scheduled for three in the afternoon. Who changed it?"

"Gramps." Mitch grinned that wide, alluring smile. "He wants to take Hope on a honeymoon trip to Paris. The plane leaves at three."

Melanie gaped. "Paris," she whispered, her mouth sagging. "Lucky Hope."

"Well, she doesn't know yet, so don't tell her, okay? Gramps wants it to be a surprise, and he'll tear a strip off me if she finds out."

"All right." Melanie could barely say the words. Nothing was sane in the world anymore!

"The thing is, I've got their lists, and the invitations need to go out right away. I wondered if you'd help me address them all. I could help you wrap those candy things later if you want." He looked like a little boy begging, and Melanie couldn't help the smile that curved her lips.

"All right," she agreed. "I'll help you for a while tonight, but first I've got to set up Mom's VCR. There's a program on that I want to tape for Mr. Harper. He just loves Westerns, and there aren't that many on anymore." She set the controls and then poured a cup of coffee for each of them.

Melanie could feel his eyes following her, watching her every move.

"You really care about those people, don't you?"

Melanie didn't understand why he seemed so surprised. "They're my friends," she told him. "Of course I care about them." She began writing out names and addresses with the thin-tipped gold fountain pen Mitch had given her. They worked companionably together for several minutes before Mitch spoke again.

"We got a letter today." He waited expectantly, and Melanie's eyes flew to his. "Here, let me read it. 'Dear Miss and Mr. Stewart, Papa John's Peanut Butter has come to a decision regarding the prize money of fifty thousand dollars that was to be awarded in regard to our recent peanut butter contest. Our client has requested your presence at our office on Friday next to discuss the resolution of this issue. Should this time be unsuitable, please feel free to contact us as soon as possible.'"

"But that's the day after tomorrow," Melanie said.

"I know," he admitted. "Can you make it?"

"You bet I'm going to make it," Melanie told him firmly. "Twenty-five thousand dollars is a lot of money, and I need every dime of it for Sunset. And, believe me, I intend to collect every cent."

"Melanie, it might not be that easy," Mitch cautioned. His voice had dropped.

Melanie stared at him. "What do you mean?"

"Well," he began reluctantly. "If they're going to award the money, why didn't they just send the checks? Why make us go in there and discuss a 'possible resolution'?" He shook his head. "It just sounds odd to me."

"Oh, you worry too much," she teased. "I know that God has sent that money just when we needed it most. He'd hardly take it all away now." Her thoughts meandered. "I can hardly wait to start improving the place. They've waited for so long."

Mitch said nothing, but she could tell he was still thinking about the letter. An hour later he stamped the invitations they'd addressed and carefully packed away the rest, folding the lid closed just as Charity walked through the door.

"Thanks for the help," he murmured, walking beside Melanie to his car. "I sure appreciate it."

"Oh, you're welcome." She smiled. "I want everything to go off without a hitch for those two. Goodness knows, they've waited long enough."

He stood staring at her until Melanie flushed a dark red.

"What are you staring at?" she demanded at last.

"A very beautiful woman," he whispered. "One who isn't afraid to give to other people and just keeps on giving, no matter what." He leaned forward and kissed her, his arms tight and compelling around her. Then, in a movement so quick she had no time to protest, he was in his car.

"Good night, sweet Melanie," he murmured before shifting gears and pulling away.

He disappeared down the street and around the corner, his

car softly purring in the stillness. It wasn't until another car passed that Melanie realized she was still standing on the street, staring.

"Good night," she whispered, brushing a finger over her tingling lips.

Chapter Ten

"Today's the big day, Mother. You'd better pray extra hard this morning. Sunset needs that money now more than ever."

Having thus ensured that someone would be talking to the Lord about her problems, Melanie glugged down her coffee. She wanted to be on the road as early as possible. Since Mitch had neither offered her a ride nor asked to come with her, she felt free to leave when she wanted. Why wasn't that a pleasant thought?

Charity's hand on her arm was the only thing holding her back.

"My dearest girl," she murmured with a smile. "If God wants those folks to have things, they don't have to depend on Papa John's beneficence. God will make His own way."

"I know, Mom. The Lord will provide." They grinned at each other as she recited their favorite saying from years gone by. "But He already has, otherwise I wouldn't have won."

"You don't actually have that money yet, Melanie. Please let God work this out in His own way." Charity's usually smiling face was sober.

Melanie kissed the smooth parchment cheek and hopped

into her car, waving one hand. Just down the street she could see Faith and Hope striding toward her. Their faces were strained, and Hope seemed to be crying.

"Bye," Melanie called and drove away, wondering what the problem was. *Why doesn't life ever seem to go smoothly?* Unfortunately, the answer evaded her.

At WMIX, Mitch had already arrived and was seated in one of the comfortable leather chairs. His blue gaze swept over her quickly before he looked into her eyes. She couldn't read his. They were closed off, shuttered.

"You made it," was all he said as Papa John's lawyer offered her a seat.

"Of course I made it." She stared at his elegantly suited figure. "How come you're here so early?"

"Business," he told her. "Melanie, I need to talk to you. Privately."

His face was white with strain, and he looked distant. This tall, cool man who sat across from her was suddenly a stranger. And it hurt. Oh, he treated her with courtesy and respect, but there was no sign of the man whose big hands had rubbed suntan oil onto her back, who had massaged her tired shoulders when she had been depressed and beaten, who had held her when she'd lost Jonathan. Melanie searched his blue eyes, looking desperately for the man she had come to know over the past few months. But he wasn't there.

"But not now. Now we'll settle this prize thing. If you're ready?" the chilly-voiced stranger inquired coolly.

"Yes, go ahead." She tried to pretend his cool civility didn't hurt.

Papa John sauntered in, grinning brightly from ear to ear.

"Ah, my two prospective winners," he bellowed in that down-home voice he assumed for official duties. "Let's chat, shall we?" With a flick of his wrist he motioned the corporate exec types out of the room.

Melanie was confused. Chat? Weren't they supposed to award the prize now? And what was this *prospective* business? She glanced at Mitch for confirmation, but he shrugged, unable or unwilling to shed light on the situation.

"I wanted to speak to you two alone for a few minutes," the old man began, glancing from one stiff figure to the other. "I foresee several problems that never occurred to me before and I wanted your input. You, Mitch, will know all the legal implications of this."

Melanie frowned. She didn't like the sound of this. Not at all.

"The thing is, folks..." Papa John's voice was solemn. "I have shareholders, lots of them. The board is made up of some of the most crotchety old codgers you've ever seen." He smiled faintly as if just realizing that he was one of those codgers.

Melanie stared at Mitch, trying to assess what she was hearing. But Mitch's face was a frowning mask that told her only that he, too, was dismayed.

"Cut to the chase, Papa John," he muttered, interrupting the old man's flow of words. "What, exactly, are you trying to say?"

The old man scratched his whiskered chin with one lean, manicured hand.

"Well," he began cautiously, "the board feels that the company's image with our loyal public is based on wholesomeness. If you know what I mean."

Melanie disregarded the wink he cast Mitch's way. Why didn't he get down to business?

"What is the problem?" she blurted. If he didn't soon enlighten them, Melanie was going to reach out and yank on that beard. Hard.

"We can't award the prize money to two people who are living together in sin."

The baldness of his statement shocked her. Never mind that the sentiment was hopelessly mawkish and very dated. Papa John was insinuating that she and Mitch...that they were...

Her face blushed a deep, dark red as she considered how

it must look. If not for Hope's insistence... She burst into speech.

"But we're not. I mean I moved out a few days ago. Anyway, nothing happened. You can ask—"

"Shut up." Mitch's voice cut her off midstream. She stared at him. He glared at her, daring her to say another word. "I'll do the talking here." He turned to face Papa John.

"You had two winners to your contest. Us." He pointed to Melanie and himself. "The conditions have been met, correct?"

Papa John bumbled around, but Mitch refused to let him off the hook.

"Do we, or do we not, get the prize money?"

"Well, young fella, there's no need to git all uppity. If you'll just hold yer horses..."

Melanie could feel the sizzle of anger that radiated off Mitch from her perch six feet away.

"Cut the hillbilly lingo, John. It's a put-on, and so is this bluff you're trying to pull on us here." Mitch slid his hands into his pockets and leaned against the door frame lazily. He looked like a shark deciding where to bite first. "Do we or do we not get the fifty grand?"

"Not." The word entered the room like a jolt of electricity. Melanie stood up from her chair.

"What? But I thought—"

Mitch's big hand pressed firmly on her shoulder. His voice was frigid.

"Sit down and be quiet."

She did both.

"Either you award that money to Miss Stewart and myself or we'll sue."

As she studied the rugged lines of his face, Melanie decided she would not like to face Mr. Mitchel Stewart in court. He would be a skilled opponent—razor sharp and tough as steel. For once she was glad he could hide his emotions so readily.

Papa John shook his head while his thumb snapped one suspender placidly against his rounded belly.

"No grounds," he responded sedately. Melanie could hear the ping of the metal as it hit a button. "The agreement was to award the money to M. Stewart, once we got the address problem straightened out. Miss Stewart here claimed to be the person living at apartment 108, when in fact your name is on the lease and hers appears nowhere on it. Doesn't seem to have a phone in her name, either."

Melanie noted Mitch's frustration by the clench of his hand, flexing in and out.

Papa John continued. "She didn't even move in until well after the contest drawing, did she?"

Melanie felt her cheeks burn with the implication in those beady old eyes. So this was what a harlot must have felt like. She tried to explain the situation.

"But I was just—"

"If you don't be quiet, I'm leaving," Mitch barked at her. "This is a legal issue. Papa John is legally bound to hand over that money to us. We have the reassurances of our prize-winner status on official Papa John's Peanut Butter stationery," His blue eyes penetrated her green ones, daring her to deny the facts.

But Melanie couldn't think of a word to say for, truth to tell, she didn't have that letter. Hadn't a clue where it was. Without it, she doubted they would award her anything but a jar of peanut butter. She sealed her lips tightly. Whatever Mitch could salvage out of this terrible day was the most she could hope for.

"Go ahead," she told him quietly.

"Well?" Mitch's voice was pure ice as he glared at the owner of Papa John's.

"Miss Stewart has no claim."

Melanie sucked in a breath of air, ready to defend herself as Mitch shifted those eyes to her. She subsided without a sound.

Mitch turned his attention to the older man. He let that statement go to counter with one of his own.

"And me? Why can't you award the total to me?"

Papa John stoked his chin thoughtfully. "Well, you see, there's the rub. Actually you were not an employee at Sunset, nor a resident at the apartment, at the time of the drawing. In fact, you began your job after we made the drawing, and you took possession of the apartment two weeks later."

"Nope." Mitch smiled that cat-that-got-the-bird smile and leaned backward on his wing tips. Melanie saw the satisfaction curve his hard mouth. "I was there at the television station, remember. That was two weeks after I'd arranged for residence. You haven't got a hope."

Melanie thought the old fellow looked downright smug and self-satisfied.

"Sorry, son." He smirked, tapping his toe on the soft, thick broadloom. "The draw date was twenty-eight days before the show. That was the first date WMIX could give us the time slot we wanted. And we had to inform the *prospective* winners."

Melanie heard the subtle emphasis on the word and turned to study Mitch's face. Disgust and frustration creased his forehead as he glared at the old man.

"So it was all just a game," he rasped. "A total waste of our time?"

"Good Lord, no." the old man exploded, erupting from his chair with a bound. "I wanted to award that money to you folks. Still do. But I'm not taking any heat from the board or unfavorable publicity from the public to do it." He studied them with intense scrutiny.

"What exactly do you want from us?" Mitch's low voice sounded like ice on a hot pan as it sizzled across the room. "What's the catch?"

Papa John ambled over to sink his plump body into the big leather chair behind the mahogany desk. He folded his hands calmly as he met Mitch's furious glare.

"No catch, son." He leaned back and studied the ceiling

for several moments. Then he straightened and fixed them with his watery eyes. "The only way my board will let me award that money is if the two of you are married."

"*What?*" Melanie jumped from her chair, glancing from one male to the other. "Get married? For money?" Silence reverberated through the room until Mitch's soft voice whispered in her ear.

"You were willing to live together for it. Why not marriage?"

Melanie stared. She couldn't help it. She gaped like a goldfish gulping air. "Do you mean you're going along with this? Are you crazy?"

Mitch smiled sardonically. "Oh, no," he muttered, shaking his head. "I'm not going along with it at all. I just thought it was interesting to see where you draw the line at getting that money." He swiveled to face the man behind the desk.

"Your board is going to have a little more to worry about, Papa," he said with anger. "Especially when I launch a campaign that challenges the trust your customers place in your product." He grinned at the older man sardonically.

"It's pretty bad when you can't depend on a company as big as Papa John's to deliver on its word," he continued. "I wonder what the public will think when they learn that you're not exactly who you say you are."

Melanie wondered why she had ever thought Mitch's eyes were warm. They had hardened to chips of glacial ice.

"Your lawyers will hear from us," he announced with a diamond-hard look. She felt his strong hand under her elbow. "Come on, Melanie. We're leaving."

"But...but—"

"No sense suing, son. Even if you did win, the money would all get spent on lawyers and court costs. Or else defending a libel suit. No, sirree." He shook his white head sadly. "Only thing left for you two to do is to get married."

As Melanie stumbled through the door to the hall, she heard Papa John's last words dimly.

"You let me know the date, kids. I'll be there."

"I'll just bet you would." Mitch's voice raged softly in her ear. "Can't you walk any faster?"

"Oh, suddenly you're a speed walker?" she asked furiously. He ignored the comment and whisked her out of the building and into the car before she could say anything else. It was only when she was straightening her skirt over her knees that Melanie realized they were sitting in his car.

"My car's over there," she told him, pointing across the lot. He glared at her.

"Don't you understand what's going on here? You could lose everything because of some narrow-minded old cronies." He smiled at her grimly. "The old coot's done his homework. We haven't got a chance of winning anything out of this fiasco."

"But I thought you said..." Melanie frowned at him.

"It was just a bluff. We haven't got the kind of cash it would take to start a smear campaign even if we could get away with it." His hand smacked the steering wheel. "Don't you get it? It's gone, all of it. You're not going to see a dime of that money."

It took a few minutes to absorb it, but when she did, Melanie felt the dam burst. She covered him with her fiery words.

"Yes, I'm quite well aware of that, thank you very much." Frustration clouded her judgment, and Melanie spewed out words she immediately wished unsaid.

"And I'll lose it all because of you. Come into my parlor, you said. I'll help you get the money, just move in. You— you spider!" Her green eyes snapped at him as the frustration of the past weeks poured out. "You're the one who insisted I give false information about my address. It's all your fault!"

The enormity of losing twenty-five thousand dollars hit her, then and Melanie did the only thing she could to relieve her frustration.

"Ow, ow, ow! Ooh, that hurts!" She sucked on the knuckles of her hand where it had made contact with the rock-hard dash. It had been a puerile thing to do, and she didn't feel one whit better. Her turbulent sea-foam eyes glared at Mitch.

"You're blaming this on me?" he bellowed incredulously. "This is my fault?" He looked astounded. "The only reason I ever got involved in your little Save Our Seniors campaign was because you wanted that money so badly." He shook his head in pretended amusement, but his lips were pursed tightly.

"I don't believe this. You try to help someone and all you do is get knocked down. So much for brotherly love." He thrust his hands in the air. "That's it. I give up. I quit. Do whatever you want, just don't involve me in any more of your harebrained schemes."

"Brotherly love? Ha!" Melanie yanked the door open and stumbled out. "There's nothing like that involved! Stick your head in the sand and give up, then. See if I care!"

She slammed the door of his car as hard as she could and stomped across the parking lot in red patent shoes that pinched her toes with every click the four-inch heels made against the pavement.

And all the way, Mitch could hear her castigating the male of the species. One in particular. They were nasty words that didn't explain his motives at all. And they were totally untrue!

With an angry flick of his wrist, he shifted into gear and floored the gas pedal, screeching out of the parking lot as his new tires laid their expensive tread on the asphalt. He ground his way into second, ignoring the car's protesting sounds. And to think God actually thought men *needed* women!

Seconds later, Melanie followed, honking angrily at an elderly white-haired gentleman who almost backed into her as she took the corner on two wheels.

The old fellow smiled fondly. Kids these days. So excitable. Wait till he told Nettie about this latest development.

"Mitch, I know you said you didn't want to see anyone, but I think you'd better see this fellow. He says it's urgent."

Mitch groaned, thrusting away the salad he'd picked up at the store. Salad, for Pete's sake, when he really wanted a burger and fries! Or a doughnut.

Clarence Palmer's opinion was the same as he loped through the door.

"You sick?" he asked curiously, eyeing the three kinds of lettuce, chopped celery and radishes that filled the black plastic bowl. "Got a heart condition or something?"

Ha! Now that was appropriate. Melanie Stewart definitely affected his digestion, but his heart?

"Might be," he told Clarence sullenly. "Just might be." He dumped the last of the ranch dressing into the bowl and took another mouthful. "What's so all-fired important?"

"Thought you'd want to know right away." Clarence beamed. "I don't think this Papa John fellow is the lady's old beau, after all."

"What!" Mitch jerked straight up in his chair. "But I thought you were so sure. What's changed?"

"For one thing, I got hold of some medical records. From what I know, your Papa fellow has his bones intact. Our Jean had broken his left ankle once and the right arm just below the elbow. The surgeon I talked to says he thinks he'd be able to see evidence of that on the X ray."

"After this long?" Mitch was skeptical.

"There is no sign of a break on this John guy's arm, according to his personal physician. A few other minor things seem to indicate that this LeClerc fellow is not the same as your Papa John. I've put it all in my report so, unless you have some new information, I'm closing this file."

Mitch scratched his chin in disbelief. "You're sure about this?" he demanded.

"As sure as I can be, which isn't much given the few facts in the case." Clarence eyed him appreciatively. "This one something important to you?"

"I was hoping for something that would give me a hold on the guy, yes. He's trying to do a friend of mine out of fifty thousand dollars, so I guess that does give me some interest in good old Papa John."

"So she's not getting a dime?" Faith looked aghast at the news. "But how could he do that to them?"

"He apparently wants them to get married so his shareholders don't feel that they are condoning some illicit relationship." Hope stared at her hands. "And truth to tell," she murmured, "I don't thing it's such a bad idea. Nettie seems very encouraged in their interest in each other. She says Mitch has been to the home a number of times to help out with some function or another."

"They did seem rather interested in each other after the Sunday school picnic," Charity mused. "He deliberately didn't tag her when she got that base hit, remember? That was nice."

"He also pitched it straight to her so she could hit the thing," Hope sputtered in sheer disgust. "That run cost our side the game. Love makes people so silly." The words were enunciated with disgust.

"Oh, Hope, dear, I think it's affected even you." Faith chuckled. "You were out walking in the rain last night, you and Harry. Arthur saw you," she added when it seemed Hope would deny it. "Didn't it bother you to get your hair all wet?"

Charity watched as Hope's clear, pale skin flushed a dark red. She decided to get the conversation back on track.

"The thing is, girls," she said firmly, "Melanie really likes him, I'm sure she does. And it's all so new. She's just a bit afraid of admitting it." She glanced at her friends' bemused faces. "Now what are we going to do about it?"

"I think we need to give them some time alone," Faith murmured. "I mean, Hope chaperoned them nicely in the apartment, but young folks need time together."

"So do older people," Hope sniped. "And they don't need Peeping Toms watching out the window when they go for a walk!"

"*I* wasn't peeping," Faith grumbled. "Arthur saw you on his way home from work. If you're ashamed to be seen in public—"

"I am not ashamed!" Hope's quiet voice was rising steadily.

"Girls!" Charity was firm. "How are we going to get Mitch and Melanie together again?"

"I've had them both over for dinner twice this week," Faith mused, staring into space. "I can't very well ask them again or they'll know something's up."

"And I've pulled all the little problems with the wedding that I can think of," Hope said mournfully. "They're both so efficient that they run right over all my complications and dilemmas without being deterred and without asking each other's help."

"If I ask him over here too much more," Charity said, "Melanie's going to know I'm up to something."

The three ladies sat stewing over their plans, trying desperately to come up with something new. The phone rang as Melanie walked through the front door.

"I'll get it," she called.

Unashamedly, the threesome sat listening to the one-sided conversation, their faces broadening with satisfied grins as they did.

"Oh, hi, Mitch. You are? Well, I don't think *I* took it, but I can look if you like. No, thanks. I don't really *need* any help, Mitchel."

Faith nodded at Hope, who raised a thumbs-up sign at Charity.

"Actually, I just got in the door. No, I haven't eaten but I imagine Mom's—"

"I'm going out, dear," Charity interrupted. "Special meeting of the ladies' group." She shook her head at Faith's wide-eyed dismay. "Why don't you eat out at that new Mexican restaurant tonight?"

"Sorry, Mitch. Mom was just telling me something. Oh, you heard. Yes, I suppose that would be okay. Around seven-thirty? All right. Bye."

Before Melanie could hang the receiver up, there was a flurry of action in the living room. Hope grasped her purse and her scarf and flung her sweater over her shoulders before helping Faith find her pocketbook and the list of baking she was doing for the reception. Charity struggled to slip her tired feet into the orthopedic shoes. She finished tying the laces at the same moment her daughter breezed into the room.

"I didn't know there was a ladies' meeting tonight, Mom. That's three times this week. What's going on?"

"Planning a wedding shower," her mother whispered, eyes rolling in Hope's direction.

"Oh, well, if she's going to be alone, maybe Hope would like to have dinner with me?"

"Isn't Mitch coming over?" Charity's question drew her attention from the pair by the door, so Melanie missed seeing Faith's elbow imbed itself in Hope's side.

"Well, yes, but—"

"Thank you anyway, dear," Hope murmured, her eyes watering. "But Harry and I are going to go over some renovation plans tonight. And I've just time to change my clothes." She glanced at her watch before grasping Faith's arm firmly. "Come along, Faith. I want to make sure you get home safely," she said sweetly.

As they moved through the door, Faith's light voice carried back.

"Hope, your fingernails are too long. They're digging into my arm."

"I have to rush off, too," her mother told her. "I've got so many things to do before this wedding." She was almost out the door before Melanie's voice stopped her.

"When and where is the shower, Mother? I'd like to go, if I can."

"Uh, we're just going to decide that tonight," Charity murmured, scurrying out the door. "See you later."

Melanie stared at the empty living room.

"You certainly know how to clear a room," she muttered fatalistically. Then her thoughts turned to Mitch and his offer.

She hadn't wanted to let the fearsome threesome know, but she was glad he'd invited her to go for a swim. She desperately needed to work off some of this stress, and besides, it would keep her from thinking about his ridiculous marriage proposal. After changing into a bright yellow T-shirt and dark blue shorts, Melanie sat down to view a stack of videos.

"It just wouldn't do to lose the punching bout of the century," she reminded herself. She got caught up in a rerun of the "Little House on the Prairies" series, and her eyes were full of tears when the doorbell rang. Brushing her hand across her cheeks, she hurried to answer it.

"Hi," she said brusquely, sniffing. "Come on in."

"Gee." He stared at her grimly. "I don't think I ever had this effect on one of my dates before. And we haven't even left yet." He followed her into the living room and rolled his eyes when he saw what she'd been watching.

"You've seen this thing ten times," he muttered, hitting the rewind button. "And you still bawl. Why do you watch it if it makes you so sad?"

"It doesn't make me sad," she retorted in watery tones. "It's makes me feel wonderful to be alive." She blew her nose loudly.

It was obvious that Mitch didn't share her pleasure in watching a family make it by pulling together through the tough times. And how could she tell him that the show symbolized everything she wanted in her life? He would call her a maudlin sentimentalist.

"Yeah." He grimaced, swiping at one of the tears on her cheeks. "I can tell you're feeling really great right now." Mitch sifted through the tapes scattered across the floor, his fingers plucking one from the mess. "Ah, here it is. I think." He thrust the cartridge into the VCR and waited.

"What in the world!" His eyes were huge blue puddles of disbelief as the start of a boxing match was quickly overridden by a diminutive woman with silver curls and a red-lipsticked mouth who stood on a platform.

"Men are not like women," the woman doctor was explaining. "They do not think of love in the same terms as we do. The males of our species take things literally, so if you want something from them, you have to come right out and ask for it. Don't assume anything, because men tend to think with their—''

Mitch hit the stop button as fast as he could, his face beet red.

''What happened to my boxing?'' he demanded, looming over her. ''Is the whole tape ruined by that—that ridiculous woman?''

''She's not ridiculous. She's a well-respected therapist. Thousands of people pay huge amounts of money to get her advice.''

''Thousands of people paid huge amounts of money to see that fight,'' he said. ''And I paid a fair bit to obtain a taped copy of it.''

''Sorry! I must have grabbed that one by mistake and taped right over your show. I didn't mean to!'' Melanie glared at him, preparing herself for the battle that was sure to follow.

But Mitch didn't look angry. He looked, well, resigned. He closed his eyes and mouthed the numbers from one to ten. When he opened those big baby blues, his grin tipped wryly to one side. He squatted in front of her and took her hands.

''Never mind. I'll get another one made,'' he told her quietly.

''I really am sorry, Mitch. I taped it for one of my residents. You remember Jonathan Northrup. That doctor is his sister.'' Her voice dropped. ''He died before I got it to him.''

''Oh, yes. I understand completely. Anything for the home and the people there.'' His blue eyes moved over her like a warm, snug blanket covering her with care, his voice was smooth.

''He's the fellow who told you to try moving into today's world, isn't he? And he's right, Melanie. You can't hide out at Sunset forever.''

''Move into what? Murders, bombings, people full of hate and bitterness? That's not the type of world I want to live in, Mitch.'' Her voice was sour as she remembered the things she'd had to do today.

"What's wrong, Mel?" he asked, sitting beside her and wrapping his arm around her shoulders. "I mean really wrong."

"I'm cranky," she admitted at last, luxuriating in the feel of his big hand on her hair, soothing and gentle. "I had to order bed restraints on two residents today."

"Hmm," he sympathized, tugging her head onto his shoulder companionably. "I know how much you hate that."

"Yeah, I do. But there was one good thing. I at last managed to locate a motorized cart for Mr. Harcourt." She grimaced. "There's no way the administrator will okay an expenditure of four thousand dollars for one patient, though."

She felt his chin rest on her head as his chest wobbled under her cheek.

"What is it your mother always says?" he asked, chuckling.

"The Lord will provide." Melanie answered dully. "But I want it right now!"

"You remind me of Sara's Ben. Come on." Mitch chuckled, tugging her to her feet. "You need to get out of here and get some fresh air. I have just the thing."

"I thought we were going for a swim and then dinner." She frowned.

"We are. Now come on."

So Melanie went, noticing the soft luxury of his bucket seats and the feel of the fresh breeze playing with her hair.

"Where are we going?" she asked finally, only beginning to notice that they were on their way out of town.

"We're going for a swim. In the river. That friend of yours, Jeff? He told me about this place. Said it was quiet." Mitch parked beside a grassy spot that edged the river.

"Would madame care to sample the speciality of the day, compliments of Enjoy Gardens?"

Her eyes widened as she took in the assorted boxes and bowls he was removing from the trunk and laying out on an old quilt he'd spread on the ground. There were all manner of succulent odors emanating from the tinfoil dishes. A tiny smile curved its way across her face hesitantly. She glanced up at him.

"What's all this?"

Mitch's face was serious as he replied. "I'm tired of fighting, Melanie. I was hoping we could share dinner and discuss the situation rationally, without running away or verbally slaughtering each other." His eyes glinted with mirth. "And just for the record, that woman on the tape was only partially right. I can understand most things without having them spelled out for me in black and white."

Melanie flushed as she remembered Dr. Lana's advice. It was a good thing he hadn't heard any more than he had. Mitch had made the first move. She was a big enough person to accept it.

"Thank you. I love Chinese food." She sank onto a tattered cushion with the old-world elegance of a Victorian maiden.

"I know. Health food," he murmured, his eyes glinting. "It's one of the things I like most about you. The other is your sense of humor."

Melanie raised an eyebrow. Her fingers peeled back the lid on a container and she breathed in the fresh, sesame-scented air. As she spooned a large helping onto her plate, she looked at him through her lashes.

"What *exactly* are you doing this for, Mitch? What is it you want to talk about so badly?" Her eyes noted the light flush on his cheekbones. Melanie's curiosity grew.

"Mitch? What is all this really in aid of?" she queried, noting the candles flickering on the quilt and the paper-towel napkins he had folded into little tents. "What do you want?"

Mitch slapped a hand to his chest in affront. "I'm insulted. How can you ask such a thing?"

She grinned cheekily.

"I can ask because I'm beginning to know you." She studied him. "And I know you want something right now. That tic at the side of your mouth gives it away. What is it?"

She watched knowingly as his hand searched for the nonexistent tic and smiled when he glared at her. Nothing could have prepared her for his answer.

"What I really want is for you to marry me."

She sat there with the grass tickling her ankles, a plate of her favorite food on her lap, and wondered if she'd inhaled too much fresh air. A surfeit of oxygen was supposed to be lethal, wasn't it?

"Melanie?" His big hand was shaking her shoulder none too gently. "Say something?"

"Hello." She smiled stupidly, wondering what in the world he expected her to say to such a strange proposal. His blue eyes narrowed.

"What is the matter with you?" he asked, worried. His fingers twitched water from her water glass onto her face. It was cold, and she veered away.

"Hey! Quit that."

"Well?"

"Well, what?" Melanie made herself meet his probing glance.

"What do you think?"

She grabbed the opportunity. "I think you may be allergic to shellfish, too," she told him seriously. She watched the pulse throbbing rhythmically at the side of his temple for a few seconds before picking up her fork. "Mm, this broccoli is perfect."

He leaned back on his cushion and glared at her.

"Okay, I'll bite. Why do you think I suffer from this malady?"

"Surely it's obvious. Something has made you lose your mind." Her forehead wrinkled. "Or else it's me."

"Now that I might go along with," Mitch muttered.

Melanie frowned. He wasn't going to start *that* again, was he?

"Look. Are you or are you not going to marry me?"

Melanie strove for control. Here he was joking about the one thing she wanted more than anything. Well, she wouldn't fall into the trap. She knew better. He was baiting her, trying to trap her into saying something she would regret.

She laid her fork down and crossed her legs, hands folded carefully in her lap.

"Gee, this is so sudden." She smiled sweetly. "Why, exactly, would we be getting married, honey?"

"Well, I thought… I´mean, well… The money…it's the only way." Mitch stumbled through the speech, obviously nonplussed by her attitude.

He probably thought she would jump at the opportunity. After all, at her advanced age and everything. Ooh!

"I see." She recrossed her legs calmly, biting down the sarcastic remarks that begged to be uttered. "So you want to marry me for my money, is that it?"

"Well, yes. Sort of." He glared at her. "No."

"That's clear! Okay, and then what?"

"Excuse me?" Mitch was staring at her as if she had turned into one of those vile reptilian forms he seemed so fond of. "What do you mean, then what? We'll get them to award the money and you can get what you've always wanted."

"And then what?" She repeated the phrase, hoping he would say the only three words she wanted to hear.

Mitch stared at her. "Huh?"

"It's a simple question, Mitch. You can figure it out. What happens after we get the money?"

"I guess we could learn to live together, or whatever."

"I'm just a little leery of the whatever," she murmured. "Thank you very much, but no thanks." She slipped a spear of celery into her mouth with more aplomb than she felt.

He was dumbfounded, Melanie could see that easily enough. His mouth pursed. That meant he was close to losing control. Good! She was pretty close to the edge herself.

"What do you mean, no? Are you going to throw away all that money just because you don't like the idea of getting married? It's ridiculous. You could do all the things you had planned and more."

Melanie stopped him right there.

"Oh, I like the idea of getting married, all right. But I like the idea of staying married even more. I want a husband who wants me, not my money. I want kids and a home and a life that all that money couldn't buy." She glared at him. "I am not marrying anyone for money, least of all you. The whole thing has gone too far."

"But what about your residents, that guy who needs the cart and the new sound units?"

Melanie felt frustration well up, but she shoved it away, hardening her heart against the guilt waiting to crowd in.

"They will just have to find another way. And maybe I'll have to find another job."

Mitch was aghast. Did he repel her so much she was willing to quit her job, a job she loved doing, just to get away from him? He thought about Sara's advice.

"You've got to back her into a corner, honey. She's the type that won't give in without you saying the words. Don't give her any platitudes or grandiose schemes. Just tell her the truth."

Maybe it was worth a try. God knew he didn't think he was anything like the type for home and family, but he was darned good at making things happen. He would blasted well make sure she got that money! And in the process, he would gain the one thing he really wanted out of all this—Melanie Stewart.

"Listen to me, Melanie. I know it sounds crazy. I know we argue almost all the time. I know you think I'm just offering you a way to get the cash." He swallowed. Hard.

"But I'm not. I want to marry you. I, er, that is, I think I'm in love with you." He gulped a drink of water and wondered if he had really finally admitted it. But one look at her gaping face made him continue.

"I like it when you tell me about your day and the folks at Sunset. I like feeling your hair when it's loose and curling at the ends like that. I like the way you go all out for something you believe in.'' He grinned. ''I like kissing you, too. And I think you like kissing me.''

''Mitch, marriage is a whole lot more of a commitment than that!''

She sounded stunned, Mitch decided. Good. Now maybe he'd have a chance to get the words said.

''I know that. And I'm ready to make that commitment to you.'' He knelt in front of her. ''I don't know much about marriage, Melanie. I never had much of an example except Gramps. But I do know that it takes two people and a special spark. I think we've got that.''

He slid his hand under the heavy fall of her hair and circled her neck, leaning in to press his lips against hers. When Melanie immediately responded, he felt a rush of warmth. No matter what she said, Melanie Stewart was not immune to him!

''You can feel it, too, can't you?'' he whispered in her ear, his arms drawing her closer.

''Yes,'' she said, her arms sliding around his neck. Her eyes were dark in the dusky light. ''But, Mitch, it's going to take a lot more than attraction to make a marriage work. What about the money?''

He felt the grim chill of reality, and suddenly wished he had never heard of Papa John's Peanut Butter.

''Melanie, the money doesn't have anything to do with this. It's just a byproduct of us getting married, it's not the main reason.''

But Mitch could tell she wasn't listening. She had withdrawn into that shell that protected her from pain.

''I can't get married because of some prize money,'' she whispered. ''Marriage is a serious commitment between two people and God. It's what I've believed all my life, and I can't just forget my principles because there's money involved.''

''But money isn't the reason I'm asking you,'' he told her. ''I care for you. Really.''

''Do you?'' She looked skeptical, at best. She was placing

the covers on various containers. "I think we'd better go now," she murmured. "I've got several loose ends to tie up before the wedding next week."

There was nothing to do but follow her lead for now, Mitch decided grimly. But she'd come around. She had to.

"You'd better pay attention to all those details," he told her on the drive back. "You're going to need to remember them when our day rolls around."

"Don't start on that again," she pleaded. "Please?"

"You are going to marry me, Melanie. Sooner or later you'll realize that. So make up your mind to it because there's no way you can talk me out of it."

"I'm not marrying you, Mitchel. No way. So don't think you're going to bully me into it." Melanie got out of the car and stomped up the front steps. "I'm not getting involved with you for the money."

"No," he agreed. "We're not getting married for money. Not at all."

He pulled her against him and covered her mouth with his. Within seconds her arms wound round his neck and she was kissing him back.

He grinned. She did want to marry him. She was just too stubborn to admit it. Now they needed to get down to business. And he knew exactly how to do it.

He grinned as Melanie flew into the house, to the safety of her private space. He waited about ten seconds and drove off, content that Melanie wasn't immune to him, despite what she claimed. Not at all immune, if that kiss was anything to go by.

As he drove toward his apartment, Mitch thought of Nettie Rivers's words to him at their last meeting.

"If there's anything I can do to help you and Melanie, Mitch, you only have to ask." She had smiled a coy little grin. "After all, I do have some influence, you know."

He hadn't been exactly sure what she'd meant then, but maybe it was time to find out. He could use all the help he could get.

Chapter Eleven

"It's just a ceremony, Melanie. It's not condemning yourself to death." Charity looked at her daughter in amusement. "It's a promise for the future."

"It sounds like a death sentence. Why does Hope want all these silly things in her vows, anyway? Is there something wrong with the good old-fashioned kind?"

"Maybe she wants to express her feelings especially to Gramps," Mitch murmured from his position opposite her. His big fingers struggled with the narrow ribbon as he fluffed and tied a tiny bow around the mint satchels they were making. "Every couple experiences things differently. And they have waited a long time. I'm sure she just wants everything to be wonderful."

Melanie sighed tiredly. Mitch was like a dog with a bone. He would not give up this marriage idea. Whenever she refused to consider it, he started kissing her. Then her knees turned to mush and her brain blew a fuse and she couldn't understand what he was saying for ages afterward.

"Just think about what you're going to say to me at that altar," he whispered in a voice loud enough that neither Charity nor Faith could fail to hear.

"Oh, I am," she assured him grimly. "I'm thinking of a lot of things that I'm going to say to you. But mostly in private."

Mitch had tricked her into blood tests by requesting, through official administration channels, of course, that she have a full range of blood work to update her files and make sure her insurance coverage was up to date. It had been so skillfully done that Melanie hadn't even seen his hand in the thing until he'd presented her with their license.

"Blood tests all done," he'd crowed, waving the papers in her face Sunday morning before church. Thankfully, she'd hushed him up, although it had meant sitting next to him all through the long service. Melanie had been fully aware of the speculative looks, the press of his knee against her leg and the warmth of his hand when he'd clasped hers so tightly.

"I need some encouragement," he'd whispered when she had tried to tug away. "After all, as you pointed out, marriage is a big responsibility for a man."

And his hand had stayed under her arm, under her elbow, holding hers until he'd walked her to her mother's. He seemed totally unperturbed when Melanie threatened to dump her entire glass of iced tea into his lap just after lunch. He merely coaxed her into sitting on the patio.

"I've told you a hundred times," she said, "I am not getting married. Not to you, anyway."

Mitch leaned across and kissed the tip of her nose.

"Yes, dearest Melanie," he insisted, "we are. Sooner or later."

Melanie shook her head firmly. "I won't be there."

"Oh, yes, you will. Shawna and Sara will be there. Your mother and her friends, too. I think it would be nice if Gramps walked you down the aisle, don't you?" He smiled fatuously. "What do you think of autumn colors for the invitations?"

"Invitations?" Melanie tried to remember discussing that, but her mind drew a blank. He had told her so many things she couldn't keep track anymore. It was like being pestered by a whirling dervish. He was constantly on the go, planning something or other.

"These are some of the people I want to invite," he told her seriously. She unfolded the piece of paper to find a wedding invitation inside with a long list attached. "Unless you'd rather elope? I'm all for that." He kissed her again.

"How could you choose invitations when you don't have anyone to marry you?" She deliberately avoided his arms.

His blue eyes peered into hers. "Don't I?" he whispered softly into her ear. Seconds later she forgot what they had been talking about as his mouth teased hers in mindless abandon.

"You did say your favorite color was green," he whispered, tickling her earlobe. "I thought maybe a dark spruce tone would be nice."

Melanie burst out laughing. She just couldn't imagine him walking into a bridal shop and demanding to see their spruce-colored wedding invitations. The man had nerve, she admitted. Lots of it.

"I didn't realize you were into sweetheart roses," Melanie murmured, struggling out of his arms. She agreed the invitation was very nice, and he accepted the issue as settled, which it wasn't but she wasn't risking another one of those sock-stealing kisses. It was hard enough to keep away from the man.

"I'm going to see Nettie now," he murmured two hours later when the mints were all wrapped. "She has something to discuss with me, she said."

"You two seem to spend a lot of time together," Melanie said grumpily, knowing he wouldn't tell her the subject of their discussion. "If you two are so thick, why don't you ask her to marry you?"

She grinned triumphantly, but Mitch wasn't in the least put off.

"She's already involved with someone," he told her, pressing a kiss on the end of her nose. "Besides, she thinks we belong together. I'm Prince Charming, remember?" He grinned smugly. "Bye, Charity. Thanks for a wonderful lunch." He pressed a flyaway kiss to her mother's cheek and proceeded down the line to encompass Faith and finally Hope in his magnificence. "Just four more days, Gramps," he chided, smiling. "Can you wait that long?"

"That boy sure is pleased about something," Faith said when the door closed. "Why, his spirits have just lifted to the skies. Melanie?"

"Yes, Faith?"

"Do you have any idea what Mitch is so happy about?" Melanie caught the knowing glance her mother exchanged with the other members of the fearsome threesome.

"Not a clue," she lied airily. "He lives a fantasy life most of the time. Hope can tell you about that. She saw it as well as I did." Melanie glanced at the other woman for confirmation and instead found Hope shaking her head.

"I always thought he was very down-to-earth and sure of himself," Hope murmured. "Didn't you, Harry?"

"He certainly is now." Harry chortled. "And I think the thing he's decided on is Miss Me—" His booming voice died away in a sudden coughing spurt.

"I've got to get those thank-you notes from that shower finished this afternoon." Hope broke the silence. "Come along, Harry. You can help me. See you later, girls."

They were gone, soon followed by Charity and Faith, who were picked up by Arthur for a drive in the country.

With nothing left to do and no one to talk to, Melanie found herself glancing through the bridal magazines Hope had left behind. She laughed outright at several of the most improbable pictures, but stopped at the center section.

"It's perfect," she whispered.

The dress was long and elegant with not a flounce to be found. The sweetheart neckline draped gracefully over the model's shoulders, ending at the opalescent sheer sleeves that formed a delicate point at the wrist.

Melanie could almost feel the heavy silk caress her skin as

she studied the tiny row of buttons up the back and the beautiful full train that trailed behind.

"Her hair's wrong," she murmured, imagining a soft upsweep that would emphasize the tiny Juliet cap with its delicate pearls and fluff of netting.

"Yes, you're right," a voice whispered in her ear. "This is definitely your style. I can see you coming down the aisle carrying palest peach roses."

Melanie came awake with a jerk as Mitch's mouth nibbled on the corner of hers.

"What are you doing here?" she demanded, startled and embarrassed. "I thought you had an important engagement."

"I did." Mitch grinned his lazy well-fed-cat smile, his fingers wrapping around one tendril of her hair. "And then I came back to you. Miss me?" His eyes sparkled like blue diamonds in the sun.

"Of course not," Melanie muttered, shutting the magazine with a thud. "I'm just going out for a walk."

"Wonderful idea," he agreed. "A little exercise with my bride-to-be. Just what I need."

She smiled, remembering his last venture in walking.

"It's everybody at their own risk," she warned, bending to tie her shoes. "I've got a very stressful week to prepare for."

To her dismay, Mitch beamed with delight.

"Perfect! I can hardly wait."

Melanie deliberately started out at a far faster pace than was good for her, hoping he'd drop out and leave her alone. To her amazement, Mitch kept up, jogging, even talking to her as they went. And all without a sign of breathlessness when she could hardly draw in a lungful of air for the pain in her chest.

She asked Sara about it later.

"How's it going with you and Mitch?" Melanie asked tentatively with just the right note of compassion. "Any problems?"

"Problems? With Mitchel?" Sara had repeated. "No, since

you left he's been a model host. He's up before dawn to jog for forty-five minutes, has his shower, eats his Wheaties and then he's off, whistling, for work!''

"Wheaties?'' Melanie stared at the phone. "Mitch only eats doughnuts for breakfast.'' *And lunch and dinner,* she repeated to herself. "And he hates jogging.''

"Not anymore, Melanie. He says he's turned over a new leaf, and I believe it. The kids don't get their usual junk food treats from him anymore, you know. Now he brings home apples and grapes and popcorn. *Popcorn,*'' she repeated with amazement.

"Well, I, for one, don't believe it,'' Melanie murmured. "What's wrong with him, anyway?''

"I don't know,'' Sara told her seriously. "All he's saying is that I'll know when he makes the big announcement.''

"What announcement?''

"Beats me, Mel, but I can tell you there's a lot of fishy stuff going on here.'' Sara's voice grew faint as she called to her children. "Yesterday, for example. Just as I was leaving, a little old lady showed up here. Said she had an important meeting with Mitch. It was weird, I can tell you.''

"At least that explains this afternoon.'' She quickly described her jogging and Mitch's unexpected ability to keep up. "He's up to something,'' Melanie asserted. "I can feel it.''

"Well, whatever it is,'' Sara said, "I like it.'' She went on to tell Melanie about her husband's imminent return from his peacekeeping duties overseas. "The kids and I will be so glad once we move in to our own place. Not that we don't feel welcome here, but after all, it isn't home.''

That night as she lay in bed, Melanie dared to ask God once more for direction.

"I love him, Lord. But I'm just not sure that he loves me. At least not enough to spend the rest of our lives together. Please, could You help me with this? Send me some little sign?''

It was rather providential that a dozen red roses arrived the next morning at work, addressed to her. Tucked inside was a card. *Marry Me!* it ordered in bold print, underlined for effect.

"That's not exactly the kind of sign I meant," she said. Melanie stuffed the card into her purse and refused to answer the questions with which her staff bombarded her. Mrs. Rivers strolled past her office in the afternoon and, sighting the roses, buried her face in their fragrant petals.

"Oh, Melanie, I knew Mitch was your true love," the old woman told her softly. "I just knew the two of you were meant to be together. God let me see it so clearly."

Melanie stared. With vivid accuracy, she remembered the day she'd met Mitch, when Mrs. Rivers had said those exact words. She tried to laugh it off.

"Oh, Nettie, I don't think he's my true anything."

The old face crinkled with dismay. "But he loves you, dear. Very much." Nettie nodded. "I've seen it."

Melanie excused the old woman's silliness. After all, she suffered from dementia. Nettie Rivers could afford to indulge in fairy tales, Melanie thought. She needed to focus on the duties of the day.

The next afternoon, right after lunch, Melanie returned to her office to find someone had delivered chocolates, a monstrous box of the expensive Belgian kind she especially adored and seldom bought. The card inside was identical to the one that had come with the flowers. *Marry me,* the card insisted. She filed it away in her purse with the first.

Melanie hated to do it, but she didn't want any reminders of him around to poke and probe at her conscience, so she passed the delicacies around to her staff, watching sadly as, one by one, the delicious tidbits were eaten.

Mitch showed up for an afternoon coffee break that day, full of bouncing good humor. Melanie found herself envying his sparkling eyes and obvious good health. She hadn't slept at all well for days.

"Anything interesting going on?" he asked cheerfully, flopping down in the chair next to hers after he'd brushed her cheek with his lips.

"I wish you wouldn't do that in public," she told him angrily. "Now the entire staff will be talking about us."

"They will anyway, once our engagement becomes public." He grinned affably.

"For once and for all, we are not engaged. You've mixed yourself up with your grandfather."

He ignored her cranky words and pulled two huge red apples from his pocket.

"Here, eat this," he ordered her smoothly. "Your blood sugar must be slipping. Did you eat a proper breakfast?"

"Oh, that's rich." Melanie glared at him. "The king of junk food asking me about my eating habits!"

Mitch sipped his black unsweetened coffee without reacting to her gibe. He bit into his apple with those sharp, even teeth, blue eyes twinkling.

"Maybe your problem is too much sugar in that coffee," he offered kindly. "Why don't you switch to juice?"

"Ooh! Why don't you go jump in the lake?" Melanie advised crankily. "And stop sending me things," she ordered. "You can't make me marry you." She stomped from the room. To her dismay he followed her into her office.

"I'm not trying to *make* you do anything," Mitch murmured, his hands closing around her shoulders. "And we will be married, as soon as you come to your senses."

She had a number of things to reply to that, but her mouth never got to say them because suddenly he was kissing her and she had wanted that for so long, she couldn't help wrapping her arms around his neck and enjoying every moment of it.

"I knew I was right!"

Melanie heard the words through a fog and turned to see Nettie Rivers standing in the doorway, her faded eyes bright.

"What do you mean?" Melanie unwrapped her arms and moved away from Mitch.

"My dear, you're only fooling yourself. You and Mitchel are meant to be together." She turned slowly and moved through the door. "I must go tell..." Melanie didn't hear the remainder.

"Now look what you've done," she said to a grinning Mitch. "She'll tell the whole world that you were in here kissing me, and everyone will be staring at me!"

She could have screamed when he smiled before using a tissue to wipe a smear of pale pink lipstick from his mouth.

"I think the kissing was mutual." He snorted in amusement. "And as wonderful as that was, I did come here for a purpose." He straightened his tie and flicked back the errant lock of hair that seemed perpetually out of place. "I wanted to ask if you'd come to my place tonight."

"Are you kidding?" she asked. "I'm up to my ears with this wedding tomorrow. I'm certainly not going to open myself up to any more of your silly tricks."

"Okay." He shrugged agreeably. "I'll just have it delivered to you and come to your place." And with a grin and a wave he was gone.

"Of all the rude, pushy, overbearing..."

"I like rude and overbearing men." Bridget giggled from the doorway. "Especially if they're also tall, dark and handsome." She eyed the flush on Melanie's cheeks and the agitated motion of her hands. "Give in, my dear, and admit you're head over heels in love with the guy."

"I am not," Melanie muttered, snatching the schedules from Bridget's hand. When the older woman simply smiled, Melanie glared. "Don't you have anything to do?"

Bridget shrugged.

"Grumpy and out of sorts. Refuses to admit the truth. Yep, you're in deep, Melanie, my girl." And whistling "Here Comes the Bride," she strolled out of the office.

That afternoon a package arrived for the Director of Care, Sunset Nursing Home. Melanie eyed it warily, suspecting Mitch of some trickery. But the plain, brown-wrapped package looked innocent enough, so she signed for it and tore away the paper. Three CDs were nestled inside the box, all of them wedding music.

Melanie stuffed the items into her purse before anyone saw. The enclosed card with its peremptory edict she filed with the others. The day dragged after that, and Melanie found herself scurrying home, wondering what he was up to.

By seven-thirty it looked as if there might be some respite. She checked through her list three times, organized the bows, bells and other fripperies and generally piddled around until the doorbell rang. It was a delivery man. Or rather, a delivery boy.

"Hi," the young voice greeted her. "I'm to deliver this into your hands." The youngster thrust a large, plain white box into her hands before loping off down the street. Melanie pushed the door closed with her foot as she tried to peer into the box. The thing was huge and weighed a ton, but the box was securely fastened, and she had to set it down on the dining room table before she could free the sides.

She gaped at the contents.

"Oh, my, now he's really done it," she muttered.

A square one-layer wedding cake sat nestled inside covered with a thick white frosting. Misty green tulle curled in soft gathers around the bottom. The cake had a trellis pattern on the sides. On top a tiny bride and groom stood below an arch with the tiny scripted gold letters PJPB on it. Across the top in pale green script were inscribed the words "Melanie and Mitchel."

She let him have it when he came through the door.

"Are you crazy?" she squealed. "You're going around planning a wedding and you don't have a bride! This wedding cake must have cost a fortune. It's custom-made, you know, and they're not cheap." When he kept on smiling, she tried reasoning. "You're going to be very embarrassed when you end up standing at the altar all by yourself."

Mitch studied her seriously while Melanie wondered about the odds in a marriage where only one half of the couple, the bride, for example, was in love. But, in the end, she refused to dwell on it. She prepared to do battle instead.

"I do have somebody to marry," he told her seriously.

"And I don't want anybody but you." He looked at the cake. "They've obviously mixed up the orders. I'll call them first thing tomorrow morning. Hope's cake is much more elaborate than this." He picked up on her sigh of relief.

"Don't get any notions about trying to keep this a secret, Melanie," he told her sternly. "I've already asked your administrator if you can have two weeks off after the wedding." He added the kicker with a smirk. "I also told her the reason why."

Melanie studied him with a thoughtful frown. What reason? she wondered curiously. Had she missed something here? Why was everything spinning so wildly out of control?

"Are you going in for a lobotomy?" she demanded irately. Honestly, if the office people at Sunset knew about this wedding, then not only Sunset but the whole town would soon know. "What reason?" she asked, dazed.

"Our honeymoon, of course," he announced, obviously pleased with himself.

Melanie desperately wished she could have slapped that grin off his smug face. But there didn't seem to be much point. The whole world had apparently been informed of their blissful status. Sighing loudly, she rested her head on her folded arms atop the table, wondering if he would let her sleep through it all. Maybe she would wake up to find it had all been a dream, a very bad dream.

Instead, Mitch tugged her into his arms. He flashed his brilliant smile at her. Perhaps it could work, she considered. Perhaps, one day, Mitch would come to love her.

But then reality intervened and she remembered the PJPB on the cake. He was still thinking about that money! She floated to earth with a thud, to an engagement that wasn't and a wedding that would never be.

"By the way," she asked, "where is this grand occasion supposed to take place? You've done all this planning, and I'm certain you have not forgotten that tiny detail." Her tone was only half joking.

"Uh, actually, I don't have it all arranged yet," he told

her, clearing his throat. "Once I get the order in to the florist, I'll look after the place and the time."

Melanie knew he would not tell her until he was ready, so she gave up, wisely deciding to focus her attention elsewhere.

"What kind of flowers are you ordering?" When he stared, Melanie flushed. "Not that I care, since I *will not* be there. I was just curious."

"I know." The big oaf was grinning like a fool. "And you do know what happens to cats that are curious?"

"Yeah," she replied pertly. "They die." She shook the curls off her face and smirked. "They don't get married."

His lip turned down. "That's not nice, Melanie. I'm doing this all for you."

"Then stop." Melanie whooshed out a puff of air in exasperation. "I am not marrying you for money. I'm not even getting married. Period."

Nothing disconcerted Mitch. He sat down with his gargantuan list and began studying brochures. Although she asked questions constantly, Melanie got very little satisfaction from his vague answers.

She knew he was planning a reception, but she didn't know where. She knew he had planned on a honeymoon, but Mitch wouldn't say where they were going. She knew he had chosen someone to give her away, but he refused to tell her who. And on and on.

"Why don't you just plan everything? I'll just show up when you tell me to," she muttered in frustration.

"Exactly what I'm doing," he told her smugly.

Despair filled her as Melanie realized she had fallen into his fantasy trip. She jumped up from the table in frustration, wishing bleakly that her topsy-turvy world would right itself.

"I am not, not, *not* marrying you."

Mitchel Stewart barely glanced up from the funeral wreath he was studying with interest. Melanie shuddered at the glistening black roses entwined with baby's breath. She could only hope he wouldn't go for that! Nobody deserved black roses. Not even for this peculiar marriage.

"I think you're protesting too much." He leered. "I think you like me a lot, too."

"Mitchel Stewart," she snarled. "Sometimes I don't like you at all."

Ignoring his smug grin, she turned away. It was only with the firmest resolve that Melanie got herself away from that room and into Charity's office. He was going to have a rude awakening, she told herself. And it would be all his own fault because he didn't or wouldn't understand that she had absolutely no intention of marrying him.

Half an hour later his knuckles rapped on the door just before his head peered round the corner.

"I'm starving." He grinned. "Want to go out for supper?"

Melanie shrugged. Why not? It would be nice to get out of the house and away from all these stupid wedding plans, she decided. Besides, there were a few things that needed to be discussed about the real wedding tomorrow.

"Okay. Where?"

"Why don't we go out for dinner and dancing," he asked her softly. His blue eyes shone in the dimmed light. "We'll celebrate." With a wink, he disappeared, leaving her to stare after his retreating figure.

"Oh, no, you don't," she muttered. "You can buy me dinner and dance with me, but that's all that is going to happen here. I'm not getting involved any deeper in this hallucination of yours. Just keep a level head, my girl," she told herself over and over. "And watch out for those lips."

She needed this break, Melanie told herself later, studying her new aqua outfit. An evening of fun dressed to the nines was just the thing to take her mind off that elaborate overdone wedding cake sitting on her mother's dining room table.

Mitch whistled when he saw her, his eyes moving from the tousled curls on top of her head to the slim, straight lines of her dinner dress.

"You look very, er, nice," he stammered, his eyes slipping over the shimmery silk as it hugged every curve.

"Thank you." Melanie giggled, enjoying the rise of red in his face. "What kind of dancing do you like?"

"Close ones!" His comeback was quick, and he drew her into his arms. "Ones where I can hold my partner and do this." He brushed his mouth over her cheek, stopping just short of kissing her.

Melanie moved back slowly. She wanted to remember tonight, savor it for all the dull, lifeless future days without him. Tonight would be the last time she had anything to do with him, she decided. She was determined to put an end to this foolish dream of his if she had to camp out at the nursing home to do it. The whole thing had already gone far enough.

"Ready?" he whispered in her ear, and Melanie nodded. "Lead on, MacDuff."

Where he led her was to the restaurant they'd visited the night Sara had appeared. A pianist was again the featured artist. The decor was slightly different if still rigidly formal and very posh, but good old Kramer was there, waiting to take their order.

"Welcome back, Mr. Stewart, Miss Stewart," he murmured softly. His stern face creased into a smile. "Are we celebrating tonight?"

"No."

"Yes," Mitch overrode her. "Miss Stewart and I are getting married soon. We're here to escape all the madness for a few short hours."

"Congratulations." Kramer bowed. "Champagne?" He said it with a French accent that made it sound exotic, and Melanie fell into a daydream about Paris and young lovers, which only reminded her of her current predicament.

"You shouldn't have told him we're getting married, Mitch. This is getting way out of hand."

Mitch grinned, holding up his crossed fingers. "Oh, ye of little faith," he murmured. "Relax, Melanie. That's what tonight is all about, relaxing and enjoying the calm before the storm. And don't make any mistake—we are getting married."

Melanie peered at him, trying to read the dark flashes in his expressive eyes. Calm before the storm? Was she missing something here? If that's how he regarded marriage, why was he so determined to go through with it?

Kramer ended up bringing a lovely nonalcoholic champagne that was every bit as delightful as the real thing. Melanie sipped it, enjoying the tickles of the bubbles against her nose.

"I'm having a steak," Mitch told her, eyes wide with innocence. "I have a feeling I'm going to need all the energy I can get tonight."

She frowned. "For what?"

He winked, and it only added to the worry that was settling around her. He was up to something. And that wasn't good!

"For whatever comes along. Like dancing," he added, obviously noting the suspicion crossing her brow.

"Oh, right. Dancing." She stared at the menu while her pulse drilled. "I guess I'll have the pheasant," she decided at last. "And those potatoes I had last time," she added, glancing at Kramer. "They were excellent."

"Oui, madame."

"Oh, she's not madame yet, but she soon will be!"

Melanie pursed her lips at Mitch's boisterous voice but refused to take the bait.

The salads arrived almost immediately, and they munched away in silence. To her surprise, Melanie found she was hungry. Kramer kept filling their glasses with the bubbly concoction, and Melanie was glad it wasn't alcoholic. She would be under the table by now, she considered, recognizing the signs of nervousness as she took yet another sip.

As usual, the meal was exquisitely prepared. They ate silently, enjoying the Chopin flowing from the nearby baby grand. The evocative notes made her introspective, and she drifted off into a dreamworld where everything was wonderful. Slowly the music changed, flowing into a slow, dreamy number that released all kinds of wonderful thoughts in her brain.

"Come on, let's dance." Mitch's deep voice was suddenly behind her. She turned to find him holding her chair.

"Oh, thanks for asking," she muttered as he escorted her to the floor. "Don't mind if I do." She glowered at him. "Do you ever ask before you steamroll everyone into doing your will?"

"Sometimes. But only when I know I'll get the answer I want. Tonight you're cranky, and I wasn't sure."

He sounded funny, Melanie decided. Like he was choking or something. She pulled her head from his comfortable black shoulder and squinted into his face. It looked like the face of a smugly satisfied male, she concluded.

"Well, you should try it more often. Asking, I mean."

With a whirl, Mitch steered her onto the patio. The brick terrace was surrounded by flowers that gave a soft, welcoming perfume to the chilly night air. She wondered absently how they kept the blooms from freezing during these autumn nights.

"I'm glad you feel that way," he was saying. "Because I wanted to ask you something quite important."

She waited timeless moments for him to continue until the fear and nervousness in her unruly stomach could not be quashed any longer.

"Well, ask then," she ordered peremptorily, fed up with all this silly suspense.

Melanie's eyes grew huge with astonishment when Mitch pulled the brilliant diamond solitaire that sat perched on a wide gold band from his shirt pocket. She stared at it stupidly, watching the light reflect off its many facets. He pushed the golden circlet onto her finger. It was a perfect fit.

"I really am very fond of you, Melanie. And I want to marry you. Will you please say you'll be there, ready to walk down the aisle? If you don't, I'm going to be terribly embarrassed."

That hangdog expression was the pièce de résistance, she decided. He looked so woebegone that she stifled her hysterics and tried to speak rationally.

"I've told you, Mitch. I don't want to be married just so I can collect twenty-five thousand dollars." *Please say that's not why,* she begged silently. *Please tell me you love me.*

"What if it were the full fifty thousand?"

Melanie yanked her hand out of his, pulled off his lovely ring and thrust it into his hand. She hurried into the restaurant, her heart breaking. Moving swiftly, she gathered her handbag, picked up her stole and swept outside. Mitch followed minutes later.

"Melanie? Where are you going?"

"I'm going home. Either you can take me or I'll get a cab," she said sadly. "But whichever way it turns out, I am not, repeat *not* marrying you. Not even if it involves a hundred thousand dollars. I am not marrying anyone for money."

Fortunately, a car pulled up to the entrance just then and Melanie's friend Jeff came loping down the stairs to accept the key from the valet. She hurried across the damp pavement, calling his name. "I need a ride, Jeff. Can I tag along?"

"Mellie? What are you doing here?" Jeff stared at her.

"I'll take you home, Melanie. You don't have to go with him." Mitch sounded frustrated, but Melanie ignored the plaintive tones, rounding on him fiercely as she swallowed her pain. She couldn't deal with this. Not now.

"You're right, for once, Mitchel Stewart. I don't have to do anything. Including marry you. And I am not going to!" Whirling, Melanie flung herself into the front seat of Jeff's car, oblivious to everything but the need to get out of there. Now!

But as Jeff drove her home Melanie didn't feel victorious or smug. What she felt was a sharp, stabbing pain in the middle of her heart. She was alone. Again.

One little four-letter word was all it would have taken, she thought. *Just one tiny word. And he couldn't say it.*

At home she avoided the fearsome threesome in the living room and scurried up to bed. But she lay for a long time before her eyes closed, and when they did, all she could dream of was Mitch and the things that would never be.

Chapter Twelve

"He's besotted with her." Faith giggled enthusiastically. "I've seen him watching her, and I'm positive Mitch loves our Melanie every bit as much as she loves him."

"That may be," Charity muttered, fastening Hope's beautiful pale peach dress with difficulty. "But she hasn't told him, and if I know my daughter, she probably hasn't even admitted it to herself. And I'm positive that he certainly hasn't told her any such thing."

"I'm so happy myself, I can hardly imagine anyone being sad." Hope smiled sympathetically. "I just wish there was something I could do."

"You can pray, dear. We all can. The Lord will make a way through this mess. He is in control."

"Faith's right," Charity murmured. "And this is your special day. Don't let anything or anyone spoil it for you, Hope. Not when you've waited so long."

There was a pounding on the door, which sent all three ladies scurrying.

"Who is it?" Charity called out just before Faith opened the door. They all gaped at Mitch's grim countenance and Melanie's white face as they stood together in the doorway.

"Uh, I'm sorry to bother you, Hope. Really, I wish this could wait, but it can't. I have to talk to you right now." Mitch's voice was low and husky.

Charity advanced like a mother hen protecting her chick, but Melanie forestalled her. "Leave them, Mother. This has to be said."

Mitch led Hope to a seat and knelt in front of her.

"I'm so sorry to do this, Hope," he murmured, holding her small, fine-boned hand between his brown paws. "I've had a private investigator checking into Papa John. He assured me a week ago that Papa John and Jean LeClerc were two different men, but today I received a phone call that seems to prove the two are one and the same."

Hope's face grew white and still. Faith scurried up to support her with a comforting arm around the shoulders while Charity rushed to get a glass of water.

"But I thought that wasn't possible," Hope whispered. "I understood there were records or something that totally disproved that hypothesis?" She stared at Mitch in confusion.

"So did I," Mitch murmured. His eyes were dark with sympathy, and Melanie was glad he was there to help her deal with it. "But Clarence just phoned me with information about fingerprints. Apparently an old set was found from long ago, in France, and they match Papa John's."

"And John?" she asked quietly. "What does he say?"

"He says he's very sorry," John murmured from just outside the door. His white head was bowed, his eyes full of sadness. "I would explain it if I could, Miss Langford, but I simply don't remember. Not you, not our plans, not the war. I have only confused fragments of the time in hospital, a date and the name John."

Hope stood, a slim, delicate figure in the bright afternoon sunlight.

"And Harry," she murmured in confusion.

"I'm right here, Hope." Harry Conroy moved forward to enclose her in a hug that crushed her dress and made Charity frown.

"All these men in the bride's room." She fussed, straightening a pillow with a surfeit of energy. "It's just not fitting."

Harry pressed Hope onto a nearby sofa and sat down beside her, gathering her hands in his.

"My darling Hope, I'm still here. I always will be. If you want to call this shindig off and think about things, we can do that. I know it will take a while to assimilate everything."

"You're so dear, Harry," Hope whispered, cupping his cheeks in her palms. "Such a dear, wonderful friend when I've caused you so much…"

"Happiness," Harry finished for her. "Nothing has changed, my dear. I still love you as much as I always have. All I want is for you to be happy and content. If it means that you have to talk to this fellow, think things over, then that's what we'll do."

Melanie watched as a thousand different emotions flitted across Hope's face. Hope glanced from John to Harry and then back to John as if she couldn't quite grasp this latest development. Then she moved forward to grasp John's arm.

"I'm so glad you're alive," she whispered. "So glad. If only I'd known sooner…" Her voice died away. Harry stood, walked to the door and silently pulled it open.

"Where are you going, Harry?" Hope asked, her voice stronger.

"You'll need some time to discuss this, absorb what it means to you. I'll just go to the church and tell everyone to go home." The judge's tones were quiet.

Charity gasped in surprise while Faith issued a wail of dismay. But Hope stared at her fiancé.

"Are you backing out on me, Harry Conroy?" she demanded.

"No, of course not, but—"

"Yes, you are," she told him severely. Then her face creased in a smile. "That's an awful thing to do to a woman who's waited until her late fifties to get married," she teased. "And I'm not letting you get away with it." Hope held up her ringed finger in front of his face and spoke in a sure, steady voice.

"I loved Jean once, Harry. And when he never came back, I locked my feelings away and decided that love wouldn't be a part of my life. I thought that if I were stoic enough, God would give him back." She shook her head.

"But after Anna died, and you and I got involved in the seniors' center and the choir at church, I realized that Jean had left my heart. Yes, I remembered him fondly, but I wanted something real, someone alive in my life. And finally—" she kissed his cheek "—finally I realized that I loved you."

Harry's face was a beaming circle of happiness as he hugged Hope.

"I'm not waiting any longer, Harry. It's now or never for me."

"Then it's now," Harry boomed, and led her from the room.

Those in the room heard two voices whispering outside, then Hope scurried into the room to stop in front of Papa John.

"I'm very glad that you're safe and alive and have gone on with your life," she told him sincerely. "And while things might have been different, God has led me down a new path." She stood on her tip toes to kiss his cheek.

"Be happy, Jean. Make your life as full and rich as you can. And don't worry about me. I'm going to be very happy." And smiling through her tears, she glanced around the room at her friends.

"Are you going to miss my wedding, girls?" she chided, giggling like a schoolgirl.

Charity bustled forward and scooted the men from the room.

"No, we're not," she said firmly. "But everything must be done decently and in order. Mitch, you get your grandfather to the church right away."

It was Faith who led Papa John from the room. Melanie

tried to listen in on their conversation but all she heard was Faith's quiet voice inviting the elderly man to the festivities.

"And bring your lady friend," she encouraged brightly. "Hope will be glad to know you have someone special in your life, too."

Melanie drove to the church and checked the pew bows, the flower arrangements and the bridal bouquet, but she couldn't help repeatedly seeking out Mitch's tall, dark-suited frame.

"It seems that everyone has someone special in their lives," she murmured to herself as the organ music started and her mother led the procession down the aisle leaning heavily on Frank Bellows's muscular arm.

"Everyone, that is, except me."

Life should have settled down in Mossbank, back to its usual boring routine of work, eat and sleep, but Melanie couldn't truthfully say that she got much of the latter. Not since Mitch had cornered her after the reception, saying it was urgent that he talk to her.

"I have something extremely important to say to you," he said.

But his important business had to take second place. A telephone call demanded her immediate attention at the nursing home, and not wanting to spoil the festivities, Melanie kissed Mr. and Mrs. Harry Conroy, gave them her best wishes and hurried away, Mitch trailing behind.

"Why is it that whenever I want to talk to you, you take off?" he demanded, grabbing her by the arm. "What's so important this time?"

"Sunset's on fire," she told him grimly. "I've got to go." When he insisted on coming, Melanie didn't argue. She couldn't seem to find her car keys, and he was as efficient as she might have wished for.

Melanie was doubly glad he had come when she saw the red flames licking up the south wing. And he was a bulwark of strength, propping up her shaky body when she saw the damage.

"It's okay," he muttered, brushing his hands over her hair gently. "Everyone got out, the fireman says. They have it almost under control."

Melanie stared past him unseeingly, her mind fixed on the blackened, ragged edges of Sunset and on her residents. As each of the clients came to mind, Melanie finally broke free of the stupor holding her inactive.

"I've got to see them," she whispered, hurrying toward the wing of the hospital nearest the home. "Please God, let them be okay."

"He'll have them safe, honey. Don't worry."

Mitch was right behind her, and he stayed close as they worked to organize the residents, calming and settling as they went. Nettie Rivers was white and pinched with fear as she sat clutching the cat she spoke to constantly.

As Melanie watched, Mitch coaxed the elderly woman out of her chair and to her room, tucking the covers around her carefully after she had swallowed her medication.

"Please stay with me until John comes," the old woman whispered in a thready voice. Mitch sank onto the chair beside her bed, still holding the blue-veined hand. "Someone phoned him, and he promised he'd be right here."

"I'm not going anywhere, Mrs. Rivers." Mitch patted her shoulder reassuringly. "I'll sit with you until Papa John comes. After all, you are my biggest client."

Melanie frowned as Nettie patted Mitch's shadowed cheek. Client? What was that about, anyway?

"You're such a dear boy," she told him. "The most suitable mate for our Melanie. I know you don't think I should have done it, but I was so sure that you two would be the perfect foil for each other. All of us did."

"None of that matters now, Nettie," Mitch murmured, helping her to lie back. He tossed a sideways look at Melanie and shrugged. "Just rest."

The paper-thin lids closed as Nettie breathed out a sigh.

"Melanie needs a man who will challenge her," she whispered. "Someone who's not afraid to dare her to take a chance. She's buried herself here for so long, seeing to our needs. I just knew God would send someone very special. If only..." The words died away as Nettie drew a deep breath and slept. Melanie stared at Mitch.

"What was all that about?" she demanded softly. "You'd think she had some hand in our meeting." His skin flushed a deep pink. "Never mind," she murmured. "I've got to go check on the rest. This sure would be a good time for Papa John to hand over that money."

The pained look on Mitch's face drew her immediate suspicions. "What now?"

"That's what I was trying to tell you earlier, Melanie. I have notified him and his company that we have no further interest in them or their prize money."

"What?" Too late Melanie remembered to keep her voice down, but Nettie seemed undisturbed. "Why in the world did you do that?" she asked angrily.

"Because you said you thought I only wanted to marry you because of the money," he told her softly. "I was trying to prove to you that it simply isn't true." Mitch's deep blue eyes blazed with something Melanie couldn't or wouldn't define.

"I don't have time to deal with this right now," she told him furiously. "I'm in the middle of a crisis here."

"I know. We can talk about it later. I've got some more ideas for the wedding, anyway." He smiled that heart-stopping grin that shook her to the core.

"We are *not* getting married," she enunciated clearly, whirling from the room. "And you have just made doubly certain of that by ending what little chance I had to improve Sunset. Now if you don't mind, I'd like to get on with my job."

And so she did. She worked steadily using a matron's office to phone families and friends of those who had been displaced by the fire. Miraculously, there were only a few.

When Melanie and the fire chief toured the building, it seemed that most of the home was undamaged. Smoke and water had rendered the southern end unusable. This was the area Melanie had been trying to convince the board to replace. The task of erecting temporary walls was made much easier.

Her staff had handled the situation with the quick-thinking aplomb of troupers, and Melanie made it a point to congratulate them on their speedy solutions. Doggedly, Melanie continued on, refusing to give in to the ache of tiredness that edged its tentacles toward her body. There was too much to do. Besides, she didn't want to think about what might have been.

By seven in the morning the seniors had all returned safely to their rooms. Tired and discouraged, many had agreed to go to bed and rest a little, while a stalwart few demanded breakfast.

Melanie sighed as she pushed the heavy fall of hair off her face and took a deep breath. She sank into her plush chair with a sigh as Bridget carried in a tray of coffee and toast.

"You had better sit and eat this before you fall down," the older woman chided her. Bright gray eyes studied her thoughtfully. "You can't do it all yourself, Melanie. We can manage. Faith and Charity are coming over, and they'll give us a hand settling everyone down. Go home. Get some rest. Then you can pitch in again when you're feeling better."

"You know, Bridget," Melanie said with a sigh, leaning her head back thankfully, "this is one time when I'll welcome the fearsome threesome's presence. Even if they are minus one." She grinned. "They'll be a ray of sunshine here."

"Yes, they will," Mitch said quietly from the doorway. "Come on, I'm taking you home."

"I have a lot to do," Melanie said tiredly, not wanting to face him and his pressure tactics. "I should probably—"

"Come with me." He grinned, tugging her from the chair. "That's what I said, and I meant it."

"And I agree with him," her mother said from the doorway.

"We both do," Faith added, grinning from ear to ear as she set a bouquet of flowers on Melanie's desk. "And these are from Hope and Harry. They'll be back in a few days to help, but they send their love and thanks."

"Oh." It was the only thing she could think of with everyone standing there staring at her.

"Now do I have to get the wheelchair?" Mitch teased, with a glint in his eye as he rolled up his dingy, smoke-crusted sleeves. "Or are you going to come willingly?"

"Yes, I'll go," Melanie acquiesced at last, yawning widely. "I could use a few hours' sleep."

Mitch ushered her down the hall and out the door, steering her away from Nettie Rivers and her companion, Papa John.

"It's going to be more than a couple of hours," Mitch ordered in a no-nonsense tone. "And when you wake up, after you've showered and eaten, you and I are going to talk. Without interruption." He stared at her soberly. "I have something to say to you, Melanie, and I have no intention of letting this go on any longer."

He wheeled his sports car in front of her mother's house, helped her out and ushered her inside without pausing.

"Where did you get a key?" Melanie demanded crossly. "I suppose you've wrapped my mother around your finger just like you've done with Nettie."

"Your mother and I had a…discussion," he murmured. "And she is perfectly satisfied with my intentions. So is Nettie."

"Your—" Melanie yawned "—intentions?" She stared at him, bleary-eyed. "You didn't start that marriage nonsense again, did you?" She saw his lips curve, but Mitch merely steered her toward the stairs and gave a slight push.

"Go to sleep, honey. We'll talk later."

She stepped slowly, heavily, up the carpeted stairs.

"I wish you'd stop saying that," she mumbled, tiredness tugging on every limb. "We both know it isn't true." She thought she heard him say something, but couldn't be bothered to do more than undo her once pretty party dress and crawl between the sheets.

"Please help me, Father," she whispered. "I'm so terribly confused."

Seconds later her eyes flopped closed as her body relaxed and images of a tall, dark-haired groom whirled through her unconscious mind.

Mitchel Edward Stewart was scared spitless. He'd rehearsed the lines over at least seven hundred times in his head, and still nothing sounded just right.

"I want to marry you, Melanie Stewart." No, he'd already said that. And a fat lot of good it had done him, too.

"You wouldn't have to change your name." Too frivolous.

"Why don't you just admit you love me?"

Ha! Good question. And if she came back with the same one, he was in deep trouble. By the time his grandfather and Hope stopped by, glowing with happiness, Mitch's palms were itchy with sweat.

"Just on our way to Sunset, boy. Hope and I want to check on things there. Might be able to help out." His grandfather frowned, noting the lines of tiredness creasing his grandson's handsome face. "Something wrong, son?"

"No. I'm just a bit worn out from the fire and things." Mitch stared at them both. "Wasn't Paris supposed to be in your plans somewhere?" he asked grimly.

"Still is. There's just a few things around here need straightening up," Gramps muttered with a sly look at Hope.

"Yes, Harry had one or two things that just couldn't wait," she murmured in agreement. Her fingers flipped a stray lock of hair off his forehead. "You do look worn to a frazzle, Mitch."

"Reckon you'll feel better once you get your hands on half that money." Judge Conroy chortled. "I should think twenty-five thousand dollars would put a smile on that face."

"I'm not getting the money, Gramps. Neither is Melanie." Mitch hated saying those awful words. He knew how much she'd wanted her half of the prize to buy equipment for her friends. Now, because of him, she would never get it.

"But I thought—" The judge's booming voice was interrupted by his wife's softer but firmer one. Mitch had to smile at the meek look on Harry's face.

"This isn't the time, Harry. Look at him. He's dead on his feet." Hope whirled around and glared at her new husband. "He's tired out and needs to be left alone."

"Yes, dear," Harry agreed, patting her hand gently.

Hope lifted Mitch's unshaven chin until her faint blue eyes met his darker ones.

"You go to your grandfather's, Mitch. There's no one there, and you'll be able to rest. Your grandfather and I will stay here and make sure Melanie isn't disturbed."

"No." Mitch shook his tired head, his hair flopping forward onto his face. "Thanks, anyway, Hope. But I have to be here when Melanie wakes up. I need to talk to her."

Mitch studied the two of them for a time, wondering how much he should say. But he was tired of carrying this burden around by himself for so long. What would it hurt to share it with these two? It wasn't as if they could do anything about it. He'd have to settle that himself.

"You see, Papa John actually did agree to give us the money. But only if we get married."

"What? I didn't know that." Hope frowned. "Why must you get married?"

"He says it has something to do with his company's image and moral standards. Besides, we don't have a leg to stand on. I think Nettie Rivers entered my name in their stupid contest. And I took possession too late for qualifying." He shook his head tiredly. "It's all rather complicated and confusing, but the bottom line is we have to get married to get the money, and Melanie blames me for the whole fiasco." He grimaced.

"I wanted her to get that money. She has so many plans for those residents, and I knew how much it meant to her. I figured if I helped her out everybody would benefit. I'd get twenty-five grand myself, she would get her bed alarms and new sheets and stuff, and everybody would be happy.''

"That was a perfectly generous thing to do." His grandfather nodded benignly. "I knew he'd turn out all right," Harry muttered to Hope. "And I was right."

"You see, when things started getting complicated, I did tell her she might have a better chance if she moved into my apartment. I thought I was helping her." Mitch sighed. "And now that's the stumbling stone. 'Living in sin,' he called it, and now Melanie thinks I've ruined her reputation completely, even though I offered to get married."

The newlyweds stood staring at him as if he'd grown purple horns from his ears, and Mitch couldn't blame them. The whole crazy thing sounded ridiculous, especially the way he'd just phrased it. He wasn't even sure Melanie had entered that crazy contest, either. What was it Papa John had said? Something about the handwriting? When you added that up with Nettie Rivers's strange comments, well...

"It's not just the money, though, is it, Mitch? There's something more to your proposal now, am I right?" Hope's face was a study in thought, but her eyes were bright and curious as she waited for Mitch to return to reality. At his nod, she smiled. It transformed her stern face.

"I thought so," she burst out, hugging him tightly. "I've wondered for weeks when you'd finally admit it. You're in love with Melanie, aren't you?"

"What?" Harry stared at both of them as if they'd lost their minds. "In love? Mitch? He's not in love. Doesn't believe in it."

"Honey?" Hope's voice was quiet. But there was a thread of compelling determination in it. Harry stopped speaking and stared at her. "I'm not finished."

"But you said..." Harry took a second look at his new wife's face and then swiveled to stare at Mitch. Finally he sank into the nearest armchair, shaking his head in amazement. "I never thought I'd see the day," he mumbled.

Hope ignored him and concentrated on Mitch, who could feel her steady gaze penetrating his tiredness.

"You can't talk to her now, Mitch," she murmured at last. "You're far too tired to explain this properly. Go and rest and when you've shaved and showered and eaten something, you can talk to Melanie and get the whole thing straightened out."

It was tempting, and Mitch almost gave in.

"No," he muttered finally. "I should be the one to show her this." He tugged the rumpled letter from his pocket. "It's from the peanut butter company, accepting our notification that we are dropping all claims to their prize money."

"You renounced all your legal rights?" Harry bellowed, starting up in his chair. "Haven't you learned anything, boy?"

Hope whirled, her hands on her hips.

"I'm sorry to have to say this to you, Harry," She spoke firmly. "But it needs to be said. Hush, will you? This is not your courtroom."

Harry's face flushed as Mitch stared at Hope with a glint of admiration.

"But the boy doesn't understand—"

"He understands more than you think." Hope smiled, pressing a kiss on top of the balding head. "Now just hush while I sort this out."

Justice Harry Conroy, Esquire, hushed.

"Now you go to your grandfather's, Mitchel, and you get some rest. The time will come for you to talk to Melanie. But that time isn't right now. She's got a whole lot of work to do to get things on an even keel, and I expect she's running on empty right now." Hope led him out the door and down the steps.

"You rest and relax. If you really want to do something about this situation," she advised firmly, "you start praying. God will provide a way for things to happen according to His will." She opened the car door and stood waiting for him to climb inside.

Instead Mitch wrapped his big arms around that slim, immaculate form and hugged for all he was worth.

"Hope Langford Conroy, I think Gramps knew exactly what he was doing when he married you." He laughed, kissing her smooth, flushed cheek. "You're a martinet, but I mean that in the nicest possible way. Welcome to the family."

"Thank you." She blushed. "Now go and rest. I'll see if I can recruit a few prayer warriors for you, and we'll talk to the Lord about this."

Mitch drove toward his grandfather's old bungalow with a heavy heart. She meant well. And no doubt Faith and Charity would be called in to help out with the heavenly petitions. But Mitch was pretty sure that even the fearsome threesome couldn't work miracles in the iron-hard rock of Melanie Stewart's heart.

"I guess it's all up to You," he prayed tiredly, as his head sank against the crisp cool sheets. "I guess it always was." He turned and stared out the window at the bright, sunny day.

"Please show me the right way," he whispered. "There has to be something I can say, something I can do that will show her how much I love her."

But whatever it was, it eluded him. At last his eyes closed, and he allowed the blanket of sleep to override his aching body and whirling mind.

"Charity, I'm telling you that we have to do something. They've broken things off, and Mitch is desolate. I don't think he's going to keep asking her. Your daughter has rejected that boy once too often." Hope listened to her friend's voice for a long time, nodding and murmuring from time to time, until finally her face cleared and her lips smiled.

"Are you sure this will work?" she demanded finally. "I still want to go on my honeymoon, you know."

Again there was a reply that made her smile.

"All right. I'll handle that. You and Faith go see Nettie. And keep praying. Hard!"

"Hope, dear." Harry came up behind his wife and tapped her on the shoulder. "I was just feeling a bit peckish," he murmured apologetically.

"Harry Conroy," Hope burst out, grasping his lapels, "you help me with this and I'll buy you the best steak dinner you've ever eaten."

"Done," he agreed, kissing her cheek. "Now, what's up?"

Chapter Thirteen

Melanie rolled over and squinted at the bedside clock. Her room was lit by a few golden rays of sunshine, and while a little breeze blew through the curtains, the room wasn't hot. She wondered what had woken her and realized the phone in the hall was pealing a summons. Rubbing her eyes, Melanie padded out to pick it up, praying there hadn't been another incident at Sunset.

"'Lo," she mumbled, yawning widely.

"Melanie, darling, it's Mother. How are you feeling, dear?"

"Tired. I just woke up."

"That's good, dear. You don't want to sleep too long after these things. Best to get up and get back into the scheme of things."

It was the last thing Melanie wanted to do, but she agreed anyway. "Yes, Mother. I'm far too tired to go anywhere, though. Where are you?"

"I'm with the girls. We're having a little coffee party." Charity's voice changed, lowered to a whisper. "Faith wants to come over and see you, dear. She has something she wants to say."

"Oh, Mom! I'm not fit to receive visitors." Melanie grimaced at her tousled reflection in the hall mirror. "Whatever Faith wants, can't it wait?"

"Why, no, dear," Charity murmured. "I don't think it can." There was a pause and some whispering before she came back on the line. "She'll be over in fifteen minutes. Okay?"

"I suppose," Melanie mumbled ungraciously. "It's not as if I have any choice about it, is it?" But Charity had hung up and Melanie was talking to herself. "It figures," she complained. "That's the first sign."

With a lot of effort and only by resolutely ignoring the bunch of fresh-picked daisies standing on her dresser with a card that carried Mitch's scribbled signature, Melanie managed to shower and dress in fifteen minutes. As she did, snatches of the last evening she'd spent with him returned.

He'd refused the prize money!

The thought shocked her into stillness. Just when she had him figured out, he went and did a silly thing like that, throwing all her preconceived notions out the window.

But why? That was the question. It wasn't because he didn't need the money. Nobody in their right mind refused twenty-five thousand dollars. Of course, if you believed he wasn't in his right mind... No, she wouldn't go there.

Melanie was still puzzling when Faith breezed through the front door, her arms loaded with fresh-baked cinnamon buns.

"Hello, dear." She beamed happily. "I thought perhaps some calories might make you feel better." Quick as a wink, the older woman had made coffee, whisked out two of the steaming, dripping concoctions and set places for them both.

"Oh, Faith." Melanie breathed, closing her eyes as she inhaled the fresh cinnamon scent. "You didn't have to go to all this trouble. I didn't need a lot of fuss. I could have had a piece of toast." She slipped a bit of cream cheese topping into her mouth and smiled. "But this tastes much better."

"Oh, piffle! Of course I wanted to fuss over you," Faith said sternly. Her blue eyes were narrowed. "People want a chance to fuss over you, Melanie. You're always doing something for someone else, and we just want a chance to pay you back.''

"I didn't do anything special," Melanie said. "I was just doing my job to make sure everything was settled down after the fire."

"You always do your job. That and more," Faith murmured. "It's almost as if you're afraid to stop and let us love you."

Melanie jerked in her chair as she stared at her mother's dearest friend. There was something different about Faith today. Some strange look in her eye.

"It's not that," Melanie denied softly. "It's just that I feel it's my..." She couldn't express it exactly.

"Your duty," Faith added steadily. "Melanie, do you think that we could love you any more or any less just because of what you do or don't do for people?"

"Of course not!" Melanie burst out, red flags of embarrassment warming her cheeks.

"No, we couldn't, but my dear, you spend so much time going the second mile that you never let anybody minister to you," Faith murmured softly. Her hand affectionately stroked Melanie's loose auburn waves.

"I'm sorry," Melanie said stiffly. "I never realized that I was bothering anyone. Someone should have said something."

"That's not what I'm saying at all, dear," Faith told her firmly. "And I think you know it." She waited, watching carefully for the grudging nod of admission. "We love you, Melanie. All of us. Your mother, Hope, me, your friends at the nursing home, the people you always have time to give an ear to. We all think you're a very special person, and we are very grateful for the many things you've done for us all."

"You don't have to say this," Melanie blustered, feeling insecure and slightly childish, as well. "I'm only doing what I should. 'It is more blessed to give than to receive,'" she quoted staunchly.

"Piffle," Faith exploded, standing. "That is the most mis-quoted piece of scripture I have ever heard. And it's never referred to by the people who need it most."

"I, uh, don't know what you mean." Melanie frowned, pouring herself another cup of coffee. "What people?"

"Greedy souls who can never see another person's need." Faith's usually sweet voice was harsh. "No." She held up a hand. "Don't get me started on that or I'll get sidetracked and never say what I came to say."

Melanie blinked several times, trying to focus on the conversation.

"What did you come to say?" she urged quietly. Her nerves felt taut, stretched.

"Melanie, do you love Mitchel?" Faith demanded outright.

"I, er, that is, well..." She looked into Faith's green eyes. "I don't know."

"Yes, you do. If you look deep inside yourself, you'll know whether or not Mitch is the man you want to wake up to in the mornings. If the thought of him makes your skin crawl, then you'll know he's not the one."

Melanie blushed at the straightforward words, assessing the older woman with a different perspective.

"He doesn't make my skin crawl," she admitted, looking at her tightly knit fingers. In fact, the thought of kissing Mitch and having him kiss her back made her skin react in an entirely different way altogether, Melanie acknowledged privately.

"No, I suspect he makes your heart beat faster and your breathing quicken whenever he's around, doesn't he?" The older woman nodded wisely. "And when something interesting happens at work, or you hear some special bit of news, you want to share it with him first, don't you?"

Melanie didn't answer. She couldn't. She was busy remembering those special moments for herself.

Faith let her think for several moments before her worn, tired hand with its sparkling gold band slid over Melanie's.

''Why won't you admit that Mitchel Stewart is the one and only man for you?'' she demanded quietly.

''Because he's not,'' Melanie told her, dashing the stream of tears from her eyes. ''I've prayed and prayed about it, and whenever I ask for some guidance, another obstacle comes up. God doesn't want me to get married. He wants me to continue with the work I'm doing and be content with my life.''

''So now you know the mind of God?'' Faith snapped her fingers in disgust.

''But, Faith, it's true. I've prayed and prayed.''

''So there were a few problems. So what?'' Faith sank into a chair across the table and stared straight into Melanie's eyes until the younger woman was sure Faith could see clear through to her heart.

''Darling Melanie,'' she began, shaking her head in dismay. ''I believe you love Mitch far more than you've even admitted to yourself, but you think you're not worth loving, or some such silly nonsense. You think that you need to earn love when love is freely given, whether you will accept it or not.'' She smiled sadly. ''Let me ask you something, Melanie. What did Mitch have to do to earn a place in your heart? Did he have to invite you to stay in his apartment? Did he have to take you out to dinner so many times or spend a certain amount on flowers?'' Faith's voice rose. ''Was it important that he be a lawyer and have a good job so he could buy you things or drive you places in that flashy new car? What list did he have to fill to be worthy of your love?''

''I don't have any list of criteria for men,'' Melanie spluttered, aghast at the thought. ''There wasn't anything specific that he did. It's just who he is.'' She was getting frustrated.

''So it wasn't because he was tall, dark and handsome,'' Faith offered. ''He earned your affection because he was willing to help you get that money?''

''He didn't earn it,'' Melanie almost yelled. Her chagrin with the deliberately vague woman overflowed. ''I fell in love with him just because of who he was.''

As soon as the words had left her mouth, Melanie's eyes widened. She clapped a hand over her mouth in dismay but Faith was beaming from ear to ear.

"Exactly." Faith's countenance glowed with satisfaction. "And who do you think put that love in your heart and let it bloom and grow if it wasn't your very own personal God?"

Melanie stared at her.

"Do you know the scripture that tells us to ask God for the desires of our hearts because He wants to give us them more than we know?"

Melanie frowned. "But that's being greedy and concerned about ourselves, isn't it?"

"No, dear. That's admitting that we're human and we like company through our life." Faith closed her eyes and leaned back in her chair. "You know," she reminisced, "I recall the way you used to play, years ago. You were always so intent on playing family. It didn't matter what the other kids wanted, you always returned to your favorite game of a mommy and a daddy and their children." She sat up and grinned.

"I used to think it was because you hadn't had a really good home life and wanted that for yourself. But you know, Melanie, I believe that even then, God was working in you, creating and building on the desire for a family because that's what He intended for you to have. Do you think that He would ask you to forget about what He's specially planted in you?"

"But I don't know how to be a mother." Melanie grasped at the only straw she could think of. "Or a wife, for that matter. I never had very good role models. Charity's been wonderful, of course, but she had already raised her children when I arrived. She knew what she was doing. I haven't got a clue what to expect. What if I mess up?"

Faith burst out laughing.

"Oh, my darling girl," she gasped. "If you only knew how many phone calls Charity made to us asking if we thought she was being too soft or too strict, if we thought you should be allowed to go out with the Whalen boy or not, if we would pray for you when Charity's husband died and you blamed yourself.'' She wiped the tears away.

''My dear girl, if you mess up in life, you clean up the mess and move on!'' She grinned. ''It's time for you to take a break and relax, Melanie. Have a day off. Contemplate your navel.''

''I don't know about that,'' Melanie whispered in a gurgle of tears and laughter. ''It sounds hedonistic.''

''Maybe a little hedonism is what you need right now.'' Faith giggled. ''Nobody knows the future, Melanie. All we can know is that we can trust in God because He thinks we're worthy of it. After all, He paid the same price for all of us.''

''Yes, but this isn't the same thing,'' Melanie wailed. ''Mitch doesn't love me. He keeps insisting on this proposal because he wants the money. I want someone who wants me for myself.''

''Proposal?'' Faith's birdlike glance lighted on Melanie for a moment while she digested this. ''What exactly did he say, dear?''

Groaning at her slip, Melanie gave her a shortened version of Mitch's tactics, ending up with tears rolling down her face. Angrily, she dashed them away.

''He just wants the money,'' she reiterated. ''And he'll do anything to get it. He's rude and pushy and overbearing and bossy and—and—'' She stopped to sniff.

''And wonderful and handsome and the man you love more than anything,'' Faith finished with a smile. ''And he doesn't want to marry you for the money. Of that I'm sure.''

''Why?'' Melanie demanded. ''What has he said?''

''To me, nothing. But think, my dear. Think of the childhood he's had and his attitude toward marriage. I don't think money could motivate him that strongly when his old girlfriend with the rich father didn't stop him from finishing school, do you?''

Melanie stared.

''How do you know about...'' She stopped and shrugged. Some things were just unexplainable, and the fearsome threesome's knowledge of everyone and their history was one of those things.

"Furthermore, Mitch is a legal eagle. If he intended to marry you simply for the money, I'm sure he would have drawn up a prenuptial agreement that would set you both free without any unnecessary encumbrances." She raked a hand through her white curls, sending them every which way.

"Besides all that, he isn't getting the money, is he? He's told Papa John that neither you nor he will accept it. That's because he wants to start on the fresh, firm foundation of something much stronger than money. Love." She crowed triumphantly.

"And that's another thing," Melanie grumbled. "How can he just up and tell them to stuff their money without talking to me? I wanted that cash."

"I know." Faith nodded. "For Sunset." She studied Melanie. "I wonder," she murmured.

"Faith? Yoohoo!" Melanie waved her hand. "What were you thinking?" she asked when the green eyes finally focused once more.

"Oh, I'm just wondering if you weren't just a little too wrapped up in that money and God needed to get your attention. It's possible, you know, that Mitch wanted that money out of the way so he would know you wanted to marry him for himself and not because you'd get some cash."

Melanie thought about that for a long time, tossing the idea into the air and then discarding it as her own wants and not fact. But then, according to Faith, she didn't know which end was up anymore. And, strangely enough, right now Melanie would have agreed with that assessment!

"In a way, you're right, Faith," she admitted at last. "All this time, and I've really only fooled myself into believing money was the most important thing. And it wasn't." She smiled grimly. "I wanted that money so badly that I forgot to let God handle it. I thought I could force things, get what I wanted my way." Melanie grimaced in remembrance. "I wanted to matter to someone so much that I even thought I could fake living with Mitch if it meant I'd get that money and be the lifesaver for Sunset.'' She shrugged miserably. ''I forgot who's really in charge.''

''We all do from time to time, dear,'' Faith said encouragingly. ''Then the Lord has to catch our attention. Now that you're listening again, you can ask Him for more directions.''

Melanie sat thinking about those words of wisdom.

''I must go,'' Faith said, staring at her watch. ''Arthur's coming home tonight, and I want to make myself look good.'' She preened in front of Charity's kitchen mirror. ''He likes me in autumn colors, you know.'' Her voice held the girlish giggle of a young woman meeting her beau. She turned to Melanie and patted her hand.

''Think over what I've said, my dear. Relax, enjoy a day off. Go to the park and take a walk to clear your head while someone else takes over at Sunset.'' She smiled hugely. ''It's time for you to let others enjoy the gift of giving while you learn the fine art of receiving. Open up your heart and let the sunshine in. Ta, ta.'' And with a whirl and a swish, Faith was off down the steps and into the street, whistling merrily as she skipped along.

''Learn the art of receiving,'' Melanie repeated. ''It makes sense. In a strange, weird kind of way.'' She cleared the dishes away, wrapped the cinnamon buns in plastic wrap and wiped off the table before grabbing her jacket from the closet.

''Maybe a walk is the best thing,'' she told herself as she strode down the street. ''Maybe I do need to go out and see the world differently. The truth of the matter is,'' she lectured herself, ''I've been trying to *get* for a long time now. I don't need that money. Sunset will manage just fine. The important thing is that I'm doing the job I was put here to do—with whatever God gives me to do it with.''

So intent was she on her voyage that Melanie failed to notice the three pairs of interested eyes peering out the sheer curtains at Hope's. Nor did she pay particular attention when a white-bearded gent stopped in front of a house across the street and escorted an elderly woman up the front walk. But the arrival of the couple set off a flurry of activity that Melanie would have done well to pay attention to.

Chapter Fourteen

Melanie tipped her face up and enjoyed the warmth of the sun as it shone down brightly, lighting the trees from above. The dark green leaves were fading and would soon take on their autumnal reds and yellows.

No children played on the sidewalks and streets since school was back in session, and the luxuriant park grass was empty except for a busy squirrel who chattered madly when Melanie passed too near his cache of nuts.

She took a path and followed it around through the underbrush, between the picnic sites and far beyond the playground. On and on she went, across the ball diamonds and past the pond where she sat staring into the still, reflective waters for a long time. Now and then a trout jumped to catch a mosquito, making her glance around the peaceful enclosure again.

But no matter how hard she prayed, how diligently she stormed heaven's doors, Faith's words kept rolling around her brain.

"You love him, Melanie. Give him a chance. Find out if this is a gift to you from God. You'll be sorry if you deny yourself the love of a lifetime because you're too stubborn to give in.''

"Okay, Lord," she whispered at last, rising to her feet and studying the bright, clear sky. "You're in charge here. You direct events. I sent him away once and I don't think he'll be back, but that's up to You. I'll do my best to listen for Your direction. And if You give me another chance, I'm grabbing it with both hands.''

Peace, calming and steady, flowed through her mind as she walked up the roadway from the lake. It wouldn't be easy, but she would wait until God showed her the next step.

Melanie reached the small grove of evergreens before she saw him. He was unmistakable, even in brand-new, immaculate jeans and a brilliant blue shirt. He was crouched in front of a pit, building a fire.

"That's the most pathetic fire I have ever seen," she told Mitch truthfully, peering in at two fat logs that sat atop a piece of crumpled and barely smoking newpaper. "Weren't you ever a Boy Scout?''

"Melanie!" His face lit up, his eyes a bright blue, only to dim seconds later. "I wasn't sure you'd come.''

"Since I didn't know I was coming myself, that would have been difficult to predict," she admitted acerbically. "What are you doing here?''

"But I thought—that is, they said…" His voice drifted away as he stood staring at her. Finally he shrugged. "That doesn't matter, I guess. I want to talk to you, Melanie.''

She was nervous and sort of frightened, and her palms were sweaty, but Melanie was determined none of that would deter her from hearing him out.

Still, she needed to do something, so she bent and with a few swift strokes of his ax, built a pile of kindling. Pushing his nonburning creation to one side, she built a fire from a piece of his newspaper, added several tiny wood chips and then coaxed the flames upward with ever larger bits of wood. When it was blazing nicely, she pushed the big log on top, dusted off her hands and stood straight and tall before him.

"Talk about what?" she asked calmly.

"About you and me. Us. The future, Papa John, everything." He frowned. "Are you okay? You look tired."

"Let's just skip the compliments and get to the heart of the matter," she muttered, annoyed. "I understand you told the peanut butter man to stuff his fifty thousand dollars. Fine. It's done. What more is there to say?"

"I had to," he said simply. "It was getting in the way."

"In the way of what?"

If the Lord was directing her down this path, Mitchel Stewart was going to have to spell it out good and clear, Melanie decided. She wasn't taking any more chances.

"In the way of us." He moved to stand in front of her, his face pale in the bright afternoon sun. She noticed that the daredevil look had disappeared from his face. Mitch looked completely serious. And more vulnerable that she'd ever seen him.

"I know I haven't handled this very well. I never explained anything or gave you an acceptable basis for my actions," he admitted softly. "But I had a good reason for it."

"You did?" she asked, gulping when his hands came out to clasp hers.

"Well, I thought it was pretty good at the time," he murmured. "Now, after listening to some good advice on the subject, I guess I was just scared."

He was rambling, babbling about some advice he'd gotten, when all Melanie wanted to hear was the reason he was scared. *Say the words, Mitch,* she ordered subconsciously. *Just say the words.*

"Aren't you going to say anything?" His harsh voice finally penetrated her thoughts.

"Say anything about what?" she asked, blinking in confusion.

Right before her eyes, Mitch's chest puffed out like a bantam rooster's and his face turned several shades of angry, frustrated red.

"I just thought that when a man tells you he's in love with

you, you might possibly have something to say," he said in a wounded tone. "Is that asking too much?"

There were several comments she wanted to make, but something in his face, some tiny spark of worry that flickered in his eyes, made her relent.

"No, not at all," Melanie murmured at last, grinning from ear to ear. "The only thing is, I didn't hear you talking about love. Would you mind repeating it? Please," she added as an afterthought.

His grin reappeared, wide and white and full of that bad-boy sparkle that never failed to tug at her heartstrings. He walked slowly to where she was standing and deliberately wrapped his arms around her.

"I said, I love you, Melanie Stewart. More than any money or peanut butter could ever make up for. I love you so much, I want to marry you. That's why I had to get it over with, this whole fiasco with the prize money. The money doesn't mean anything. We can earn our own money. And we'll find some way to get that stuff for Sunset."

He was talking ninety miles an hour and only stopped because Melanie placed her index finger over his lips. He arched one eyebrow.

"What?"

"Do you know you talk too much?" she told him firmly.

"You asked me!" He looked offended. "Besides, I was only explaining." He stopped explaining immediately when Melanie's lips touched his, and he didn't bother to begin again until a long time later.

"I love you, Mitch," she whispered when she could get her mouth free. "I have for a long time. But I didn't want to face it because I thought love like this couldn't possibly be meant for me."

"Why in the world would you think that?" he asked, his lips nipping at her earlobe. "Someone as lovely as you should have been snapped up long ago."

Melanie drew in a deep breath and let out all the worry and fear that had been trapped inside for so long.

"I thought I wasn't good enough," she told him clearly. "I thought God wanted me to continue the way I was going, single and alone, because I wasn't worth loving. That's why I've spent so much time working, I guess, pouring myself into the home and its needs. I was trying to avoid my own desires."

She stared at him, grimacing.

"Then you came along and that windfall of money clouded my judgment. Whenever I prayed for guidance, another problem would come up. I took it to mean that God didn't want us to be together. That I was trying to have something that I didn't deserve, wasn't worthy of."

Mitch set her gently away so he could stare deeply into her eyes.

"You can't earn love, my dearest Melanie. Of all people, I know that the best." He smiled grimly and turned away. "I have to tell you something, Melanie, and you can't stop me until I'm finished. Is it a deal?"

She frowned, worried by the dull gray look in his wonderfully sensitive eyes.

"It's all right," he murmured, brushing a hand over her head gently. "It's nothing for you to worry about. I just need to say it."

"Say it, then," she agreed finally, but her fingers curled around his for comfort.

"You know about my mother from Sara, don't you?" he asked, and watched her nod. Mitch felt the prick of pain he always experienced whenever the subject came up, but he damped it down.

"Okay. Well, suffice it to say that I had a rather awful childhood. My mother couldn't stand up for herself or me, and the alcohol was her escape route." He swallowed hard and continued. "My father used to beat her up and she'd never say a word to us except that he was our father and we should obey him. We owed him that, she said." Mitch frowned. "I didn't owe him anything and I hated him with everything in me. Eventually he got tired of us and moved on and I was glad. My mother drank some more. She was in and out of three marriages in about as many years, and each one was worse than the last.''

"Oh, Mitch." Melanie squeezed his hand. "You don't have to tell me all this."

"No interrupting." He grinned crookedly. "Anyway, in all that turmoil, there never seemed to be a place for me to fit in. I tried everything I could think of to earn a little bit of her love, but I never really felt like she cared." He stared at their entwined fingers.

"Even after I went away to school, I'd come home and be the odd man out, trying to fit in where I didn't belong. By then I was cold and cynical and I looked for a fight with everybody. I usually found it with my stepfathers."

He breathed a little easier when Melanie wrapped her arms around his waist and snuggled her head on his shoulder.

"I made up my mind that never, not ever, would I be a soft, easy target like my mother. Nobody was going to hurt me like that. I was pretty sure I could get through life without loving anyone, but underneath the fear wouldn't go away." He smiled grimly.

"I coasted through college and got into law school without any commitments. Until Samantha."

"Mitch, I know about Samantha," she whispered. "You don't have to say it."

He was grateful for that. "Well, anyway, after Samantha dumped me, I was humiliated and ashamed. It was just as usual, I had let myself be conned by love, and in so doing, lost my scholarship, a year at school and my standing at the top of the class. I resolved not to ever get my heart involved again."

He bent and kissed the top of her head.

"And then you came along. Somehow nothing was ever cold or calculated with you around. Here I was just learning about God and His care for me and there you were, insisting you get that money for Sunset." He chuckled at her dismayed look.

"I told myself to keep it cool. I'd help you out, make sure you got that cash, listen to you talk about your seniors, but I wasn't going to get involved." He snorted. "Ha! I was up to my neck in involvement! I had you and Hope in my apartment and an assortment of people coming and going. I watched you with them, Melanie. And envied them."

"Envied them? Why?"

"Because they belonged. You belonged. Even Gramps belonged. But the closer I tried to get to you, the more I realized that I didn't belong. Again. You weren't the type to tolerate my no-commitment rule. You talked about families until I realized that that was what I wanted, too, underneath it all." Mitch's voice was soft. "The thing is—" he hesitated, looking at her "—I don't think I'm a family man, Melanie. I don't know how to be." He stopped speaking, his face drawn and white.

"Do you know what my father said once when he was finished punching the daylights out of my mother?" Melanie shook her head. "He said, 'You hate me, Mitch, but one day you'll be just like me.'" His face was pinched. "I can't let that happen, Melanie. Not ever. I won't."

"Mitch, you're nothing like that! You're you, and you would never do that to a woman or a child." The assurance was heartfelt, and Mitch stared at her, trying to believe.

"But I don't know anything about raising children, how to be a proper father." He looked utterly shocked when she started laughing. "What's so funny?"

"I said almost exactly the same thing to Faith this afternoon," she admitted. "And thank goodness, she made me see how silly I was being." Melanie wrapped her arms around his neck and pulled his head to hers.

"We'll pray and learn about it together," she told him seriously. "After all, we've got the Creator for a teacher. We'll start with Him as the head of our family."

Mitch was distracted. He wanted to tell her the rest of it, but he also wanted her to keep on kissing him. Still, there was something niggling at his brain.

"Faith?" he asked a moment later. "But she was over at my place. She's the one who suggested I come to the park this afternoon."

"No doubt about it." Melanie grinned. "The fearsome threesome have been busy today. For once, I don't mind their meddling. They've been at me to get married for so long that I'm looking forward to telling them I'm taking their advice. They can be grandmothers for our kids. I'm sure they'll tell us exactly what it is we're doing wrong!" She only stopped speaking because he put his hand over her mouth.

"Melanie," Mitch complained dryly. "Dearest, darling Melanie. I hadn't finished, you know. I haven't even proposed yet, and you're discussing our children!"

"You've said all I want to hear right now, Mitchel Stewart." Bright and teasing green eyes glittered at him. "You love me and I love you and we both love God. That's all we need to start out with." She kissed his chin. "And you did propose, Mitch. Remember? Several times." She grinned teasingly. "I'm just a little delayed in my answer." She reached up and wrapped her arms around his neck.

"Yes, please. I will marry you. Because I love you and trust you and want you for my husband."

There was a large gap in the conversation while Melanie convinced him that she was serious about becoming his wife. Mitch's head was reeling when she finally stepped away. He glanced down bemusedly when her pointed nail tapped him on the chest.

"What?" he asked, noticing the brightness of her eyes and the glow on her face.

"Could I have my beautiful ring back please, dearest fiancé?" she pleaded softly. Her eyes grew wide and anxious when he continued to stare at her. "Mitch?"

"Only if you promise one thing," he told her seriously.

"What's that?" she demanded, sensing he needed to hear her say the words.

"That you promise to love me for as long as I love you

and never, ever doubt that love again.'' He watched her steadily.

"Yes! I remember you once telling me that if and when you got—tied up was your phrase, I believe—you would only consider it under conditions of a very secure lifetime commitment.'' Melanie chuckled. Her face teased him as she watched him in the deepening gloom.

"And I have no problem with those stipulations, counselor. Where do you want me to sign?'' she asked archly.

But Mitch was ready for her shenanigans, and he scooped her up in his arms to settle onto one of the log seats by the fire.

"Right here,'' he ordered, tipping his head down and pointing to his mouth. "In triplicate.''

"No problem. I love you, Mitch.''

"I love you, Melanie. Now hurry up and kiss me before your fire goes out and I don't get my dinner.''

Melanie stopped to glance at the cooler on the picnic table. "What's in it?'' she demanded warily.

Mitch shook his head. "First things first,'' he told her.

Between kisses Melanie heard him whisper delightfully teasing words like hot dogs and potato salad and marshmallows. It all sounded divine to her. But nothing was as wonderful as the feel of Mitch's arms holding her tight.

Chapter Fifteen

"I've always dreamed of an autumn wedding," Melanie said, staring at her mother's garden. "Thank you, Lord, for another prayer answered."

The sun shone down warmly as a tiny breeze danced, releasing the last few red and gold leaves. Bright and blue, the sky promised a fine start to her new life together with Mitch.

"Melanie? Come down here." It was her husband-to-be. His face was wreathed in a grin as big as all get out. "I've got something to show you."

"No way. You're not even supposed to be here this morning. It's bad luck." Her mouth tilted as he roared with laughter.

"As if any silly old superstition could keep us apart. Now come on. I've got things to do today, you know. For one thing, I'm supposed to be at a wedding at two."

"Yes, I remember." She got lost thinking about it until he whistled. "I'll be right there," she called, and scurried down the stairs to find the fearsome threesome arguing.

"He shouldn't be here," Hope was saying. "He'll spoil everything. I'm going to have Harry speak to that boy."

"Oh, piffle," Faith argued. "You saw Harry on your wedding day before the ceremony, Hope, and it hasn't hurt you two any. Leave the children alone.'' A dreamy look wafted across her face as she noticed Melanie standing on the bottom step, her hair in big fat rollers and covered head to toe in a thick gray terry robe. ''Such a beautiful bride.'' She sighed.

''It must be something important,'' Charity said, peering out between her lace curtains. ''Otherwise why would he have come so early?''

''Relax, all of you,'' Melanie ordered calmly. ''This is my wedding day, and nothing is going to spoil it.'' She kissed each one lightly and hurried to the door. ''Back in five,'' she called.

Mitch was waiting by the chrysanthemums, and he scooped her up into his arms, kissing her soundly before he set her down.

''I come bearing news.'' He grinned. From his breast pocket he pulled a small piece of paper.

''What's that?''

''A check, my dear. Made out to Mr. and Mrs. Mitchel Stewart and dated for tomorrow. In the amount of fifty thousand dollars.'' Mitch waited for her cry of surprise, clearly worried when it didn't come. Instead, she was frowning fiercely. ''What's the matter?''

''Not again,'' she told him firmly, shaking her head. ''I'm not going through all that again. I thought you told them to keep it.''

''I did!''

''Well, then, send it back. I'm finished with Papa John and his peanut butter money.'' She watched his face with a tinge of worry. He was up to something. She knew that look. It always spelled trouble. ''Mitch? What are you thinking about?''

''How much fifty thousand dollars can buy.''

Melanie's heart sank. Then she slapped him on the shoulder.

''That's not funny.''

''No,'' he murmured. ''I mean it. Buzzers, bed linens,

those mechanical carts. Think of it, Mel. We could get a good start on outfitting Sunset." He stared at her with a question in his glittering blue eyes. "What do you think? Shall we make it out to Sunset and let your board of directors deal with it?"

It took her thirty seconds to decide, and then Melanie flung her arms around his neck and hung on for dear life, hugging him tightly.

"I love you, Mitchel Stewart," she whispered, tears running down her cheeks. From his response, the three onlookers assumed that he loved her, too.

"Now, children," Charity murmured, patting Melanie's shoulder. "You'll have lots of time for this later. Right now we need to get on with your wedding preparations."

Somehow the three of them managed to get Mitch on his way and Melanie upstairs. Shawna and Sara arrived moments later to help Melanie dress in Charity's beautiful silk wedding gown and while they did, the fearsome threesome stood around babbling.

"Melanie, dear," Hope murmured, flicking a nonexistent piece of lint off her dress. "I...that is, er, the three of us want to say something."

"Are we going to tell her about the prize now?" Faith demanded.

"I already know." Melanie grinned. "And everything's wonderful."

"You know about Nettie sending in the contest entry?" Charity frowned. "That she arranged it all from the beginning? That Faith and Hope and I only helped a little at the end?"

"So that's how our names got in there," Melanie exclaimed. "I knew something was odd about the whole thing. I might have known. How did she know Mitch?"

"That's the strange part, dear. She didn't. Hadn't ever met the boy." Charity rubbed her earlobe thoughtfully. "It really was the oddest thing that your phone call went to him."

"With God all things are possible." Faith smiled serenely. "Hadn't we better get you ready for that wedding?"

"My dearest daughter." Charity sighed and hugged her gently. "You look so beautiful, and I'm so very happy to give you to Mitch. He loves you, dear. Never doubt it."

"I won't," Melanie whispered.

"Turn around now, dear," Hope ordered, fastening the last of the tiny buttons down the back. "This rich ivory suits your skin so well. And the fit is fantastic. Faith's done a wonderful job altering it."

"Piffle," Faith blustered proudly. "You can't go wrong when you've got such quality material to work with. Charity bought the best way back then."

The dress left Melanie's shoulders and neck covered only by a film of sheer silk while the strapless bodice lovingly molded Melanie's full curves, dipping out to a billowy tulle skirt below her hips. A short veil fell to shoulder length, held in place by a row of delicate, fragrant lily of the valley.

In her arms she carried a cascade of glowing yellow roses, a gift from Mitch. He'd insisted on choosing the bridal bouquet himself and surprising her.

"I picked out the invitations and the cake," he'd asserted proudly. "I can do this, too." Melanie had finally acquiesced, praying desperately that his taste didn't run to the black roses she'd seen him studying.

There was a tiny card attached to the green ribbons, and Melanie laughed when she read the words. "Marry Me Today!" it ordered. In small letters on the bottom Mitch had printed, "I Love You."

In the deepest recesses of her mind, Melanie knew she would never doubt his love again, but she tucked the card into her dresser drawer to remind her in the future. Then she slipped on the silky blue garter Sara held out.

"Something old, Mother's dress. Something new, my shoes. Something borrowed, my veil. Something blue, the garter." She grinned at her friends. "I guess I'm ready," she told them.

When the limo came to pick the bridal party up, Melanie was eager to go. Shawna and Sara spent a few moments preening before the mirror in billowy sea foam dresses that matched. Sara's children were beautiful in their tiny wedding outfits. Ben wore a minuscule black tux, complete with cummerbund and bow tie that made him certain he was one of the big guys. Becky was the picture of daintiness. The women carried a parasol of golden mums and white daisies, while Ben gingerly held two gold wedding rings on a satin cushion.

"Mitch picked these," Melanie told them proudly when Shawna commented on the flowers. Sara grinned.

"My ex! He is pretty special." She giggled, enjoying Melanie's grin.

The car was full, with Faith and Hope taking turns fussing over her dress while Charity tried to remain calm. When they drove up to the Sunset Retirement Home, Melanie's mouth formed a perfect Oh of astonishment.

"We agreed that we should be married here," she whispered to her mother. "But I never expected this."

Pots of bronze, gold and pale yellow chrysanthemums nestled along the edges of a white carpet, which guided her to the privacy of the courtyard. Through the doors, Melanie could see the rest of the wedding party waiting.

Smiling gently, she kissed her mother's cheek and watched Charity hobble down the aisle on the arm of Sara's husband. When Charity was seated, Sara drifted forward slowly, followed by Shawna. The birds sang happily overhead as a wedding march played softly in the background. Then Melanie urged the children forward, surprised to see them scattering rose petals as they went.

"Thank you, God," she whispered.

As Melanie moved forward, she felt an arm grasp hers. Glancing down, she stared into Nettie Rivers's happy face. The delicate, petite figure was covered in gracefully elegant autumn hues that enhanced her parchment skin as it glowed in the afternoon sun.

"I am going to give you away, my dear," she told Melanie

shyly, her white-gloved hands slipping under Melanie's arm. "After all," she whispered, beaming from ear to ear, "it's due to me, and John, that you two are together. With the Lord's help."

There was no time for Melanie to puzzle it out. It was time to go. Slowly, carefully, she walked beside the tiny woman, moving over the white carpet toward Mitch.

He looked elegant and heart-stoppingly handsome in his black tuxedo. Clear and deep, his blue eyes met hers and telegraphed a message that left her blushing. Melanie turned her head to identify an older man standing at Mitch's side. Amazed, she recognized the features of Papa John, who was resplendent in a black suit and white bow tie. Well, he certainly was a best man, she supposed. Today, nothing surprised her.

At the front, Mrs. Rivers placed Melanie's hand in Mitch's and nodded to Judge Conroy, who stood in his official robes waiting to marry them. Then the two seniors moved to the side, to take their place beside Faith, Hope and Charity.

Melanie focused on Mitch. Even through the filmy clouds of her veil she could feel his love shining through. His big hand squeezed hers as they turned toward the minister to repeat their vows before the God they had entrusted their future to.

Oblivious to the crowd of residents watching from the chairs crowding the lawn, unmindful of the beautiful piano solo Sara was playing, Melanie and Mitch focused on each other. They repeated their vows, exchanged rings and smiled all through the hearty congratulations. They were far too busy enjoying the good wishes of their friends to hear Hope whisper to the man at her side.

"Bless you, Jean. That was a wonderful wedding present for them. Thank you for all you've done." She patted Mrs. Rivers's hand with a friendly touch. "I know the two of you will be very happy together."

"God has given me the desire of my heart by giving me

John,'' Mrs. Rivers murmured softly, beaming at the man by her side. "Just as Melanie has hers."

The fearsome threesome turned and stared openly at the tender kiss the handsome bridegroom placed on his pretty new wife's smiling lips.

"That's another success to our credit." Faith giggled, her face wide with satisfaction.

"Yes, it is." Charity beamed with motherly satisfaction as the bride laughingly tossed her bouquet over her shoulder. "An inspiration to us all. Now, about that nurse you mentioned…"

*   *   *   *   *

Don't miss the third book in Lois Richer's series,
FAITH, HOPE & CHARITY.
Watch for SWEET CHARITY.
Available in July from Love Inspired.

Dear Reader,

Thank you for picking up book two of my
FAITH, HOPE & CHARITY series. I hope you enjoy
Melanie and Mitch's love story. When I was writing
A Hopeful Heart, my husband's father had to move into
a nursing home. Although so much of this proud man's
long-held freedom was lost, he still took great pleasure
in the little things of life: the tart, greenish taste of a
crabapple, the fresh, clean scent of a pine needle and
the childish giggles of his grandchildren. He reminded
me of my grandfather during his stay, years earlier.
Both of them loved to go for a car ride with the sun
beating down through the windshield as they studied
the crops and named them one by one. It was a small
thing, yes, but it gave so much pleasure.

The Bible says that if God only gives us a cup of cold
water, then we are to use that to help another. We have
so much in our lives and so little time, it seems. Will
we regret, in ten, twenty or thirty years, that we didn't
exert that extra effort, go that second mile, take that
extra time to make someone's days on this earth a little
bit better? I believe God has given each of us just one
life to live and that He intends that life to count for
something eternally worthwhile.

My wish for you is a generous life, lived to the max
and brimming with His love.